# The Scriptures

DRGN

Kingston Imperial
4050 Sheridan Ave, #360
Miami Beach, FL 33140

For information address Kingston Imperial
Rights Department,
4050 Sheridan Ave,
Miami Beach, FL 33140

First Edition:
Book and Jacket Design: LiteBook Prepress Services
Illustrated by: Keron Grant & Joshua Wirth

Manufactured in the United States of America

Cataloging in Publication data is on file with the library of Congress
Title: The Scriptures: End of Days   DRGN

ISBN 9781733304122 (Hard Cover)
ISBN 9781734892512 (Ebook)

# PART ONE

## The Word Is Given

# JD – 200 Days

The Hummer bounced along what could only loosely be called a road, the surface rutted by mortar blasts and studded with fallen masonry, the wrecks of long abandoned vehicles and used ordnance. The battle had finished months ago, but the desert had not yet started to reclaim the aftermath. Sergeant John Struthers studied the wreckage with something approaching despair.

*What the hell are we doing here?* he thought to himself. *The locals don't want us, the enemy is as elusive as a weasel and the folks back home couldn't care less. I signed up to fight, to be a warrior. There's little honor in this.*

They were a long way from base, right on the edge of hostile territory, and it was a while since any of them had got a rest, never mind a good night's sleep. The strain showed on the men's faces, and Struthers knew that they should be heading back to the relative safety of the barracks.

Ten minutes ago, he had been intent on doing just that—even got as close as a mile away from a beer and a burger before the call came through that turned them around. Aerial support reported something going on in the hills to their west, and Struthers was ordered to head over and investigate.

Sammy Brown had driving duty and he wasn't happy at being taken off the main desert road.

"I'm just saying, Sarge," he said. "The roads are bad enough round here, but this is just asking for trouble. If we hit a rock of any size at all, you can wave goodbye to the back shaft. It's rusted to hell and back and ready to go at any time."

The wind blew sand in whirling vortices that spattered against the windows like gunshot. The other four men in the back of the Hummer seemed oblivious, lost in a game of poker that had been going on for days now.

The *comm* whispered in Struthers' ear.

"You're getting close," the pilot in a chopper high above them said. "Two klicks further. Whatever it is, it's kicking up a shit-load of sand. I can't make out a thing."

Struthers turned to the men in the back.

"Saddle up lads, it's show time."

The cards disappeared fast, and the metallic clang of weapons being readied filled the interior of the Hummer.

The *comm* whispered again several minutes later. "You're there. It's right in front of you."

The view cleared enough for them to see where they were headed.

"Holy shit, Sarge," Sammy whispered. "What the hell is that thing?"

Struthers had no answer. He stared at a wall of blackness—a deep, almost pitch-black vortex that spun, counterclockwise, in a football stadium sized area straight in front of them.

*Tornado?*

It looked almost like something he'd once seen in Oklahoma, a storm passing over the plains. But he only had to have one look at this thing and he knew immediately it was no natural phenomenon.

*It could be a new weapon?*

He'd heard stories. Who among them hadn't? The men in white coats were close to perfecting the HAARP weather modification system and rumor had it that they had successfully tested it in Alaska.

*Maybe this is an enemy attempt at something similar. Or maybe it's one of ours that the brass forgot to tell us about?*

But it didn't just look wrong—it felt wrong. It felt like something that was completely out of place, out of time. It shouldn't be there.

*And neither should we.*

Struthers didn't want to have anything to do with it.

"Back off, now," he shouted.

Sammy didn't need a second telling. He flung the Hummer in reverse. Tires screeched and sand flew. The back shaft took that moment to live up to its description and gave way, sending the vehicle lurching to one side. Struthers fell sideways, body pressed tight against the passenger door, as Sammy struggled with a steering wheel that bucked in his hands.

The black wall was getting closer, as if drawn to them by their accident. Metal screeched against metal as Sammy tried to turn away from it. It was too late. The blackness engulfed them, falling on the Hummer like a wave crashing on an inexperienced surfer.

Everything went dark.

Struthers felt like a cat in a dryer as the Hummer rolled and tumbled. Only his seat belt kept him from knocking his body against the doors and the roof. Someone screamed behind him, and he heard the unmistakable crack of bones breaking, but he couldn't move to turn as the vortex sucked them deeper inside. The sensation of traveling grew stronger, as if the vehicle was flying through the air at sickening speed. It felt more like being in a crashing chopper than a road vehicle—and if they came to a sudden halt now, Struthers guessed the result might be just about the same. He closed his eyes—the spinning was too dizzying, too severe. He prayed for it to stop.

Then, as quickly as it had come, the vortex was gone.

The Hummer came to a grinding halt in a squealing flurry of sand and dust. At first Struthers did not realize the ordeal was over—he couldn't see anything but blackness beyond the windows. But at least they had wheels on solid ground and, miraculously, seemed to be still upright. When Sammy turned off the engine, and the dust settled, they looked out onto a desert scene. Sammy had to put on the headlights—it was dark out there.

*It's nighttime. How long were we in that thing?*

A moan from the back seats reminded him that he did not have time for rumination. He looked around.

"Everybody okay?"

Greg Lacont had an egg sized bruise on his forehead, Jimmy Scott was rubbing a mashed, bloody nose, and Ewan Kaminski held one arm in the crook of another, inspecting it for breakage.

Thad Wilkins had got the worst of it. He'd been the only one without a seatbelt. He lay draped over the rearmost seat, bent at an angle that immediately told Struthers that the man's neck was broken. The dull lifeless stare only confirmed it. He had no time to grieve. That would come later. For now, the living was what mattered.

"Sammy. Can this thing go anywhere?"

The little man took his hands off the wheel and shook his head.

"It's totally screwed this time, Sarge. We're either waiting to get picked up, or we're walking."

Struthers tapped at the control on his headset, expecting to hear the familiar crackle and hum. All he got was dead air.

"Try the *comm*," he said to Sammy Brown.

Sammy shook his head.

"Ahead of you there, Sarge. It's dead. And look at this."

He pointed at the dashboard GPS system. It showed only a blank green screen.

"It looks like everything's down. Probably a result of that… whatever it was."

Struthers nodded.

"Okay—saddle up, people. Time to be going."

"What about Thad?" Kaminski asked from the back.

"Leave him," Struthers said softly. "We'll be back for him later. First we need to get the lay of the land. We're fish in a barrel if we just sit here."

He led the squad out into the desert night.


The first thing he was aware of was the quiet. The only sound was the ping of metal as the Hummer engine cooled.

The sky overhead was filled with stars and the arc of the Milky Way stretched across from horizon to horizon. Struthers got his bearings and turned to look west, towards Baghdad. The lights of the city should have been clearly visible, lending a dim red glow to the skyline—but not tonight. The western horizon was as dark as any other part of the sky.

Sammy saw him looking.

"Could that storm that hit us have knocked out all the power when it was at it?"

Struthers nodded, but he had a cold feeling in the pit of his stomach.

*The stars are not right.*

He wasn't about to tell the squad, but something was off—way off. Several well- known marker stars were not where he'd expect them to be. And he clearly remembered a crescent moon the night before, but a full smiling face had just risen off to his east.

*I don't think we're in Kansas any more.*

That feeling was confirmed by a new sound in the night – the dull thwup—not a chopper, but of wings, beating.

*Vulture?*

An accompanying shriek put a lid to that idea. It sounded like nothing less than a man in mortal agony, and came from back where they had left the Hummer.

"Thad! He's still alive," Kaminski shouted, and broke into a run before anyone could stop him.

Struthers looked around the other men. They were all staring at him, waiting on an order. He sighed.

"Well don't just stand there. Get after him."


They arrived back at the Hummer only seconds behind Kaminski and at first Struthers did not understand what he was looking at.

A tall bipedal figure loomed over the vehicle, darker than the night itself. There was something misshapen about it, as if its back were hunched. It bent over the body of Thad Wilkins who lay half-in, half-out of the Hummer. His head lay at an alarming angle to his body, lolling like a broken doll. But that wasn't the worst. The corporal's mouth opened and he screamed, long and hard, the sound running across the desert like the wind.

Kaminski raised his weapon.

"Put him down, motherfucker."

The dark figure turned.

Struthers forgot to breathe. The hump on its back opened out into a pair of wings so large that he could no longer see the Hummer behind them. Red eyes flared in a face that was no more than a deep pool of blackness. The thing drew itself up to its full height, standing some eight feet tall. It carried Thad Wilkins in one arm, as if he weighed no more than a baby.

"Put him down, right fucking now," Kaminski shouted again. He fired a warning burst over the thing's head.

The black wings beat, twice, and suddenly it took flight, heading up into the sky above them, taking the dead soldier with it.

"No!" Kaminski shouted.

He fired a burst after it.

Thad Wilkins' body fell with a dull thud at his feet.

Overhead the black wings thwupped and a shadow moved, heading away with the wind.

Then all was silent.


The squad was in turmoil, all speaking at the same time, all asking questions to which Struthers had no answer.

He bent to check on Wilkins. The corporal was dead. Then again, he was already dead when he checked him earlier.

Sammy Brown came and stood beside him.

"What was that thing, Sarge? Ain't never seen anything like it."

Struthers didn't want to speculate. To do so would open doors to fears he was afraid to give rein to lest they sent him screaming. That didn't stop the men though—their voices were raised, and he heard fear there—near hysteria. He silenced them with a shout.

"The plan hasn't changed. We're moving out, headed West. Lacont—you're on point. Sammy and I will bring up the rear. Shag it, guys."

Kaminski couldn't take his eyes from the dead body.

"We can't leave him here, Sarge."

"Put him back in the Hummer and lock the doors—it's the best we can do for him for now—we'll get a chopper down for him as soon as we get through to base."

Kaminski waved the others away when they tried to help with the body.

"I've got this," he said. The big man lifted Wilkins gently, as if he weighed no more than a pillow, and put him in the Hummer.

When it was done Struthers started to walk away.

"He's not going anywhere now. And I'm not hanging around to wait for that winged beast to come back. Now, move soldiers. That's an order."

Their training took over. As a unit, the squad moved out.

They walked for nearly an hour before Sammy mentioned something that Struthers had already noticed, but kept quiet about.

"Where's the road gone, Sarge?" he whispered. "We should have reached it by now—we should have reached it a klick or more back."

Struthers had been trying not to think about that. With the stars being out of position, a winged demon torturing an already dead man, and the fact that there seemed to be no other living thing apart from his squad out here, he was storing up a lot of things he'd rather not think about. He was saved from answering this one by a call from Lacont up ahead.

"We've got something here, Sarge. A building of some kind."

Struthers joined Lacont on a ridge looking over a long valley. On the valley floor, in what looked to be a long, dry riverbed, a squat white building sat next to an ancient dead tree. There were no lights visible.

"It'll be dawn soon enough," Struthers said. "And we can't walk far in the heat of the day. That looks like a good place to hole up—and there might be a well down there. Take point again, we'll be right behind you."

They followed Lacont down what seemed to be a goat trail and reached the building several minutes later. Struthers had the squad stand quiet, but there was no noise from within. He silently motioned Lacont forward. The man gingerly opened a warped wooden door and slipped inside. They heard him moving around, then he cried out.

"Sarge. Get in here. You need to see this."

He left Kaminski and Scott on guard and with Sammy at his back went inside. He thought he was prepared for any eventuality.

He was wrong.

Lacont stood just inside the door of the only room. His face was pale, eyes wide with shock and, something else—something that looked like awe. Struthers saw why when the man moved aside and he stepped into the room.

An angel lay spread-eagled on the floor at his feet.

At first Struthers took it for another of the winged things they'd seen earlier. But where that had been dark, this one was light, almost luminescent. The body itself was over eight feet long, but thin, even anorexic. The wings, long and feathered like an eagle, lay beneath it. It—or rather, he, for the gender was also obvious in his nakedness, had taken a blow to the head. Blood matted the blond hair and pooled on the stone floor beneath it.

"Is it—is he—dead?" Lacont whispered.

"I hope not," Struthers muttered. "We need some questions answered here."

He bent to check on the body. A pulse beat rapidly at the angel's neck, its breathing fast and shallow. He checked the eyes and found they were rolled up in their sockets, only the whites showing.

"He's alive."

"What is he—or should that be, it?" Lacont whispered.

Sammy Brown laughed sarcastically.

"What does it look like? Have you never seen an angel before?"

Lacont turned angrily on him, and it might have come to blows if a loud call hadn't come from outside right then.

"We've got incoming."

Struthers arrived at the door just as Kaminski and Scott started firing. The noise of the automatic weapons was deafening after the quiet that had gone before. Muzzle flares lit up the outside of the building like disco strobes.

At first he couldn't see their targets, then something moved across the face of the moon—something large, with eagle's wings. More dark shadows stood up on the ridge above the goat track—shadows with hunched backs.

"Down," Scott shouted, and Struthers ducked. He felt a whoosh of air and heard the thwup of wings just over his head.

Scott screamed, just once. Struthers looked up just in time to see the man get lifted in the air and swept away. Automatic fire came from a distance seconds later then all went quiet.

"No!" Kaminski shouted and started to fire indiscriminately at the shadows on the ridge above. As one the shapes unfurled their wings and took to the air. They swooped down the valley wall, wings bent back in attack position.

"Back inside," Struthers shouted. He had to grab Kaminski and drag him toward the door.

"Those things have got Scott," Kaminski said.

"And they'll get us too if we don't take cover. Get in there—right fucking now."

They didn't quite make it.

Lacont and Sammy Brown were inside, but just as Struthers got Kaminski to the door one of the black shapes swooped down and hovered, like a hawk seeking prey, just feet above them. The sound of sarcastic laughter echoed around the walls of the building.

"So, you are the defenders? This should not take long."

The winged figure looked like a negative photographic image of the angel lying inside. The body was sleek and black, shimmering like oil on water. The wings were darker still, and beat slowly in a steady thwup. The motion brought sand and dust up from the ground such that Struthers had to cover his mouth and nose before he could breathe.

Red, fiery eyes stared from a black hole where the face should be and the head was surrounded by a halo of jet- black tousled hair that wouldn't have looked out of place on a rock star.

Kaminski raised his gun.

The demon laughed. It raised an arm and a long-sword appeared in its hand, first silver, then red as flame ran along its length.

"Let me show you a real weapon, human" the demon said. It drew back the sword for a strike.

Struthers joined Kaminski in sending a volley of rounds into the demon's face. The head blew apart like a stone hit by a heavy hammer. There was no blood, but there was a satisfying thud as the body crashed to the ground in a tangle of broken wings and feathers.

Kaminski spat on the corpse.

"You were saying?"

"Incoming," a call came from the doorway. A burst of fire flew close to Struthers' ear as another demon swept towards them. The bullets drew a line across its chest and it screeched, then veered away in a straggling flight, lost in darkness in seconds.

Everything went quiet again. Struthers scanned the valley but there was no sign of movement, and no darker shapes on the skyline.

"What the hell is this, Sarge?" Kaminski said, kicking at the corpse at his feet. "Some kind of black ops baloney? Have they got us fighting against flying fucking Muppets now or what?"

Struthers was thinking about the blazing sword.

*Black ops might be the right words for it.*

"I don't know," he said. "But I know who might."

He left Kaminski on guard and went back inside. He had an angel to question.

The winged figure still lay in the same place on the floor. Lacont was standing above it, looking down, and couldn't take his eyes off it. Indeed, he seemed almost hypnotized until Struthers shook his shoulder.

"Take inventory," Struthers said. "Then go and spell Kaminski. And stay frosty. We don't know what we're dealing with here—but we do know that we can kill them. That's enough to go with."

Lacont left with one last look at the angel.

Sammy came over and stood by Struthers' side.

"He still hasn't moved, Sarge," the smaller man said. "But he's alive all right."

Struthers bent to check the extent of the head wound. One of the angel's hands came up and grabbed at Struthers' wrist—and suddenly Struthers was somewhere else, somewhere dark. A voice intoned, as if reciting from a book. At the same time pictures ran like a cinema screen in his mind:

"*And the Lord sent a horseman, a pale rider, and his name was Death. And his skin shone silver and his hair spread behind him in a great cape. But his eyes were like pits of blackness in the depths of space, and no smile touched his features.*

"*And the horseman carried with him the key to the gates of life and death. And the gate was unlocked and death came forth in its blackness and spread across the face of the earth. And where it passed the sons of Adam fell before it, and the cities lay quiet and the noise of the works of the Adamities was heard no more.*

"*And there came a second rider, and his name was Darkness. And he threw a great cape over the burning orb of the sun. And the heat went out of it then, and when the cape was lifted there was only the sky and the stars.*

"*There was a chorus in the heavens as of the chant of a great throng, and the Lord called for his first made to come forth.*

"*And the earth trembled and shook, and the works of the Adamities fell into its cracks and crevices. And there was a great churning and crackling on the face of the earth, and a wind arose, a wind that scoured and cleansed wherever it passed. And when the wind fell all traces of the Adamities had gone.*

"*And the Lord called the host of angels to sit by his right hand.*

"*And when they were standing before the Lord the great ledger was brought forth, in which all their deeds were etched forever in the fabric of time. And each was judged, and each repented of the deeds of life.*

"*And there came a third horseman, who was called Repentance, and he carried a flaming sword. And his likeness was also as of an angel. And he called from under the ground the old adversary, the great serpent. And the serpent came, in fire and in thunder. And there on the dust under the stars they fought, as ages passed, under the sight of the Lord.*

"*Great was the battle, and great was the blood spilled. And the serpent sprouted many heads, and each was struck from its body by the force of the sword of Repentance. And where the heads fell there sprung from the earth imps and demons that harried and tore at the flanks of the great horse, even as they were dashed under the black iron of its hooves.*

"And the serpent was who weakened first, and fell to dust in defeat, pierced by the sword of Repentance. And the Lord shackled his old foe, binding him to the ground until such time as the last judgment be called.

"And so that all men would know of it, he placed a tree atop the place where the serpent dwelt, and sent a warrior to guard him, lest he be wakened before his time."

# JD – 199 Days

Struthers came out of it slowly. He realized he was staring into a pair of golden eyes. He also realized he'd understood everything that had just been said, despite the archaic language. He held the angel's gaze.

"You are the guardian?" Struthers whispered.

The angel nodded, his eyes rolled up in his sockets and he fell back into his stupor.

"Are you okay, Sarge?" Sammy said from behind him.

"I may never be okay again, Sammy," Struthers replied. "But I think I'm finally getting an idea as to why we're here."

He led Sammy outside to join the others and told them of the vision the angel had sent.

"Baloney," Kaminski said. "There's no such thing as angels and demons. And I'm not about to start taking the word of that circus freak in there."

Struthers kicked at the body that still lay outside the hut.

"Have you seen this thing we killed? What does it look like to you?"

He bent and spread out one of the black wings, pointing at where it was seamlessly joined to huge muscles on the demon's back.

"Does this look like a Muppet to you?"

"Baloney," Kaminski replied, but he wouldn't look Struthers in the eye.

"So what are you saying?" Lacont asked. "We've been brought here as some kind of warriors for God to stop some demons that want to get Satan out of Hell?"

Struthers managed a laugh.

"Well, if you put it like that…"

Kaminski spat on the corpse below them.

"Fucking black ops crapola," he said. "That's all this is."

Sammy Brown looked down, then back at Struthers.

"He's got a point, Sarge. At least black ops is believable."

"It's believable what you want, is it? How long has it been since we hit that big black wall—four hours maybe? In case you haven't noticed, the moon is still in the same spot as it was when we first saw it. It's not going anywhere—and neither are we. I don't think there'll be a dawn any time soon."

He turned to Kaminski.

"And how does a black ops unit make a monster like the one you blew the head off—one that didn't bleed? Can black ops do that? Can they conjure up a blazing sword out of nowhere?"

"Don't talk crap, Sarge," Kaminski said, but it was more of a plea this time, and yet again he wouldn't look Struthers in the eye.

Lacont took his turn in looking down at the corpse.

"I've never been one for all that holy-Joe stuff," he said. "It must be some kind of CIA mind games bullshit. We're probably all strapped into a virtual reality machine somewhere."

Struthers looked over the man's shoulder and laughed.

The black shadows were back on the ridge.

"In that case, get your game face on. We've got incoming again."

The now familiar shadows stood on the western ridge of the valley—and Struthers stopped counting at twelve.

"Get inside," he shouted. "I hope you found something useful in that inventory Lacont. We're going to need it."

They got inside just in time. The flock of demons rose from the ridge with wings splaying, and as one launched down into the valley.

They took a window each, one in each quadrant of the room.

"Here they come," Lacont shouted. He had the west window, directly facing the slope where the demons had been waiting. He shot off a volley—the noise was deafening. The demons scattered, shadows flitting across the stars. It didn't look to Struthers like he'd hit anything.

Struthers found himself reminded of childhood summers shooting turkey. But these were no easy pickings. The demons were black targets against a black sky, and they swooped as fast as any bird of prey he had ever seen. He quickly realized that they weren't going to do much damage until they could get the things on the ground.

"Save your ammo," Struthers shouted.

Sammy Brown laughed, and Struthers was dismayed to hear a touch of hysteria in it.

"Yep. Wait until you see the whites of their eyes."

Kaminski turned away from the window he'd chosen to defend on the north side.

"So what's the plan, Sarge?"

Struthers laughed.

"Don't get dead."

Then there was no more time for talk. Something heavy hit the roof above them, sending dust down onto their heads. Struthers had a quick look around. There did not seem to be any access to get up there from the room they were in. And he had no time to worry about what might be above him—out of his own window he saw three demons that had landed less than ten yards away and were advancing towards him. He sent three rapid shots into the nearest and saw the bullets trace a line across its chest. The next three blew feathers in a flurry from its left wing. It barely slowed.

The red guidance laser targeted the black void just beneath the red eyes and Rodgers fired, blowing the head apart in less than a heartbeat. The wings beat, just once, then the headless body fell to the ground.

The sound of automatic weapons rang all around the round,

interspersed with the shouts of men lost in a fighting fury. The air smelled burnt and dead.

"Go for the heads," he shouted, unsure if he was being heard.

By the time he swung his weapon to the second demon they were almost within reaching distance of his window. He was surprised when they veered away to his right just as he attempted to target them.

*The door. They're going for the door.*

Lacont had spotted it. He trained his weapon on the doorway just as the door was pushed open. Muzzle-flash lit up the room.

"Fire in the hole," someone shouted, and before Struthers had time to react he was thrown to the ground by the blast from a stun grenade. The light stayed behind his eyelids for long seconds. When his head cleared he saw that the doorway had been reduced to little more than a smoking hole. Two dead demons lay blocking the entrance, and burning feathers floated in the air.

He didn't have time to celebrate. A figure moved beyond the window he was defending and a blazing sword struck the wall outside. Stone hissed and sizzled, the blade cutting into the wall like an oxy-acetylene torch. He sent three shots out to where he guessed the head might be but the stone was already starting to crumble around the window frame, and the sword strokes became more frenzied as the attacker pressed harder.

Lacont fired, again and again, through the doorway. He saw Struthers looking at him.

"Virtual reality," the private said. " I told you, Sarge, this is all just a game. We can't die here. But we can at least have some fun."

He started to move closer to the door, and Struthers guessed his intent.

"Lacont. Get back here. That's an order."

Lacont looked over his shoulder and smiled.

"See you back in the real world, Sarge."

He marched towards the door.

"Come and get it," he shouted.

A piece of stone the size of Struthers' head fell from above the window frame as the demon's attack on it strengthened—Struthers was forced to turn back to the defense. Someone—it sounded like Kaminski, screamed in pain, but Struthers couldn't afford to look around. He took a grenade from his belt.

"Fire in the hole," he shouted and dropped the canister out the window. This time he was ready for the blast, but even then the concussion almost sent him down into the darkness of unconsciousness. His ears rang as if someone was banging on a gong in his head. Somewhere in the distance he thought he heard the *thwup* and flutter as the demons took flight.

Then everything went quiet once more.

Struthers checked out his window. There was no sign of movement, either in the vicinity of the building or further out along the ridge. Only then did he feel safe in checking on his squad. Kaminski's face showed a long burn that ran from the side of his left eye all the way to the point of his chin, but he managed a smile and gave a thumbs-up when he saw Struthers looking.

Sammy Brown was getting up off the floor by his window.

He looked groggy, but otherwise uninjured.

Lacont hadn't been so fortunate. His body lay spread over the top of the demons in the doorway, his facial features lost beyond recognition, charred and blackened. Struthers hadn't seen it happen, but he could imagine it—a stroke of one of those blazing swords would be more than capable of the damage he saw.

He had the others help him clear the doorway.

They left the bodies, demon and man alike, outside—there were three more of the winged figures lying dead around the building.

"We can't just leave Lacont like this," Kaminski said, but Struthers waved him away.

"There'll be time enough for ceremony and mourning later—if we make it."

Sammy Brown stood looking at the bodies, then up at the valley rim.

"We need to get out of here, Sarge. This is just a killing field. We need to get back to the Hummer – back to reality."

"And which reality would you prefer?" a voice said behind them.

The angel stood in the ruin of the doorway, bent over to avoid the lintel, the wings folded behind him giving the impression of a hunch. Golden eyes shone from a face as smooth as old ivory, the white broken only by the darker area of bruising and dried blood around his wound. He looked almost too frail to be standing, and had to hold onto the doorjamb for support.

He looked Struthers in the eye, and Struthers felt suddenly calm, as if he'd just learned that all was right with the world, and always would be. He had to drag his eyes away. He couldn't afford to feel that way—not in the middle of a battle.

"Thank you," the angel said. "You have kept it secure. For now at least."

Kaminski stepped forward and looked up into the angel's eyes.

"Is this some more baloney about guarding the pit to stop the Devil from getting out? I'm telling you now, that's not going to wash. All of this shit is your fault. You brought us here, didn't you?"

"Yes," the angel said. "I brought you here. After I was injured Murmus pressed his attack and I knew I could not repel him without help. You were in the area, and right minded. I am sorry that it came to this, but I had no choice." "In the area? Right-minded? What the hell does that mean?" Kaminski was getting angry. "Where exactly are we?"

The angel smiled.

"You are here. Where else?"

Kaminski raised his weapon.

"I've had enough of this crapola."

Struthers stepped forward and put his hand on Kaminski's shoulder.

"Take guard—you and Sammy both. I'll see if I can get to the bottom of this."

Kaminski glared at the angel, then finally backed off, but not before spitting at the feet of the winged figure.

"You can take your right-mindedness and shove it where the sun don't shine," he said. "I'm here for the Sarge and the squad. I wouldn't take a leak on you if you were on fire."

Sammy Brown led Kaminski away and they disappeared around the corner of the building.

The angel looked down at Struthers.

"You must understand—I had no other choice," he said. "I needed warriors. And you were all that was available."

Just the act of speaking seemed to weaken him further and he slumped against the doorjamb, pain etched across his face. Struthers stepped forward and took the angel's weight, leading—half-dragging—him back inside the building. The angel let himself be lowered gently to the floor where he sat, cross-legged. He looked up at Struthers, and once again Struthers felt a strange calm sweep over him.

"This Murmus you mentioned," Struthers said. "He is leading these attacks against you—against us?"

The angel nodded.

"Ever since your war in the East, the dark ones have been growing in strength and becoming emboldened. They sense the coming of the end of days, and know that they have to release their master before then if they are to have any chance at all."

"Chance of what?"

"Of toppling the throne of Heaven. That is what this is all about. The evil prince wants the throne and only a band of perfect knights can stand in his way. Do you not read the old stories? It is always thus. As above, so below."

The angel's head fell forward and Struthers thought he might have passed out again. He was about to step forward when the head rose.

"Murmus is a Grand Duke of Hell. If the old one is freed, Murmus will stand by his right hand, and be master of all he surveys. You think you have seen hell, Sergeant Struthers? You have touched but a part of it. There will be much worse to come if we do not prevail right here, right now."

"And this Duke has a squad of his own?"

The angel smiled grimly.

"He has thirty legions of demons under his command."

"And that's a lot?"

This time the smile was one of sadness.

"Somewhere around one hundred and fifty thousand of them. The number varies. I have destroyed many—as have you—but a Grand Duke of Hell is never in want of followers."

From just outside the window Struthers heard the murmur of voices, one, heavily accented, raised in anger.

"And you brought us here to fight for you?" Struthers asked the angel.

Every word seemed to be a strain for the angel. He looked Struthers in the eye.

"No. I brought you here so that you, Sergeant John Struthers, might understand what is needed. I recognized you. You are the one who will go forth from here and spread the word of God—the word of the coming."

"The coming what?"

A shout from Sammy Brown put an end to the conversation. "Sarge. You'd better come and see this."

The angel kept his gaze on Struthers.

"Murmus has come. It is time."

The angel tried to stand. His legs buckled beneath him and his wings fluttered feebly as they tried, and failed, to unfurl behind him.

"Stay here," Struthers said, and left the room at a run.

Sammy and Kaminski stood just outside the doorway staring, mouths open, at a dark shape that sat some fifty yards away. Huge wings stretched on either side, the tips touching the valley walls. The body of the figure seemed massive and bulky and it sucked in light from all around, the darkness obscuring its features. But there was no mistaking its monstrous strength.

It was only when a body detached itself and started to walk towards them that Struthers realized that the winged creature had merely been the carriage, a great vulture-like bird that now waited patiently as its master strode towards the building.

The demon that had dismounted and now walked towards them was taller than the ones they'd killed so far, and nearly twice as broad. In form and substance it was little more than a huge, man-shaped area of darkness, but the red eyes that stared at them were the size of plates, and glowed with an inner flame.

Its voice boomed and echoed in the narrow confines of the valley.

"So he has brought you here to wage his battles for him?

My fight is not with the likes of you." "Tough shit," Kaminski said, and fired.

Once again he aimed for the head, but this time he did not get the result he wanted. The bullets seemed to vanish into the pool of blackness that was all they could see of the demon's face.

"You will find I am not so easily vanquished." Its booming laugh echoed around them. "My turn."

The demon raised a hand and a long sword grew in his grip, a blade nearly ten feet in length. Before any of the men could react the blade blazed with red fire. It came down on Kaminski in a stroke that smote him all the way to the ground, cleaving him from left shoulder to right hip. Small flames rose the full length of the wound and Kaminski fell forward, already dead as his face hit the dirt.

Sammy Brown lobbed a grenade into the dark body of the beast.

It swallowed it.

The flaming sword came up and went down. Sammy Brown joined Kaminski, face down in the dirt.

The beast raised its hands in the air.

"Come, Father, you have slept long enough. I am here to stand with you once again, as we did of old."

The dead tree at the side of the building started to tremble. The ground shook, shocks radiating out from around the old house, tremors building until the valley floor bucked and seethed like a wind-swept sea.

"Stop," a quiet voice said.

The angel stood just outside the doorway of the building.

Everything fell quiet.

The demon, Murmus, looked at the angel and laughed. "Your time is over," it said. "You can barely stand. You do not have the strength to defy me."

The angel walked slowly over and put a hand on Struthers' shoulder.

"Are you ready to fight the good fight?"

Struthers looked at the demon, then down at the bodies at his feet. If he did not act now, the death of his men would be for nothing. He turned and looked the angel in the eye.

"Ready when you are."

The demon raised the sword above the angel and brought it down fast. Struthers met it with his rifle. The blow jarred all the way up his arm, turning it as cold as stone.

But he did not burn.

Once more he felt infused with calm. With the angel's hand still on his shoulder, he raised his rifle again. It elongated and flattened, turning golden yellow, a long blade that hummed with power. Sparks flew as it met the demon's blade.

The ground trembled and shook again beneath them.

"Hurry," the angel whispered in Struthers' ear. "It must be done now if it is to be done at all."

Struthers felt invincible. It was only as he strode forward, his weapon raised, that he realized he was staring at the demon almost eye to eye.

The demon raised the blazing sword for a strike, but Struthers didn't give him the time to deliver it. He stepped inside the blow and thrust his own sword deep into the heart of the blackness.

The demon shrank, tendrils of shadow wafting frantically in the air. Struthers raised his sword again and Murmus retreated, fleeing for his mount.

Seconds later the great vulture took off in a flurry of wings and feathers. A scream racked the air as the creature, and its rider, swept over the lip of the valley and off, out of sight.

Struthers was left alone on the valley floor.

The ground slowly grew quiet beneath them. Struthers could feel the old one stir once, then settle. He knew the truth of it now, knew that the greatest beast of them all was there, deep—way down deep—under his feet.

"The time is close—he is almost awake. Will you serve?" the angel said.

Struthers looked around the valley, at the bodies of his squad.

"Haven't we given enough?"

"This valley is not the world," the angel replied, as if that was an answer, then reached out and touched Struthers' head with a long forefinger.

Struthers went elsewhere.

# JD – 100 Days

"We're here tonight with John, who has a message for us—a message we all need to hear."

John blinked—the lights in his face were almost blinding, and the studio—a grand word for what was little more than a barn with pretensions—was too warm, even more stifling than the desert he'd left behind these three months past. But he had to start somewhere—and he knew it was not going to end here—not after he showed them the truth—not after he'd given them the Word.

He smiled. A woman in the front row gasped—she'd seen a little of what was now inside him, what would be released, what could not be denied.

It was going to be glorious.

The presenter in the chair opposite John across a small, cheap coffee table looked like he too was feeling the heat—he had a glistening sheen of sweat all over his too-big, too-red face and his polyester suit gleamed, too shiny under the lights. The cheap glue he used to keep his wig in place was also wilting under the heat and had started to dribble out just in front of his right ear. He looked like he was ready to melt as he turned from the camera to John.

"So, John—you've been making something of a name for yourself in faith-based circles these past weeks. Are you a religious man?"

"I wasn't," John said. "My family was Southern Baptists from way back, so I had to learn it young. But it never took. Until recently."

"It is being said that you correctly predicted the escalation of the Syrian crisis—and the tsunami in Japan. Is that correct?"

"These things did happen, yes—but they were not predictions, they were the Word, as I was given it, as it shall be given in return."

"You claim this is the word of the Lord? That it was given to you in the desert?"

"That is correct," John replied. "But it is not a claim. It is truth. Those who have eyes, let them see."

He already knew what was coming next.

"You walked into the U.N. advance operations center after a month in the desert, barely alive. It is said that you were babbling, speaking in tongues, and acting like a crazy man."

John smiled.

"The word of God is a lot for a man to take in. I had to be properly prepared."

"Forty days? What had you been doing all that time?"

"I was receiving the Word." John said simply. "Then, I was getting well enough to spread it. And now, as you see, I am here amongst you."

The presenter looked slightly confused at that, but he was reading from a teleprompter and plowed on.

"You have said that the events in Syria, and the tsunami are the long awaited signs, that the rapture is imminent. That's got a lot of folks here pretty darned excited, as I'm sure you know. And we are led to believe that you were given this word by an angel of the Lord during your trials in the desert?"

John smiled—he was getting practiced at it now, and it came more naturally the more often he looked into a camera. He would only improve, the further he went up the food chain.

"That is correct," he said. "I have fought the good fight and prevailed. Now I am here to bring you the Word that will lead you all through the tribulations to come. As it was given to me, so shall I give it to you in return."

John knew that in the days—weeks—months—ahead before the Day, he would face presenters who would not believe him, who would mock his every utterance, but here, now, the shiny-suited man across the table beamed a smile of his own.

"Praise be," the sweating man said, and the small audience—some forty of them, replied in turn—hushed voices that didn't sound much like praise to John's ears.

The presenter's wig was definitely slipping now, but he'd forgotten that, forgotten the teleprompter—John saw fervor—and need, and longing—in the man's eyes—he wanted to believe, but needed to be shown.

*I think I can oblige there.*

"Would you like to hear the Word of our Lord?" he said.

The audience responded with a murmur.

John spoke louder, almost shouting.

"I said, would you like to hear the Word?"

They were used to this kind of prompting—this time they clapped and shouted.

John waited for quiet, and felt the power come into him as he spoke. It felt like it came up, rising from a point in his chest, and he felt again the touch of the angel on him as the words spilled out.

"Those that have ears, let them hear. Blessed are they that hear the words, for the time that was foretold is at hand." The silence that fell over the studio was almost complete, as if everyone had taken a deep breath at the same time. John kept speaking as the power filled him and the truth of his words went out and into the studio and through the lens and into all of those who might be watching—now, or later.

"He hath prevailed to open the book, and to loose the seven seals thereof."

"Praise be," the polyester suit said—and this time he sounded like he meant it. When the audience replied, it sounded like a prayer.

The presenter had tears in his eyes that sparked as they dripped onto his polyester suit. He turned back to John. His wig had fallen sideward, almost covering his left ear, but all theatricality was forgotten now—the fervor of the Word had gripped him, and gripped hard.

"You really think it is time?" he asked, little more than a whisper.

John nodded and looked straight into the camera, smiling. "The signs are there for those with eyes to see—it is coming—and it is coming soon.

Repent, and give yourself to the Lord's will, for the day of Judgement is at hand, and only the righteous will stand."

"Praise be," the crowd shouted. They were all into it now, wide eyed, red faced and bellowing out their reply. Normally at this point in proceedings, the presenter would be asking for his cash donations—and they'd be only too willing to give—but John wasn't here for the money; John was here for the Word, and it was time it was given. He spoke loudly, his voice carrying above the excitement of the crowd.

"The Lord our God is a merciful God, but the day that was foretold has come. I, John have been chosen for I have stood in a dark place and seen the light, I have heard the great beast stir in the pit where he is chained—stir and awaken for even he knows the truth of it. The great ledger will be brought forth, in which all our deeds are etched forever in the fabric of time. And each of us will be judged, and each will be asked to repent of the deeds of this life.

"I was sent tonight to give the Word, and to bear witness of the truth of it—for the world to see the truth in me. Tonight, the first sign will be given. Look to California. Look now, and remember it as it is, that gaudy glittering jewel to Mammon—for it will not be there in the morning."

He waited, two beats, then intoned the words—angel words—holy words—California's doom.

"And the earth trembled and shook, and the works of men fell into its cracks and crevices. And there was a great churning and crackling on the face of the earth, and a wind arose, a wind that scoured and cleansed wherever it passed."

"Praise be," said the crowd.


The earthquake—9.6 on the Richter scale—hit California the next morning. The San Andreas fault slid, San Francisco went sideways, and tens of thousands died in the first big shake. Dams broke, power lines fell, bridges buckled and geography was rewritten. It was the big one everybody had always whispered about but nobody had really expected. And it was worse—far worse—than any Hollywood portrayal could ever be. News channels ran with a rolling ticker of reported casualties. The number kept growing as the aftershocks kept coming and response teams themselves got into trouble.

The state fell into chaos. Recriminations flew, and blame was sought. Politicians blustered, scientists were trooped on screen and asked to give simple explanations to complex geology—and somebody, looking for a fresh angle, remembered seeing John on a cable channel the night before. His appearance on the small-town show went viral online.

John's face, smiling, showed in homes and offices across the world. He was the Revelator now, and the Word was given in ten-second sound bites.

"Repent, and give yourself to the Lord's will, for the day of Judgement is at hand, and only the righteous will stand."

# JD – 50 Days

It took a couple of weeks for the mainstream media to take note of the Word.

John spent that time in a round of interviews and news spots of Evangelical pastors and small cable channels. It did not matter that their audiences were small—at this stage in proceedings all that mattered was that the Word was spread—it would find a way.

It was the angel's promise that his service would be meaningful, that the war was not yet over. He knew that already—he'd come out of the valley and into the desert with the knowledge—the certainty—that his time was limited and that the Word had to be heard by those who needed it. He had first spoken it in the hospital bed where they put him to try and find out why he was still alive, and in the detention rooms where they questioned him about the fate of his men. He told them that the bodies would never be found, that the Lord had taken them—and it wasn't incredulity he saw on some of the faces—it was a realization that they'd heard—and understood—the Word. He'd seen it in almost everyone he'd spoken to from desert to airport, from homecoming to online fame.

He knew that fortune could be had too, if he had desired it. But the Word was his only focus now—interviews, meetings, broadcasts and podcasts—the Word had to be given.

It wasn't until he predicted—correctly and to the exact minute—the first use of nukes in the Middle East conflict that the larger news sources really started to pay attention to the Word. Now they had a truth they could not deny, in blossoming clouds that reached all the way up to the very heavens.

He was suddenly the most sought after man on the planet, his every step followed by rushing people with microphones and cameras and shouting voices, demanding that he speak. He chose the ones with the biggest, most widespread audience, where the Word could blossom itself and grow.

Now here he was, waiting to go on one of the world's biggest stages, waiting to give the Word to people that didn't yet know they needed it. Events were happening fast now—almost too fast for the media to keep up.

John sat in the Green Room waiting to go on while the top-of-the-hour news broadcast was displayed on the screen across from him. The presenters were making a valiant—but vain—attempt to cram a decade's worth of catastrophe and mayhem into five minutes so that the public might be able to understand.

The images came almost too fast for their scope to be comprehended.

The Middle East was a ravaged war zone—that in itself was hardly new, but the use of a tactical nuke in the latest battle zone—and the deaths of tens of thousands of civilians—had raised the stakes to a new level. Egypt, Saudi Arabia and Israel were all watching Syria and Iraq—and each other—and the first wrong move from any of them would send more missiles flying. Pundits were trying to calculate the odds of a full out nuclear conflict, peacekeepers were invoking the need for calm, fundamentalists were calling for jihad or holy war, and the world's press was wondering how it might all end. Nobody had asked John about that yet—but if they did, he could give chapter and verse on just how it was going to go—he only really needed one word.

*Badly. Very badly.*

Likewise, nobody had asked him yet about the new bleeding plague coming out of the Congo—mainly because wherever it hit, no news came out of. Large swathes of Equatorial Africa had already gone quiet and nobody apart from a few of the smaller news sources had noticed it yet—but they would.

The North American networks were mainly concerned with two other matters—one was the perilous state of things in the Western Pacific. North Korea was saber rattling, setting off missiles, moving troops to the borders and making accusations of persecution. Same as it ever was. But this time China, Russia and Japan were getting twitchy, and South Korea was on the verge of demanding that the UN declare all out war in the region. John had a word for that too, if anyone had asked him.

*Futile.*

The other matter concerning the networks was much closer to home. The situation in California was desperate. Huge aftershocks kept coming—and coming—each of them a major earthquake in its own right, each thwarting any attempt by the authorities at getting control of the situation. Brushfires raged, dams weakened by the constant run of quakes threatened to burst, communication with major populated areas was still sketchy at best—and there were strange reports of a sickness in remote areas—red, bloody, sickness that was killing faster than the quake had done. The quakes had also set off a rumbling, venting, chain of volcanic activity up through Oregon that required mass evacuations all up the coast. Seismic monitors showed micro- quake clusters up the Pacific Seaboard as far as Anchorage—there were now worries that the whole North—and South—American side of the ring of fire might all blow at once.

*Inevitable.*

John watched the mayhem unfold on screen—it had no emotional impact on him at all, as if it were all just another blockbuster movie to be watched and forgotten. He wondered whether he should feel more concern, but was aware that something that made him human had gone—it had been burned out of him with the touch of the angel, back in the hut in the desert valley, when he had agreed to serve. But the loss did not bother him unduly. He had gained far more than he had lost—before he went to war he was an only son of dead parents. Now he had family everywhere. He felt the glory of the Word in him, rising, ready to be heard, rising just as surely as the old enemy was now rising out of his slumber, just as surely as the day was coming.

They called his name across the tannoy—five minutes, and the cameras would be waiting to suck up the Word and send it out to the ears of those who would listen.

*Soon.*

"Surely you cannot ask us to believe such a story? A U.S. marine in active service is given the Word of God somewhere east of Baghdad, in a place you cannot even point to on a map, in the middle of a fight with—and these are your own words—'a platoon of hell spawn'? Is it not much more likely—indeed, is it not probable—that you were kidnapped by the enemy and subjected to some form of mind control? Or a psychedelic substance?"

The fake-tanned presenter grinned, showing off his expensive dentistry and what he thought was his modern, civilized, disdain for John's "Old Testament pretensions" as he'd called them in his introduction. He was waving a newspaper article in John's face—'Prophet, Zealot or Fraud?' it read in huge black letters, with a picture of John—taken by someone in the operations center just after he walked out of the desert—looking like a more crazed version of Charles Manson. John had finally come far enough up the chain to meet the resistance he'd long been expecting.

"It was no psychotropic drug that killed my squad," John replied, keeping his voice calm and steady. "And I am not some kind of Manchurian Candidate here to subvert the American way of life, so you can stop treating me as a danger. I am not even asking you to believe anything. I am merely here to give you the Word as it as given to me. What you then do with it is up to you."

"And I'm sure you won't be getting a book deal or a TV show out of all this publicity either," the presenter said sarcastically.

John kept his view calm.

"I am not a greedy child in need of validation," he replied, and he saw the truth of his word—and its reflected meaning fluster the presenter until he got back to his teleprompter questions. The interview wasn't going the way it had been planned.

"And the Word is that "this is the big one"? It's Judgement Day? It's the end of the world as we know it?"

John smiled.

"You see," the presenter went on, "it is your evident calm in the face of worldwide chaos that gives people doubt as to your sincerity."

"What would you have me do?" John asked. "Rage, rage, against the dying of the light? The Word is not about me, or my rage—or lack of it. I am merely a conduit through which it flows. Those who have ears let them hear. Those who have eyes let them see. Those who overcome will be made a pillar in the temple of God having the name of God, the name of the city of God, and shall dwell in the garden in the New Eden that is to come."

"See—what does that even mean?" the presenter said, addressing, not John, but the audience watching. "Forgive me, but it sounds more like Vaudeville than scripture."

"Those that have ears, let them hear," John replied as the camera zoomed in on him, and the power rose and built and came through and out and across the airwaves.

"The beast will be released from his prison and will go out to deceive all the nations of the Earth. He will gather his forces for battle. In numbers they are like the sand on the seashore, for they are Legion. The last war has begun already."

The presenter looked baffled.

"Is that a prophecy?"

John smiled.

"No—it has already started."

At almost the same instant, the presenter touched his earphone, looked shocked for a second until he regained his composure, then turned to the camera.

"We are interrupting this broadcast to bring you breaking news from Iraq."

All speculation about the Middle East was now moot. The Iraqi's started it, Saudi Arabia and Israel finished it. By the time the missiles stopped flying Iraq, for all intents and purposes, ceased to exist. The Arab world was in uproar, and Mecca was a smoking hole in the ground, the

Holiest place obliterated as if it had never existed. Jihad was called for. There was no shortage of answering voices.

They came, from all corners of the Earth to answer. The Revelator smiled.

# JD – 10 Days

There had been no sun anywhere in North America for three days and nights. The thick clouds that glowered overhead swirled—red and orange and yellow and black and angry. Sheet lightning ran from horizon to horizon, and forks whipped down to lash the ground with accompanying thunderclaps that shook whole cities. Meteorologists spent their time arguing whether it was the nukes—more than fifty had been used in one conflict or another now, and the number was still growing—or the volcanoes that were causing the phenomena—John knew that it didn't matter.

All that mattered now was the Word.

It had spread like wildfire. Since his Fox broadcast, then his subsequent prediction of the giant tsunami that took out most of Bangladesh, John had been on almost every station on the planet at one time or another—his face was as recognizable as any ruler or president, and the Word spread over all.

He had used the media to the maximum extent of their range—now it was the politician's turn—while there was still time. He'd called for a meeting of world leaders—as many as would come. They wanted to have it at the UN headquarters in New York, but that wasn't an option—for reasons John knew would be all too clear all too soon. Many of them balked at having it in the States at all—the Chinese in particular—but

John had traveled just about as far as he was prepared to, and the Word was insistent.

He gathered the politicians and the media—what was left of them—to the lawn of the White House, and the President stood, silently, at his side as John addressed the cameras.

Those present knew some of what he would say already—the bleeding plague was now a worldwide epidemic, with no cure, no vaccination, no time to stop it even if enough resources were available. The Pacific ring of fire continued to blow—and that had also set off a previously unknown chain under the Antarctic ice that was now melting enough that it would raise sea levels to catastrophic heights for centuries to come given the chance. The ongoing conflict in the Middle East was spreading—Iran and Turkey had gotten involved, Egypt was ready to blow, and refugees—tens of millions of them—were piling into Europe and causing tensions and strife to rise to a breaking point. Even before the various wars that now raged elsewhere, the human race was facing some serious problems just staying viable.

John wasn't going to mention that the Russians had, just minutes before, made all other talking points moot by launching everything they'd got at anyone they could think of—it wouldn't affect anything that was going to happen from here on anyway.

He stood in front of the staring eyes of the world and felt the Word rise up in him again, felt the power and the glory wash like a wave through and out and away.

"And I saw when the Lamb opened one of the seals, and I heard, as it were the noise of thunder, one of the four beasts saying, come and see."

Something bellowed, high in the cloud, a thunderous roar as if the sky itself was going to crack open. High up there, impossibly high, blazing lights, like stars, started to fall. One, already brighter, surged downward, piercing the gloom. The noise as it came was like a trumpet blown by a madman.

The northern horizon blazed with God's glory, the trumpet blared and a great cloud rose up to meet the heavens.

"And I saw, and behold a white horse: and he that sat on him had a bow; and a crown was given unto him: and he went forth conquering, and to conquer."

# PART TWO

## THE WORD IS SPREAD

# JD – 9 Days

*New York*

He woke into stifling heat that threatened to cook him alive. His throat burned with the taste of the hot smoke that stung at his eyes and in his nostrils. Everything was dark, and he thrashed out. His fingers met more heat—dry, baking dirt that parted beneath his touch and gave him hope that he wasn't completely trapped.

He dug, and hoped he was heading up, not down.

Alfred Collinson—although he didn't even know his name then—pulled himself through the deep pile of hot ash and rubble, clawing frantically as he thrust it aside in a burning need to reach better air. He sang as he dug, keeping the beat with his arms and hands.

> *"Well, who's that writin'? John the Revelator,*
> *"Who's that writin'? John the Revelator, "Who's*
> *that writin'? John the Revelator,*
>
> *"A book of the seven seals."*

❋ ❋ ❋ ❋ ❋

He had no idea what it meant, no idea how he even knew the words. All he knew was that if he didn't catch a fresh breath in the next few seconds, he wasn't going to know very much of anything at all.

> *"Tell me what's John writin'? Ask the Revelator,*
> *"What's John writin'? Ask the Revelator, "What's*
> *John writin'? Ask the Revelator,*
>
> *"A book of the seven seals."*

He sang, and he dug, pushing his way out of what felt like a mound of earth, as if he'd been buried alive. Then, just as he thought he'd taken his last gasp, given all that he had to give, he broke through. A hole appeared, dust rattled and tumbled and, using his legs like a swimmer, he pushed up and out, just as rubble slid away below him and he was left, gasping, flat on his back, looking up at a concrete roof and wondering how the hell he'd gotten there.

A sign above him said '33$^{rd}$ St.', but that didn't mean much to him either. He sat up, coughing—the air was cleaner here than it had been under the rubble, but it was hot, dusty and choking, swirling around like dry fog. He checked for wounds—his arms were scratched, and he'd lost most of the nail from his left little finger, but apart from that, he seemed to be okay. He was wearing loose black trousers, a sleeveless gray shirt and Converse boots that looked like they'd seen much better days. Everything was gray, covered in fine dust and dirt—he improved the look a bit by wiping everywhere he could see, but he wasn't going to be winning awards for cleanliness any time soon.

That wasn't his main problem though—he had no idea who he was, where he was—even what day it could be. He had no memory of anything at all before waking up in the earth and starting to dig. It was only when he checked his hip pocket that he got a clue to his name—an I.D. card said he was Alfred Collinson, and gave an address in the Bronx, wherever that might be. Apart from that, it was as if he'd just come into the world, and he had no notion as to what was supposed to happen next.

When he turned he discovered he'd been lying near a guitar case—the neck part stuck out of the rubble, and with a bit more digging he was able to pull the whole thing clear. It was old, battered and dusty but it seemed familiar somehow. It had a shoulder strap on it that he used to sling it across his shoulders—the weight comforted him, as if it was something solid he could grasp, something that came naturally to him.

*Maybe it was mine? In that case, I'm not stealing it—and it doesn't look like there's anyone else here to claim it.*

It was when looked around properly for the first time that he realized what must have happened—he wasn't completely new to this world, as some things seemed obvious as soon as he looked. He was in a subway station—and a bomb—a bomb to end all bombs—had gone off, either here or in the close vicinity.

It had caused mass carnage. He saw ten—twenty—bodies from where he stood, mangled and burned so that they scarcely seemed human, but rather merely large pieces of overcooked meat wrapped in burnt cloth and ash. He looked away, looking for something—anything—apart from the smoking flesh. There was a train at the platform but a huge chunk of the concrete ceiling had collapsed on top of it—anybody that had been in there was buried far more thoroughly than Alfred—Alfie—somehow he knew that now too—had ever been. And now that he'd got used to the hot dust in the air he realized something else—there was a pervasive odor hanging everywhere—he smelled the distinctive, heavy aroma of cooked meat, and his stomach rumbled.

Hungry—and nauseated at the same time at what had brought on the thought—Alfie stumbled away through the debris, heading for a brighter area to his left where thin light was coming down what was left of a set of steps, hoping to escape the stench of the dead.

He stood at the bottom of the stairwell for long seconds, looking up into more swirling, dry dust, listening for a sound that would tell him help was coming. There should be sirens, running footsteps, shouting—but there was only a deathly quiet, the only sound a soft whisper where dust hit the floor and walls in the breeze.

"Hello?" he shouted, then wished he hadn't—his voice was too loud, too strident—it hardly even felt that it belonged to him. The dust swirled faster for a second, but there was no answer to his call. He took a last look around the ruin of the subway station but it would be a long time before there was another train through here—and longer still before any of the dead answered him.

He checked his pockets—all of them—looking for a phone, but if he'd ever had one, it had been lost somewhere in whatever disaster had fallen on this place. He might find one if he looked among the dead, but he would have to be more desperate than he was now to go that far.

Twenty more seconds of listening convinced him that if help was coming, it was still some way off, and Alfie was only freaking himself out by staying in the quiet dark with the dead folks. He kept his eyes on the light at the top of the stairs and headed up.

He'd expected the air to get clearer the further up he went, but if anything the dust got thicker—thicker and hotter, dry and tearing at his throat. He pulled his shirt up to his mouth and nose and breathed as well as he could that way while climbing.

The handrail was almost too hot to touch, and heat threatened to melt the soles of his boots, so much so that they felt tacky, sticking to the stairs with every step up he took. The only noise now was the rasp of his breathing and the sound of his footsteps. There was still deathly silence from above.

Then there was a noise—a rumbling, as of distant thunder, and the dust swirled in a mad vortex for seconds before settling. The relative calm and cool back down in the dark of the subway seemed almost welcoming now, and Alfie might have thought about turning on his heels, if it wasn't for the memory of the burnt dead that waited there.

He pressed on upward and, slowly but surely, the light grew stronger and the air, if not cleaner, at least got slightly fresher as he felt a warm breeze on his face. As he reached the top of the flight of stairs and up into what should have been the street level he heard another deep rumble, more distant than the last. The dust swirled violently, then cleared, as if swept away by the breeze, giving his first clear view.

He was hardly able to believe what he was seeing.

There had been a bomb all right—many of them—or maybe just one, very big one. He knew—something else that was just there with no explanation—that there had been a huge city here—if he tried hard enough he might even remember its name—but whatever it had been called, it was gone now—leveled to little more than dust and rubble. Some of the buildings still stood—stark, ragged, fingers of tortured steel and broken glass silhouetted against a sky that burned angrily in red and black and gray and orange. But those were few and far between—it was mostly ash, smoke and gray dust as far as Alfie could see in any direction. To his left, three black figures were silhouetted—*flash burned*—into the stone of the wall of what had been a bank. In the street, dust and ash drifted like fresh snow, covering what might be cars, trucks and buses—and smaller fallen bundles, probably people.

Everything was silent, still. He caught movement in the corner of his eye and turned right, just in time to see one of the tall wrecked towers fall in on itself in slow motion. A thunderous, yet strangely muffled and deadened rumble reached him seconds later, and he just had time to cover his face again as dust rose up and swirled around him before slowly settling with a soft hiss, like sand on rock.

There wasn't another living person in sight the full length of the wide, ash-filled roadway—there was only the tumbled—and still tumbling—debris of bombed out buildings.

*How am I even still alive?*

He knew that was a question he'd be asking himself more of, for days to come—if he was spared time to think. But for now his priority was in finding somebody to tell him what had happened—and somebody to help him get out of this nightmare.

*Before it gets into me.*

He thought about shouting again, but there was something about the silence that gave him pause, as if he might be offending the dead if he raised his voice.

He made sure the guitar case was slung tight enough to not swing around too much at his back, and set off at a slow walk. He had no idea where he was going, and the cloud cover meant he couldn't use the sun as a guide. All he knew was it was easier to breathe with the breeze at his back rather than in his face.

He started walking.

The dust lay deep underfoot, but it was fine and light, easy to push through, and meant that walking wasn't too strenuous.

But the heat was going to get him long before exhaustion did. It rose up from the ground in waves, and it was like walking inside a pizza oven at full blast. His throat felt dry and rasping as if he'd rubbed it down with sandpaper, and his blood roared in his veins like boiling water. He considered leaving the center of the road, looking for cooler air at the sidewalks—but there were many more small, hunched, mounds under the ash near the walls of the tumbled buildings, and when he got too close he smelled, again, the odor of cooked and cooking meat. But he had to get some respite—sooner rather than later—for he was in danger of becoming just as cooked himself, roasted from the inside out. He looked around for shelter—there were vehicles in the road but when he opened the door of one, a blast of heat even warmer than the air pushed him backward. His thought about ovens had been closer to the mark than he'd realized—he wouldn't last ten seconds in there. He kept walking. There were no other footprints but his own in the ash—no clues as to possible shelter from anywhere. But five minutes later, he hit a spot of luck.

He passed what had been a grove of trees in a large courtyard to his right. All were flattened, little more than charred skeletons—but they'd fallen over a store front and Alfie could see through into a dark space behind the entry that appeared to have survived relatively intact. He headed over.

He had to push one of the fallen trees aside to get entry. It was still hot to the touch, but wasn't difficult to move—it had been burnt to a cinder, so light that it started to crumble and fall apart at his touch. He was able to stomp down the remnants and step through them to get to the storefront.

Any signage outside had been obliterated by the blast, but it had obviously been a coffee shop, only a few hours before. It looked like it might still be one—it had survived remarkably intact—apart from the two dead bodies on the ground in the doorway. Alfie stepped over them and made his way inside hoping to find cooler air deeper in the shadows.

There were no lights—no signs of any electrical appliances working at all. But there was a laptop sitting at one of the tables with some brightness still showing on the screen, and he took that with him as he headed through to the rear of the store, using it as a very dim flashlight.

He got lucky again—even though there was scarcely enough light to see by, he came across a cold storage room in the corridor just past the counter. Although it too was in darkness with no power, the refrigeration unit that had been running before the blast meant that the air inside was cool—not by any means cold, but a damn sight cooler than outside. And there was food here too that hadn't been reached by the heat—plastic cartons of sandwiches, milk, soft drinks and cookies. It seemed he was not fated to starve.

He tore open a sandwich box—tuna and sweet corn—and wolfed it down with the best part of a pint of milk before sitting on the floor with a second sandwich. He kept the storage room door slightly open by leaving the guitar case in the doorway, and, his hunger having finally had the edge taken off it, turned his attention to the laptop.

The screen was dim—it was in power saver mode—and there was obviously no wi-fi access to be had, but whoever had been using it had been browsing the news. The pages were still there in the browser, and the main story, front and center, told Alfie a lot of what he needed to know. War in the Middle East—nuclear war—a plague out of Africa that was spreading out of control across the Third World—more war in Korea—yet more war in Central Africa—earthquakes and volcanoes in the Pacific and Antarctica, forest fires in Canada and Siberia. One of the screens showed what they called the Doomsday Clock—both hands pointed straight up at the twelve. Alfie didn't know—or couldn't remember—where any of the places mentioned in the reports were or what his part in any of it was.

But he could have a good guess as to what had happened in this city. Wherever he was, it hadn't been exempt from trouble. Somebody had dropped a big one.

*And I've survived it—so far.*

As he played with the laptop, he realized something else—he'd been using the browser without thinking about it. He knew something about the machine and how it functioned. He could not only operate it, but knew his way around the inner systems—enough to look for satellite wi-fi to hack into, or any networks at all that might be open. He gave it a try but he found nothing—whatever was going on, either the bomb had cut all communication lines or—an even worse thought—the bombing was more widespread than just this city, and comms were down everywhere.

*I need to find somebody—anybody.*

But just sticking his head out the storage room door was enough to tell him that the heat was still stifling out there, too hot and dry for travel in any case. Here he had relative cool—for now at least—and food and drink. He closed the laptop down to preserve the battery—he might have need of the light later—and helped himself to more milk, then sat in the dark, thinking—wondering.

*Why me? I'm not in great physical shape, I don't know anything apart from how to run this laptop—and that's going to be useless as soon as the power goes. What else have I got?*

His gaze fell on the guitar case—he'd carried it with him out of the rubble in the subway, carried it all the way here—and he was using it as a doorstop. It was only now that he'd got curious enough to see what was inside.

He used the laptop to keep the door wedged open this time, and opened the guitar case.

That's when he found out what he was good at. There was a six-string, sunburst body, Gibson acoustic inside and it rang in welcome as he lifted it. It felt like a lover in his arms, it was still in tune despite the battering the case had taken, and the first chord felt like going home.

He had to play around the loss of the nail on his left little finger—it was too painful to press down on—but he chugged into a song as if he'd been doing it forever, and raised his voice to sing along. Without thinking, he'd started the same tune he'd heard in his head as he dug his way up into the word.

"Well who's that writin'? John the Revelator,"

The old blues echoed back at him in the small storage room, as if a chorus was raised in the song. It felt good—it felt right.

*This is who I am—this is what I do.*

He kept playing, and got as far as the second chorus before he noticed something else—it wasn't just the echo he was hearing. There were definitely voices raised alongside his, voices supplying the call back sections.

"Who's that writing?" Alfie sang—and somewhere, out in the city, coarse, deep voices rose in reply—a multitude, like a great host.

"John the Revelator."

Alfie let the last chord ring out and fade away. He sat, still cradling the guitar, listening—but once again the city had fallen quiet.

# JD – 9 Days

*Craftsbury, Vermont*

She shouted out words she didn't understand, a name she'd never heard.

"John the Revelator."

A ringing guitar chord faded away into the darkness from where she'd just come.

Margaret Calthorpe—although she didn't even know her name then—sat up in a bed that felt too hot, too damp. She had awoken suddenly, disoriented, and had no idea where she was. She didn't recognize the furniture, or the bed—she didn't recognize anything about the room, and the fact that everything seemed cast in a deep, glowing red made her think she hadn't woken at all but was still in the grip of a barely remembered nightmare.

She sat still for a while, trying to figure out where she was—who she was—and listening for any sounds from outside the room, waiting to see if she'd hear the guitar again. There was nothing except a distant rumbling, like far off thunder, and shifting changes in the depth and hue of the red glow that filled the window through the thin curtains.

"Hello?" she called out, but her voice was swallowed by the silence. She had to fight to get the bottom half of her body out of the bedclothes, and when she kicked at them she felt a warm dampness at her feet. She was initially worried it might even be blood, but it was just wet—probably sweat from night fevers. Once she was free she slid her legs over the edge, thinking to get out of bed, but as she did so a wave of nausea and dizziness hit her hard and she flopped back onto the too soft pillow.

*Well—I know something at least—I'm not in great shape.*

Her stomach grumbled, and her throat felt dry as dust. She checked the bedside table—there was no glass of water there, but there was a digital alarm radio. The display showed that it was just after 4 p.m.—no date, so it didn't help much—and when she tried the radio all she got was white static on all the bands. Once, she thought she heard something, distant voices, raised in a song she almost knew—a call and response with a deep bass voice and a woman answering. It was the name again—the Revelator—but when she scanned for it again it had gone, back into the dancing noise of the static. The static started to grate at her already frayed nerves so she turned it off and let silence fall.

The house felt empty and still—nothing moved. Even the curtains by the window hung straight down, unperturbed by any breeze.

*Surely they wouldn't have left me here alone if I had taken sick?*

"Hello?" she called again, but still got no answer, even when she waited for several minutes, hoping to hear a reply of footsteps outside the room. The dampness in the bed irritated her—it felt like sitting on a chair that had been left out in the rain.

*I can't stay here forever.*

She swung her legs out of bed, more careful this time, and gingerly put her toes on the floor—her feet—and most of her legs—were bare, and she noted she was only wearing a flimsy nightshirt, and it too felt damp and clammy. The floorboards felt warm—hot even—where she'd expected cold, but that was a minor issue. Her first priority was to see if she could stand and get out of the damp clothes.

She leaned forward, slowly, putting her weight on her toes. She felt a slight dizziness, but no nausea this time, which she took as a good sign, and tried putting the feet flat on the floorboards and pressing down.

She kept her hands on the mattress in case she should fall backward, then shifted her weight forward and rocked up and off the bed.

She stood upright, swaying slightly, waiting to see if she was going to faint—or throw up—before trying to take a step. The room threatened to spin away from her, and it was worse when she closed her eyes, but she was determined—she wasn't going back into a wet bed. She waited until she felt ready then shuffled forward.

The first step was the hardest, but the second was much easier, and by the time she reached the door she felt fine—already stronger—and all trace of the dizziness had gone. She was still hungry though, still thirsty, and when she called out again she felt the dryness rasp in her throat.

"Hello? I'm up," she shouted. But the house still stayed quiet.

There was a small pile of folded clothes on a chair by the door. She shucked off the damp nightshirt and when she tried on the flannel shirt that was on the chair, it seemed to fit perfectly—more than that, it was as if she recognized it. The blue jeans were equally snug, and after she'd fastened the leather belt she knew—she didn't know how—that this was her normal, everyday look. She found a small, thin wallet in the back pocket—a driver's license and I.D.—too dim to see until she took them over to the mirror. She compared the person in the I.D. to herself. Twenty-two, the card said, Caucasian, blonde, blue eyes. What it didn't say was that she was dried out tousled haired, and looked like she'd been dragged through a bush backwards.

*But I'm alive. And my name's Margaret Calthorpe—from Vermont.*

She said it again, out loud, but it still didn't mean much to her. At this point she was more concerned with food and drink. There was a pair of walking boots under the chair with heavy woolen socks tucked on top of them—it didn't surprise her at all that these too fit perfectly. She had to sit to tie them up, but there was no more sign of dizziness or nausea—whatever she'd been suffering from, it seemed to be passed.

She left the room, and went in search of someone who might be able to tell her what was going on.

She stepped out onto an upstairs landing. The red glow from outside was even more pronounced here, streaming in through a curtain-free window opposite the top of the stairwell. She couldn't see any landscape from her position, just clouds—but they were glowing—red and orange and black—angry, and swirling wildly. She might not remember who or where she was—but she knew enough to know this wasn't in any way natural.

The house lay quiet below her, although now that she was outside the room, she heard a distant, regular throbbing, like a motor running. She'd need to investigate that. But before trying her new strength on the stairs, she decided to check the other rooms on the landing.

The first was a bathroom and lavatory—empty, clean and smelling slightly of disinfectant. She got another look at herself in a mirror above a small wash basin, but there was still no recognition. She could have been looking at a complete stranger and been none the wiser.

The other room on the landing was another bedroom. It didn't smell of disinfectant—it smelled of something else entirely. She noticed it even as she stepped up to the door—it was rank—rank and sour, and it got much stronger as she turned the handle, swung it open and stepped into the doorway.

Two people lay on their backs on the bed. At first she thought their eyes had been gouged out to leave just black holes in their skulls, but as she got closer she saw that the sockets were filled with dried, crusted, blood. There was more blood—at the nose, ears and mouth and, judging by the state of the sheets, even more pooled below the bodies on the mattress. She didn't look too closely, but there were no visible signs of any wounds, and although the flesh on the faces looked puffy and bruised, the coloring seemed to be seeping up from beneath the skin rather than having been inflicted by any force. It looked like the two people—an older couple, one male and one female, had simply taken to bed, then bled out.

A thought struck her.

*I wonder if they were my parents?*

She studied the bodies, bending as close as she dared, but couldn't find anything to jog a memory, and she had no emotional reaction to the sight apart from sadness at seeing two people reduced to such dire straits.

*Whoever they were, there's nothing I can do for them now.*

She backed away quickly, closing the door behind her, but the odor seemed to travel with her, and she still smelled it as she descended the stairs to the lower floor.


The red light from outside took on a softer, almost pink, glow down on the lower floor, the swirling clouds sending washes of color over the floor and walls through the windows. As she reached the bottom step there was a flash, as if a light had been switched on and off again, then, many seconds later, a distant drum-roll that might—or might not—have been thunder. There was no sound of any rain on the windows—if this was a storm, it was a mighty peculiar one.

As she stepped off the stairs, she steeled herself against finding more bodies, but the place was quiet and empty save for the sound of throbbing—that was closer now, and she found the source when she discovered a door down to the basement.

She took the wooden steps carefully. They seemed sturdy enough, but she was alone in the house, and a fall now might mean her spending the rest of a very short life in a heap on the floor.

The basement filled the whole space below the main house. There was a gas generator, hooked up to the main panel to provide the house's supply. A cable modem was hooked up to a wi-fi router—the modem was currently showing itself to be offline. That was something else she knew without having to think about it.

*How can I remember that, but not remember me?*

Beyond the generator she found a hoard of boxes and plastic containers, stacked floor to ceiling—dried goods, water, medical equipment—and firearms, hung on a tool rack that covered the whole of the furthest wall. Whoever she was, she obviously came from folks that liked to be prepared.

*For all the good it did them.*

She was about to turn to head back upstairs when she stopped.

*What if I'm not really alone—what if I'm actually a prisoner here, stuck in this house against my will?*

She stepped over to the gun rack, strapped a holster into her belt at her right hip and armed herself with a Walther CCP. The small pistol felt natural in her hand, and she checked the mag and the slide without having to think about it. She found six spare magazines—already loaded—in a pouch and attached that to her belt on the opposite hip. She looked at the row of rifles, but decided against anything heavier—she might have to move fast. She patted the Walther as if it was a small pet, and when she went up to the living area she felt ready for anything that might come her way.

Now that she'd seen the basement and knew food wasn't going to be an immediate problem, she headed first for a drink. The milk in the fridge looked sour and off, but there were three plastic water bottles on the bottom shelf and when she helped herself—drinking straight from the bottle—the cold water did much to wash any dryness away from her throat. After that she looked for something to eat—there was a loaf of bread that was stale—but not inedible—and plenty of peanut butter that she slathered on thickly. She ate as if she hadn't eaten in weeks, and wondered if she'd ever, as a girl, wolfed anything down so avidly in the past. But after the sandwiches and more water, she felt much better than she had upon awakening. And now she was getting curious.

There was a small television set above the main kitchen work surface, but when she turned it on, all she got was more white static. She got more of the same from the big flat- screen system in the main sitting area, although when she tried channel seven she thought—just for a few seconds—that she heard the same song again, the one she'd caught upstairs on the radio.

*"'Well who's that writin'? John the Revelator."*

All of the channels, and there were scores of them, were the same—just static. The house had power from the generator, but no comms, a fact that she confirmed by trying the landline, then the laptop she found on the coffee table in front of the TV set. Nothing was coming in from anywhere.

This was starting to look like a bigger problem than just waking up from an illness.

A cell phone—she tried to use it, but there was no signal—a set of car keys, a pack of cigarettes and a lighter sat on the arm of the reclining chair opposite the TV.

*Are these mine? Do I smoke?*

Since she didn't have any cravings, she assumed not, but she took the keys, phone, smokes and lighter anyway, squirreling them away in the breast pockets of her shirt—until she knew the full lay of the land, it would be best not to let anything go to waste.

She did a full circuit of the lower floor before confirming to her satisfaction that there was no one else in the house. She couldn't put it off any longer—she'd been using the angry skies as an excuse to stay inside, but that wasn't getting her any answers.

She opened the front door and went out onto the porch. A blast of dry heat hit her in the face and almost had her running back inside, but the view from the doorstep held her transfixed.

The house sat in a small clearing in a dense pine forest, raised up on an outcrop above a running creek in a fenced off compound some fifty meters on the side. There was a barn to the left, a carport to the right, and a small animal enclosure past the barn. It looked like a dozen goats and twice as many chickens were lying dead on the ground. Even from the doorway she saw that they lay in red, wet, pools—they'd bled out, just like the bodies upstairs.

That spooked her—even before considering the raking, swirling sky—but what was, in a way, even worse, was the fact that the trees, even the tallest of them, seemed to be melting. They shed needles that were wet and somehow slimy, dripping goop to lie in steaming puddles under the canopy.

*I need to get out of here.*

She remembered the car keys, fished them out of her pocket, and headed for the carport. The keys fit a shiny, almost new black GM SUV that purred like a big cat and had a full tank of gas. She took just enough time to go back into the house, pack a traveling bag with clothes, and fill the SUV's trunk with as much as she could cart up out of the basement—food, water, backpack, sleeping bag, tent, camping stove, propane and a medical bag. She considered taking more weaponry, but somehow she wasn't happy with the idea of the heavier artillery. She only took a couple of extra boxes of 9mm ammo for the Walther.

Before she left she opened a gasoline container and kicked it over, spilling the contents over the basement floor. She tossed a lit rag down the steps behind her when she left, and by the time she got into the SUV and drove off, the house was a blazing pyre in her rear view mirror.

She was glad of the enclosed cab of the SUV as she went down the forest track away from the house. Green, smoking, slime dripped in thick globs on the hood and windshield, and the wipers were hard pushed to keep her view clear. She tried the car radio but just got more hissing static, and the almost expected far off sound of singing, like a choir in a wind. This time, she sang along, realizing she knew all the words—she had sang them herself at some point in her dim, forgotten past in the dark hole in her memory.

> "Well who art worthy, thousands cried holy,
> "Bound for glory, Son of our God.
>
> "Well who art worthy, thousands cried holy."
> "Bathed in the blood of the Lamb."

She was still singing as she drove off the forest track and onto a wider, two-lane blacktop. Here she was mostly free from the slimy drips and, with a clearer view ahead, made much better time.

The skies were darkening further as it approached sundown, so dark that she needed to turn on the SUV's lights. It didn't look like other road traffic was going to be a problem—she was the only thing on the road for a ten-mile stretch, all downhill until she came to the first sign of civilization—or what was left of it.

She passed her first vehicle at the town limits—an abandoned pickup on the side of the road, with the driver's side door lying open. She drove past slowly and had a look inside, but there was nobody there. The sign on the edge of town just past that said it was Jackson's Pass, elevation 1,400 feet, population 865—that didn't mean anything to her either—but it quickly became clear that whatever had struck the house up the hill had struck here just as hard.

Bodies lay dead on the gravel sidewalks, lying, unattended, in pools of dried blood. There were no birds feeding on the remains though—dead crows, starlings and sparrows lay beside the people just as dead, just as bloody. She passed a house where an older man sat on a porch in a rocking chair. For a second she thought he'd waved at her, but it was just a shadow moving across him, and when it moved on she saw the same, dark-eyed stare she was starting to recognize.

She drove into a small town square and killed the engine before rolling the window down, listening for signs of life. The sky lit up as a blue sheet of lightning washed across overhead, and the thunder followed right after, a bang that shook the SUV and set off the alarms of two sedans parked outside the police station. There was a light on inside the building. She drove over and parked alongside the wailing cars—there was no sign of anyone coming to investigate. She waited to see if anyone would, or if rain would follow the thunder, but neither came, so she got out, locked the vehicle—*papa didn't raise no idiots*—and went into the police station in search of officialdom.

She didn't find any—at least not alive.

There was the same telltale thudding of a generator running somewhere in the building below her, but as it had been up at the house, none of the communication lines in or out seemed to be working. A small TV high up on the wall in the reception area was only showing more of the hissing static. The cop behind the desk wouldn't be watching it anyway—he sat leaning back in his chair, his crotch full of blood and his eyes bleeding like heavy mascara in rain.

There were more dead cops in the squad room through the back—some of them looked like they been sitting, drinking or eating and had just died, falling head first onto the table in front of them—died and bled out and gone, just like that. Whatever had happened, it had been sudden.

She checked the whole building—five more dead cops in the offices, two secretaries behind computers, and three dead civilians—drunks by the smell of them—in the cells down below. If she'd wanted to she could have made away with any number of phones, radios—and firearms—but none of the phones worked, and she was happy enough with the Walther at her side—for now.

The quiet was getting her spooked though, and she backed out of the station quickly once she'd established that there was nobody alive.

*Now what?*

She stood at the doorway, looking around the small square. It was getting real murky and dark now—full night wasn't far off. She had two possibilities—drive on and keep searching, or hunker down until daylight. She'd almost decided to get in the SUV and keep moving when she saw a light flicker in an upper-story window above a bar—as if somebody had just opened a curtain and looked out. There it was again—definite this time—and the flickering reminded her not of an electric bulb, but of the sputtering flame of a candle.

*There's somebody else alive.*

She headed, almost running, across to the bar, suddenly aware of just how much she needed to find another person to talk to.

It was almost too dark to see inside the bar itself—no generator here—but there was just enough light for her to make out a set of stairs going up at the left of the main door. She put one hand on her pistol and went up them slowly, her caution getting the better of her enthusiasm—just because there was somebody here, it didn't mean they were necessarily friendly.

Once she reached the top hallway, it was obvious which room she was looking for—orange-yellow flickering showed below the door. She padded up to it softly, and rapped twice, with the knuckles of her free hand.

"Hello? Is anybody there? Please? It's Margaret Calthorpe—from up the hill? I'm looking for somebody to tell me what's going on here."

She got a pained moan in reply. She turned the handle, pushed the door open, and stepped inside—her gun hand was now curled around the grip of the Walther, ready to draw at the slightest provocation—but she wasn't going to need it. There was only one person in the room—and they weren't any threat.

An old woman sat in a chair by the window. The only lights were a flickering candle on a table beside her, and the red tip of a cigarette, glowing as she puffed. She was wrapped up in swathes of heavy woolen blankets, only her head of wispy hair, her pale, thin face, and the dry, almost skeletal hand holding the cigarette showing. When she spoke her voice was whispered and almost a croak.

"Meg? Little Meg Calthorpe? Is that really you? I haven't seen you since high school. My Lord, how you've grown." She sobbed, and tears ran down the deep wrinkles by her eyes. "I thought I was the last one—but look at you—you're not even sick—are you?"

Meg—at least she had a proper name now—stepped into the room and closed the door behind her. There was another chair on the opposite side of the table so she went over and sat down.

"So, you know me?" she said.

The old woman started to laugh but it quickly turned into a cough that brought bubbles of blood to her lips. She didn't do anything to wipe them away—just kept smoking.

"Know you? Of course I know you, gal. I taught you your letters—taught your Ma too. How is Joanna—is she as well as you?"

Meg remembered the two bodies back in the house on the hill—she'd already guessed they were her parents even before she burned them, and the house, to the ground—but that wasn't anything she wanted to tell a stranger. She kept quiet—she needed answers, not questions. But the old lady didn't seem in any hurry to talk. She sat, puffing on her cigarette.

Seeing her smoking made Meg realize something else—she fancied a smoke of her own. She got the packet out of her shirt pocket and lit up before putting the pack and lighter away again. The first draw told her it was something else she did automatically—something she'd enjoyed, back in the forgotten past. It was time to start filling in some of those blanks in her memory.

"I was sick," Meg said, finally answering the old lady's first question. "I think I got better—at least, I feel better."

The old lady laughed again.

"Ain't nobody getting better from this, darling," she said. "The Lord is calling his children home—and I'm just about ready to go."

She did indeed look like she was nearly ready to keel over, but Meg thought it would be impolite to point that out just then. She went on with trying to get answers.

"Why isn't there anyone here helping? Where's the emergency rescue crews?"

The old woman laughed again.

"Those that are alive—and I doubt there's many—are too busy keeping that way themselves. Ain't you heard, dear? The Ruskies are bombing the shit out of everything, the sickness is washing over the land like a flood and the whole damned world's going to hell in a handbasket. It's the big one—Armageddon—Ragnarok—Judgement Day—whatever way you call it, it's over—the whole kit and caboodle—gone and washed in the Blood of the Lamb. At least that's what that John fella was saying on the TV, right before the power—and everything else—went away."

"John?"

"You must have seen him—he was on everywhere just before everything went to shit. The marine that walked out of the desert with the angel's words in his head?"

Meg kept quiet again—she didn't remember anything of what the world was like before she woke just hours before—she had nothing to compare it with. She knew things felt wrong—but beyond that, there was just darkness. Then she remembered something else—a fragment of the song she'd heard through the static that the old lady had just repeated.

"Bathed in the blood of the lamb."

With the memory, came another—herself, singing, at the top of her voice, while a man—her father, presumably—sat on the porch, swigging from a bottle and playing banjo.

"John the Revelator, great advocator, get's 'em on the battle of Zion."

"The Revelator," she said. "What does that mean?"

The old woman coughed—more blood—a lot more blood—before answering.

"So you do know of him then?"

"No—I've just heard the name somewhere."

"I told you, gal—it's that John fella—he's brought the word of the Lord among us—it's the time that was foretold."

"I don't understand," Meg replied.

The old woman coughed again, and seemed to deflate, falling away inside the blankets she had wrapped around her. More blood flowed. Meg thought she was dead and gone, but her head came up again—slowly—as if it was a great strain.

"You don't understand," the old woman said—but now it didn't sound like her at all—it sounded deeper, coarser, a different voice entirely, and her eyes were set deep in the flickering shadows cast by the candle. "But you will, Meg Calthorpe—before we are done, you will understand only too well."

The blankets fell away from the body, falling to the floor with a wet thud. There was almost nothing underneath them but soft, bloody, pulp with white—too white—bone showing in places. The dark eyes looked straight at Meg and the bloody mouth rose in a smile.

"Bathed in the blood of the Lamb."

The wet, red, thing started to rise up out of the chair. It knocked the table over, and the candle sputtered, twice and went out. All Meg saw was a darker shadow, looming toward her, singing now.

> *"Daughter of Zion, Judah the Lion, "He*
> *redeemeth, and bought me with his blood."*

Instinct took over—she had the Walther out and in her hand before she even knew she'd done it, and put three quick shots into the darkest of the shadows—two in the body, one in the head—*just to be sure.*

Then she was moving, stumbling away to where she knew the door to be, and out into the corridor and down the stairs into almost pitch darkness and, definitely running now, across the square to the SUV. She had a bad moment when she couldn't find the keys in her pocket but then she had them, she leaped into the driver's seat and roared, wheels spinning, out of the town square, through quiet streets, and onto the highway—heading south.

The road was clear—easy driving with the headlights on—but no matter how fast she pushed it, the singing kept following her. She kept seeing in her mind's eye the wet black shadow that had blown apart when she put the rounds in it—the shadow that kept singing, even as it fell to the floor in wet, bloody pieces.

> *"Daughter of Zion, Judah the Lion, "He*
> *redeemeth, and bought me with his blood."*

# JD – 9 Days

*Under the East Wing, The White House*

Deep under the East Wing, the PEOC was packed far beyond the capacity it had been built for. The President, Chiefs of Staff, Vice-President, Secret Service agents, joint service military officers, non-commissioned officers, staffers, two bewildered newsmen—and John, sitting between the President and VP at the big table while they watched the world burn and fall in glorious Technicolor on the big screens.

John hadn't spoken since they'd been rushed down from the meeting on the lawn the previous day. He'd accepted coffee and sandwiches when offered, and would have answered any questions—if anybody had asked him. But the events unfolding in the outside world seemed just too sudden—and too big—for even these—supposedly—rulers of the free world to comprehend. There had been arguments, dissension, tears and shouting—mostly from the staff. The President himself had been almost as quiet as John, although when decisions had been needed, he'd made them calmly and resolutely.

The VP was far from calm—and far from happy, and was now making his feelings known to anyone there that would listen.

"What is this guy doing here anyway, Frank?" he said, addressing the President. "He started all this shit with his doom mongering and rabble rousing. As far as I'm concerned this mess is all his fault—just get one of our team to shoot him—or give me a gun and I'll do it myself."

The President didn't take his eyes off the main screen. And he didn't reply to the VP. He waved a hand at the TV, then turned to John. Finally, somebody asked him the questions he'd been waiting for.

"Is this what you expected?"

The scene showed Central London from above. A wave of water a hundred feet high washed westward up the Thames. The glittering spires of the new financial district tumbled and fell before the wave moved on, looming even higher than the old Tower Bridge, which crumbled away beneath it. It took out all the bridges in turn as it passed—the Gherkin and the Nat West Tower stood against it—for a matter of seconds, before they too succumbed. St Paul's Cathedral, the dome that had survived the Nazi bombing, was not able to withstand this, and Wren's great work was lost to what was left of history.

The wave didn't care. It moved on, taking out the Millennium Eye and Westminster Bridge and sending Big Ben tumbling into a mass of foaming debris that swept the Houses of Parliament away like sand. The wave finally made off into the distance to commit further carnage upstream, but the camera—a helicopter shot—stayed static showing Whitehall and Trafalgar Square—or what was left of it. Admiral Nelson stood on top of his column, water lapping at his toes, once more looking out, not over a city, but at a sea.

John smiled.

"I expected nothing, Mr. President. I merely pass on the Word as it was given. It is for others to make of it what they will."

"See, that's exactly the kind of BS I'd expect from a con man," the VP said, then went quiet—as did everybody at the table—when the scene changed again on screen.

Home turf this time—but U.S. cities weren't faring any better than London. Chicago had burned, San Francisco and

L.A. had fallen. The nuked cities of Boston, New York and Denver were burned out, smoking, ruins. Others still stood, but had gone dark with no news coming out of them—there were rumors—unsubstantiated as of yet—of plague up and down the Eastern Seaboard. New Orleans was under ten feet of water, as was Miami. Seattle, Portland and, up in Canada, Vancouver were clogged, feet deep in thick, choking ash from several different volcanoes.

That much they all knew already—this scene was something new again—and closer to home. It looked like it was coming from a drone, flying over D.C. just as the sun went down—and it looked like there was nobody alive in the city. Much of the area was burning or already burnt, but they hadn't been bombed—yet. The deaths were coming from another direction entirely. Bodies littered the streets—even on the lawn of the White House above them—and when the drone zoomed in, it was to show that they all lay in pools of still-spreading blood. The drone circled the Washington Monument—more bodies, more death—the same on the steps of the Lincoln Memorial. A plane had crashed in Delaware, the fuselage, tail end up, still burning. There was no sign of any emergency crews—or of anyone living at all—anywhere in the city.

"How long can we last down here?" the President asked.

One of the joint-service Colonels answered.

"A month at least, sir, if the air filters hold and there are no more attacks. We've got plenty of rations. But it's going to be real cozy—and probably a bit rank."

"Can we broadcast to the nation?"

"Yes, sir—if there's anyone out there who can still receive it."

"And NORAD?"

"Still online—and we're at Defcon 3, ready to go given the order, sir."

The President rubbed at his forehead.

"We could launch—strike back—but what good would that do us? Hell—I don't even know if there's anybody left out there to strike back at."

Nobody answered—nobody had an answer—then John spoke. His voice was soft, but it carried around the table.

"And when he had opened the second seal, I heard the second beast say, come and see. And there went out another horse that was red: and power was given to him that sat thereon to take peace from the Earth and that they should kill one another: and there was given unto him a great sword."

The PEOC fell quiet. The VP looked about fit to burst, but it was the President who broke the silence.

"Are the Russians the red horseman? And the nukes are his sword? Is that what you're saying?"

John merely smiled, and the VP couldn't contain himself. "For God's sake, Frank—don't listen to this bullshit any more—I know you've got your faith—we all have—but this is the whole human race we're talking about here—the fate of the planet."

"It is for God's sake that we do it," the President said softly. "This is a holy war now—and there can be only one winner."

He turned to the officer behind him.

"Pass me that briefcase, son—it's time."

The missiles flew minutes later—more stars in the sky, more terrible swift swords where they hit—Moscow, Baltic sea ports, Havana, Beijing, all blossomed in mushroom clouds. Many other places were also hit—places with no names, places where silos—some already empty—had sat for decades waiting for this day to come, waiting to fulfil the purpose for which they'd been built.

The VP sat at the table with his head in his hands. He looked up, tears running down his cheeks.

"Do you know what you've just done, Frank? You've read the briefings—five years of winter, lifetimes of genetic defects, mass starvation and plagues among the survivors—and for what? For God? If he's watching this, I hope he's fucking happy."

The President wept—his tears ran red as his eyes filled with blood. The VP's tears also turned red, then he slumped forward, and hit the table with a wet thud.

All around the room there were moist, wet sounds as bodies became nothing more than wet bags of blood and bone.

John, the Revelator, sat in his seat, untouched—still smiling.

"And there went out another horse that was red."

# JD – 8 Days

*New York*

Alfie came awake with a start, unaware that he'd even been asleep. The Gibson rang as it slid off his lap to hit the floor, and he had to pat around with his hands to find it again—it was pitch black, with not even a hint of light anywhere. He tried to remember which way he'd been facing when he'd dozed off.

The only sounds were of his own making as he shuffled across the storage room floor, otherwise, he might have thought he'd been struck both blind and deaf. But after finding the guitar safely—it rang again at his touch, as if welcoming him—he slid on his rear end over to the doorway and was relieved to find the laptop still wedged, holding the door open. A warm breeze from beyond reassured him that at least he wasn't about to suffocate.

Thirty seconds later he had light again as the laptop booted up—but he knew the battery wouldn't last too long.

*And I can't stay in here forever.*

He stepped out of the storage room and made a quick tour of the coffee shop. His luck was in—there was a rucksack on the floor under the same table where he found the laptop. By the time he'd gone back to the larder and filled that with sandwiches, cookies and bottled water, thin light was coming in through the main store doorway—Alfie was amazed to see that, despite his situation, he'd somehow managed to sleep the whole night away.

And now that he'd thought of moving on, he could think of nothing else, and the coffee shop began to feel too small, too dark—he jumped at every shift in the shadows in the corners.

*Time to go.*

With a bit of fiddling with straps and buckles he was able to get both the rucksack and guitar case strapped across his back. He left the laptop behind—the battery was almost gone now, and it didn't look like there was much chance of the power returning any time soon.

He took another bottle of water to carry with him, went through the shop, stepped over the bodies in the doorway and headed back out into the silent ruin of the city.


The dry, stifling heat of the previous day had dissipated to a degree—it no longer hurt to breathe, and there was no need to cover his mouth. He still didn't have any clue at all as to where he was going—and the news items he'd read on the laptop hadn't helped. If the situation was as grave as had been made out, there might not be too many places he *could* go for a very long time. But for Alfie, this felt like his first few hours alive on the planet—he had a lot to catch up on—a lot to learn.

The first thing he noticed on stepping out of the coffee shop was that the dust and ash had settled since the evening before—it wasn't so deep now, but it was firmer, more compacted and harder to walk through at any great pace.

Although the darkness had retreated, the sun itself was somewhere lost behind swirling, angry clouds of orange and red and black that looked almost low enough overhead to reach up and touch. Occasionally lightning would fork across the sky, but for now at least, there was no close thunder—and thankfully, no rain. If the thick carpet of ash and dust underfoot got damp, it would be like walking though wet clay.

Alfie looked back the way he'd come the day before—there was a single set of tracks in the ash, the ones he had made on his way down the road—and no indication that anyone else had come along since then. He looked ahead, and saw that the ash was smooth and flat—virgin—the surface only broken when he stood on it. If there was any one else left alive in what was left of the city, they were keeping very quiet about it.

He walked.

All around him was evidence that the city had been going about its business when it had been struck—there appeared to have been no emergency preparations, no attempts at escape. A school bus sat in the road—it had been full, Alfie could see the charred, black remains, but didn't venture too close. To his left was a street vendor's hot dog stand, lying on its side with two more burned bodies below it. There were more bodies in the cars he passed, more bodies lying in gutters—bodies everywhere he looked. He was grateful when he reached an area where the ash had drifted thicker. Although it was more difficult to push through, everything looked softer, rounder—less like death. The ash seemed to muffle and deaden all sound, and Alfie felt like he might be the only living thing left in the whole city—the whole world.

The silence felt like a weight on his shoulders, the thick ash making every step a chore. He started to sing, keeping time with his steps, making it into a march.

> "Well who's that writin'? John the Revelator,
> "Who's that writin'? John the Revelator."

At first he sang softly, almost under his breath, but once he realized there was no one but him to take note, he became more confident, bellowing out the words. He began to enjoy himself—so much so that he stopped noticing the drudgery of the walk, lost in the song and the rhythm—the music made its magic, and took him along with it, dancing.

He was so gone in the song that at first he didn't notice that someone had joined in on the call and response.

"Tell me what's John writin'?"

The answer came from somewhere ahead of him, and at first he thought it might be a phantom voice in his mind, trying to trick himself into thinking he wasn't completely alone.

"Ask the Revelator."

He sung the next line louder.

"What's John writin'?"

The reply came back louder still—and it definitely wasn't just in his head—it came from somewhere ahead and to his right, where there was what remained of an intersection.

"Ask the Revelator."

He sang again. "What's John writin'?"

The reply was very close now.

"Ask the Revelator."

He came to the corner and looked to his right. They sang the final line of the chorus together.

"A book of the seven seals."

There were seven of them—six had their backs to Alfie, all of them kneeling in the ash, oblivious to the dirt on their clothes. They looked like they had been office workers, maybe even executives—six men, all of them well fed, all wearing business suits. The seventh stood over them, facing were they sat, his hands outstretched as if bestowing a blessing. He looked up as Alfie rounded the corner—and Alfie couldn't quite stifle the gasp at the sight.

He was a tall white man, a good foot taller than Alfie himself, and thin with it, almost painfully so. He wore a black wool suit that was covered in ash and looked ragged, torn and even burnt in places. Below that he had a black vest—and the dog collar—strangely pure and clean and white—of a preacher. A long weeping sore—a burn by the look of it—ran all the way from scalp to chin on the left side of his face, and most of his almost pure white hair had been burned away. One of the outstretched hands that he held above the others was little more than a charred black ball of flesh run through with deep, red weeping cracks. The left eye was pale and milky, the other a deep piercing blue that seemed to see right inside Alfie's head.

"Greetings, brother," the man said. He was old—past seventy by Alfie's guess, and by rights should be troubled by his wounds—but he smiled as he beckoned Alfie forward. "Any friend of John's is welcome in the flock."

Alfie might be new to this world, but he knew better than to plead ignorance at that point. These were the first other people he'd seen—and surely they would know more than he did?

*That won't be difficult.*

The six kneeling figures did not move; not one of them acknowledged Alfie's presence as he stepped closer. All of a sudden he felt cold, a chill settling in his spine. He may well be new to the world, but it seemed that his bullshit detector worked well enough. The guitar rang in its case at his back to confirm the point.

The tall man saw Alfie's hesitation.

"Do not fear, brother," he said. "We are all lambs here."

The preacher raised his hands high over his head and bellowed, at the top of his voice.

"And it has cometh to pass; the sun hath gone in, and thick darkness hath covered the land, and lo—the Lord has sent a furnace of smoke, and a lamp of fire, which hath passed over between the places. Fallen, fallen is Babylon."

There was a gleam in the single blue eye that gave Alfie pause, and he stopped moving forward before he reached the semi-circle of kneeling figures. The preacher noticed that Alfie had stopped.

"Remember Lot's wife," the preacher said. "Do not let her sin be yours—for the Lord sees all, even in these times of tribulation."

As if to punctuate the remark, a bolt of lightning cracked in the distance—and now there was definitely thunder, a boom that sounded like the pounding of a huge drum. Now the rain came, heavy, thudding drops at first that left a spattering of holes in the ash. A drop fell on the kneeling figure nearest to Alfie—and went right through it, shoulder to hip. As more drops hit, the figures below him fell apart beneath the rain, eroding away like castles on a shore when the waves came in.

The kneeling figures were little more than piles of ash themselves.

The preacher raised his head, opened his mouth, and welcomed the rain inside him—if it was even rain at all, for it was red—red as blood—washing down the old man's cheeks, filling his eyes as he turned to look at Alfie again.

"We know you, Alfred Collinson. We know all about you. Come, join us—be washed in the blood of the Lamb."

The preacher coughed, and red watery liquid ran down his chin and over the vest—the dog collar wasn't white any longer, but was turning—pink, red—crimson, and wet.

The rain got heavier—Alfie knew he'd have to find shelter and get off the streets—the ground underfoot was going to be like molasses in a matter of minutes. But he was afraid to break away from the preacher's stare—the cold feeling sat in the pit of his stomach, like a block of ice.

"And you know us, don't you, Alfie?" the preacher said, reaching out the burned remains of his mangled hand as the six figures below finally succumbed and collapsed completely into the ash. "We can tell you all you need to know—all you have forgotten—all you have to do is take my hand."

The cold in Alfie's gut didn't lessen—and he wasn't in the slightest tempted by the offer. But he still didn't want to break his lock on the preacher's stare—his gut might be cold, but it also told him that if he ran right now, he'd be in trouble.

"You've got nothing I need," he said, trying to keep a tremor out of his voice.

The preacher laughed, a deep, gurgle of a thing that came out red and wet and sent more watery blood washing down his chin. He still had his burnt, mangled, hand outstretched. He made a fist with what was left of it, and squeezed. Thick drops of blood fell into the ash on top of the collapsed, kneeling figures—and the ash started to move, as if the blood was feeding something just below the surface.

"Washed in the blood of the lamb," the preacher said, smiled, and reached forward toward Alfie.

Alfie's will finally cracked. He turned, intending to flee. The preacher reached out and grabbed at him, but Alfie had turned so quickly that the neck of the guitar case swung around and smacked the old man on the side of the head, right over the weeping sore.

Where the case struck, fresh flame bloomed, a yellow, golden, fire that raged and ravaged up and down the preacher's body. He fell to his knees, joining what was left of his flock. His head came up, just once before the flame took him completely.

"We know you, Alfred Collinson. We know all about you. Remember what we promised—we will be waiting for you down the line a way for your answer."

Those were the preacher's last words. He fell forward onto his face and burned quickly down to join the rest then was washed away in the rain, leaving Alfie standing, alone again, in the middle of a street that was rapidly turning into thick wet clay.

He kicked at the ground where the preacher and his flock had been.

"You have nothing to teach me," he whispered, then turned and ran for what little shelter he could find.

# JD – 8 Days

*Vermont*

Meg hadn't slept. She'd driven south—thirty miles and more along the two-lane highway in the dark, no lights showing anywhere on either side of the road the whole way. She had not passed another vehicle and had the road to herself, so driving wasn't as taxing as it might have been. But she had to stop when lightning flashed overhead, a thunderclap shook the SUV and suddenly there were sheets of water flooding the view, so much rain that the wipers couldn't handle it. She slowed—trying hard to fight off the urge to hit the brakes—and parked carefully, hugging the gravel at the roadside, hoping that even now there wasn't a distracted trucker barreling along blindly, waiting to plow her down to a pile of mangled metal and crushed flesh.

The rain showed no sign of abating—but there was no sign of any other traffic either, and she seemed safe enough—for now. She had a smoke to see if it was a passing shower, but there was another thunderclap, even louder than the last one, and the rain pelted even harder against the roof and windows, like a manic drummer.

All she could do was wait the storm out. She cleaned the Walther and refilled the magazine from her ammo supply. She climbed and squeezed her way to the back of the SUV and got into the trunk to find some food, cursing herself for not thinking to move some up front in the first place. She had some beef jerky and cookies, washed them down with water, and then had another smoke—all the time trying not to think about the dark, wet, thing she'd had to shoot in the room above the bar. One minute it had been an old woman talking to her—the next—well, she didn't know what it had been—but it certainly hadn't felt right. She pushed the thought away again.

It wasn't hard to keep her mind off it—the storm was more than enough distraction in itself. Lightning cracked and crackled all across the sky, thunderclaps rocked the SUV from side to side and the rain kept coming—sheets and sheets of it. She couldn't see much of anything at all outside apart from the darker shadow of the tree line to her left—and that seemed to be shrinking, getting smaller—as if the storm was washing away the trees themselves.

At one point the whole vehicle lurched, almost six inches toward the gravel, but it stayed in the roadside, and when she remembered to breathe again they were still on the level. If she could have been sure that the road would stay as quiet as it had been, she might have taken a chance and driven further into the road itself to park. But the thought of a sleepy trucker—or one with blood in his eyes—made her stay right where she was.

She tried the radio again, hoping that, with the passage of time since her last attempt, someone—anyone—might be back on air. But there was only the hissing static—and thankfully this time there was no singing in it—she didn't think she could take any more weirdness in one night.

It was as she was turning off the radio that she spotted a pile of CDs in the well between the seats. It only took her a minute or so to figure out how to slip a disc into the machine and set the controls. She sat, reclined as far as the seat would allow, for hours, smoking and listening to tunes she didn't ever remember hearing before, from artists she didn't know— Bruce Springsteen, Neil Young, John Mellencamp, Lucinda Williams and others. She wondered if the discs were hers, but looking at the dates on the boxes, she guessed they'd belonged to the owners of the SUV—her parents. That got her thinking again about what the old woman in the hotel room had talked to her about, and she didn't want to go there—not here, in the dark, alone in a storm. She lit another cigarette, turned Bruce Springsteen up loud, and let him and his band wash everything—even the storm—away for a while.

It was getting lighter in the eastern sky before the storm abated, and by then Meg badly needed to pee. As the sky lightened, the rain slowed, and finally stopped, so she took the chance to get out of the SUV. She stepped down, stretched her back—and stood, open-mouthed, gaping at the scene to the left of the road.

Where there had been a vast tract of pine forest the night before, there was now only dead trunks, naked, dripping, branches and stumps—all of the foliage—and most of the bark—had been stripped from the trees. The result—a green, viscous goop lay in thick steaming puddles all around.

Whatever had attacked the trees, it had also gotten to the SUV—the paint job was ruined—melting off in places and completely bare in others, all the way to the base metal, giving the vehicle a dappled, patchwork look. The rear wiper was melted clean away, and the front ones were tacky to the touch, like overheated plastic.

Her first instinct was to get back in and drive off as fast as she could manage—but she still needed to pee. She wasn't about to go anywhere near that green goop though. She dropped her pants and crouched at the SUV's open door—it didn't appear that privacy was a problem she had to worry about. But now that she was lower and closer to the ground, she saw that the damage to the SUV was worse than she'd thought. The rain—acid—whatever it had been—had started to eat into the big tires, which looked as if they'd been lightly run over with a blowtorch. They still looked shiny and wet too, and although she wanted to inspect the damage, she wasn't about to get her fingers anywhere close to it. She'd just have to trust her luck and get as far as she could on them.

She cleaned herself up, got back in the SUV and started the engine—it caught on the first time, and sounded okay. There was a definite tug and drag from the tires as she started up—she had to fight a continual drift to the left—and she kept her speed well below fifty—if a tire blew out on her, she wanted to be able to control her stop.

At least there was still no traffic on the road, and the rain kept away. The clouds still roiled, dark and red and heavy overhead, but her view was clear, and she tried to concentrate on the road, and not on the carnage that had been brought to the forests on either side. After a few miles she even relaxed enough to take a hand off the wheel to light a smoke.

But just when she thought she'd got off relatively easily, the front driver's side tire went soft and started to flap, giving the SUV a lopsided lurch to that side that she had to fight against the wheel to correct. After that it was just a matter of time. She did two more, slow, miles before the other front tire went, then ground metal for a mile more until the whole front end fell forward onto the highway, the brakes gave completely and she had to coast and hope. They slid, almost side on, down a small hill for fifty yards or more, veering left all the way, and Meg was ready to throw the door open and jump out as they got closer and closer to a roadside ditch. But it didn't come to that. The SUV squealed to a grinding halt just a foot away from a steep drop off.

Meg opened the door carefully and checked out her side—she had just enough room to get out if she was careful. One thing was for sure—the SUV wasn't going any further—she was going to be walking from now on.

She retrieved what she could from the trunk, packing a large backpack with underclothes, jerky and snacks, water, ammo and a small medical bag, adding the rolled tent and camping stove to the buckles at the bottom and belting it around her waist after shucking herself into it. It was a heavy load, so she made sure none of the straps were going to chafe—she had no idea how long she was going to have to carry it—or how long she'd be able to, but she'd gone camping in these hills carrying similar weights before; she knew her limits

Then it was just a matter of checking she'd got everything she thought she'd need—smokes and lighter went back in the breast pocket beside the cell phone she'd picked up earlier, and she had the Walther snug at her hip. She was leaving enough food behind to feed her for a couple of weeks, but that couldn't be helped—she needed to move.

*And if it rains again now like it did before, hunger is going to be the least of my worries.*

Without a look back, she set her gaze on the highway and started walking.

It took her a few minutes to find her stride and balance the extra weight of the backpack, but as she walked she knew something else— this too was something she'd done before—something she'd normally enjoy—a country road, the wind on her face and the great outdoors. Only now, there was little that appeared great about it.

The breeze was warm and smelled a tang like malt vinegar, too much vinegar. Last night's storm had reduced the forest to strangely rounded shapes—stumps, trunks and branches all partially molten. The green slime covered what remained of the undergrowth, and was still steaming vapors into the air—Meg guessed that was where the nasty tang was coming from. Suddenly the green reminded her of vomit, and she felt gorge rise in her throat. She tried to look elsewhere—anywhere she wouldn't see that sickly green.

Looking up at the sky didn't improve the view—the low swirling clouds were angry and swollen and there was still the occasional flash of light in the sky, and the rumble—thankfully far off—of thunder. She crested her first small rise in the road and looked over the top, hoping for a clearer view, but it was only more blasted pines and steaming green goop as far as she was able to see ahead of her. She tried to remember if she'd passed a turning in the last few miles, another road she might take to get out of the forest quicker, but nothing came to mind. There was nothing for it but to keep on keeping on, and hope for the best.

Meg kept up a good pace—finding shelter was her top priority for the time being. It was dry, for now, but she didn't trust it to stay that way forever. She had a tent on the backpack, sure, but seeing what the rain had done to the trees and the SUV, she didn't fancy her chances in it under canvas.

After a couple more miles of mostly downhill, she hit a long stretch that snaked up along the side of a valley, and she had to put more effort into it, so much so that when she reached the top, she had to stop for water and some refueling. A chocolate bar from the pack did much to make her feel better, and she lit another smoke as she had a look over the crest of the hill. This time, being a lot higher up, she could see much further.

The land fell away to a flatter plain below—but if there was any civilization down there, it wasn't showing itself. There were more of the strangely melted trees, more glowing green goop everywhere giving off acrid, greasy vapors that danced in the air like hot oil on a skillet. In the middle distance—five miles at a guess—there was what looked to be a small town—it was hard to tell in the shimmer—but there was no chimney smoke, no traffic on the road between here and there, and no sign of anything alive but Meg herself. A breeze got up and the shimmer dissipated for a few seconds to where she was able to get a clearer view of the town. She still couldn't see any traffic, and there was a long goods train—forty carriages and more—away to the east. It had, at one time, been heading for a range of low hills, but now it was stationary. She listened, hoping to hear a long, low whistle to tell her that its condition wasn't permanent, but there was nothing—just the distant drums of more thunder.

But there was a town down there—there were houses—and where there were houses, there would be shelter. Besides, by the time she got there she'd be needing more rest—and more smokes.

She hefted the pack on her back again, and headed downhill. She had some hope now, though not much of it.

*But it's a start.*


The road was just as winding on the way down as the way up had been, snaking along the side of the valley and only descending slowly. Just as she thought she must be due a steeper downhill section toward the town she'd seen, she turned a corner, and was on top of a makeshift roadblock before she had time to hide.

Three battered pickups blocked the whole width of the highway. Five men—all barely older than Meg—sat on the bed of the middle truck, smoking, drinking beer, and passing a bottle of rye between them. Meg started to step to one side of the road, hoping she wouldn't be noticed until she'd passed them and could make a run for it, but she didn't want to go anywhere near the green goop—and besides, it was far too late for running. She'd been spotted.

"Well, hello, gal," one of the men said. He appeared to be the youngest of them. He was certainly the least pale, and was better dressed than the others, in almost clean denims, Cuban-heeled boots and a red-checked flannel shirt. His heels click-clacked on the road as he jumped down out of the pickup—Meg saw a wince on his face, as if it had given him pain, and he was hobbling, walking like a man more than twice his age as he moved toward her. "Where might you be going?"

He held his hands out, showing her he wasn't armed. She wasn't re-assured in the slightest.

"I don't want any trouble," Meg said. She stopped walking and wait-ed. She kept her hand away from the Walther—for now—there was no sign that any of the men on the pickup were packing, but she didn't know what they might have on the floor at their feet out of her sight.

The man took another step toward her.

"That's close enough," she said.

"Not by a long way," he replied. "I aim to get *real* close to you, pretty lady."

A second man got down out of the pickup—even slower and more carefully than the first, climbing off the back end rather than jumping. He was pale and drawn—obviously in pain, his eyes hidden in dark shadows, and a baseball cap pulled down to his ears. His hands were bandaged, but blood—green tinged blood—seeped through in several places. It looked like Meg's SUV hadn't been the only thing caught out in the storm the night before. This man stepped away from the pickup toward Meg, but moving very slowly, as if the pain was too much for him. There was something far wrong with this one's movements, something almost fluttery, insect like—it looked like madness, and reminded her of the red, wet thing in the hotel again. Her hand crept closer to the butt of the Walther.

*They're never going to let me pass—I'm just meat to them.*

"I asked you once already," the first guy said—he was taller than the other, bigger too. "Where are you going, missy?"

*I'll take him first.*

Once she'd had that though, the rest followed quickly. She took note of where everyone in the situation was in relation to her, picked out the weakest members of her opposition, and checked her footing wouldn't be fouled in the direction she wanted to move.

The man kept coming. His right hand went round behind his back.

*He's got a weapon there.*

Her instincts saved her life. She drew the Walther at the same moment as one of the men still in the pickup went for a rifle. She dodged right so that the younger man between them blocked the shooter's aim. She'd been right about the weapon too—the first one had a knife— long and shiny—in his hand when he brought it back in view. She fired twice—the first shot took out the knife-wielding guy, hitting him just above the nose and sending him falling away to one side. That gave her a clear view of the shooter in the pickup—he hadn't expected her to be armed, had been surprised, and hesitated over his own shot. That was all the time Meg needed—her second shot took him in the chest. She ignored the other guy on the road, the one who'd been slow to get out of the truck—he was looking at the fallen body of the first man she'd shot in bewilderment.

The other two in the pickup bent, reaching for weapons, so she stepped up beside the side of the truck and put them down—a shot each to stop them, another to make them stay down. The man who'd gone for the rifle looked up at her. She'd missed his heart but caught a lung, and blood bubbled at his lips.

"Don't," he said.

But she did—she put a bullet between his eyes and turned around.

She'd just put down four men without thinking about it and with about as much effort as she'd put into making a sandwich.

*Looks like I've found something else I'm good at.*

The fifth was still standing in the road, still staring in bewilderment at the body on the ground. He appeared to be in shock—or so she thought. But when she turned to check on him, his head came up and he looked at her from wet eyes, bleeding red runnels down his cheeks. He spoke, gurgling wetly, a gravelly, deep-throated sound, words she'd heard last night, back in the room above the bar.

"*Daughter of Zion, Judah the Lion,*

"*He redeemeth, and bought me with his blood.*"

He laughed, and more blood came out of his mouth before he spoke again.

"You've been a bad girl, haven't you, Meg. Bad girls don't get to go to Heaven—bad girls go straight to the hot place."

"Don't come any closer," Meg said, and raised the Walther. She'd fired seven shots already, and had racked the first one into the chamber before the shooting started—there was only one shot left in the pistol—but one was all she'd need.

"What are you going to do, Meg?" the man said, and took a step toward her. "Shoot me like you shot the old lady? And what about these poor fuckers—what harm did they do you? They were just having a drink and a smoke until you came along. Or maybe you'd like to burn me—burn me like you did with your Ma and Pa—would you like that Meg? Would you?"

He coughed again, and blood poured from his mouth He cupped it in his hands and drank it back down again. His mouth and chin gleamed red as he looked up.

"He redeemeth, and bought me with his blood."

Meg stepped back, not allowing him to get too close. She kept the Walther pointed at his face.

"You can walk away, right now—just let me pass in peace."

"Why?" the man said, taking another step forward.

"There is nowhere for you to go, Meg—nothing more to be seen than you have seen already. All things must pass—and your time is up."

"My time has just started," she replied. "I'm not going anywhere."

He was almost in reaching distance again. Blood poured from mouth, nose, ears and eyes, a river of it—far too much of it.

"We're all going somewhere," he said. "And we'll all go together when we go."

Meg took another step back.

"That's it—no more dancing. Either you stop there, or I'll do it for you."

Her finger tightened on the trigger as he smiled, and spat out a thick glob of blood at her feet.

"We'll be waiting for you, Meg—just down the road a way.

We'll be waiting."

Before she took her shot the man collapsed into a wet heap on the road, falling in on himself as if a plug had been pulled to let his innards drain away. Soon there was little but his face and the smile left.

"He redeemeth, and bought me with his blood."

She put her last bullet between his teeth.

She felt surprisingly calm as she clipped a fresh mag into the Walther then lit up a smoke. The killings didn't reach her at any emotional level—she saw them in the same way as they'd obviously seen her—meat—rancid meat at that, not fit for anything but to be discarded. And she hadn't been spooked like she had been back with the old lady—in daylight, with clear lines of sight and plenty of space in which to move, this was routine, a job that had to be done to get her where she wanted to go.

And now she had another job to do. She couldn't leave this mess for anyone else to find. She manhandled the dead man with the hole in his head, lifting him into the back of the pickup with the other three. There wasn't enough left of the fifth to fill a bucket so she left the remains on the road—he was already rendered down to little more than a pool of wet, red clothes and blood.

Once she'd checked there was nothing worth salvaging save more smokes and half a bottle of JD, she checked the pickups—they'd all been out in the storm, and all three suffered from the same problem she'd had with her SUV—the tires were almost completely melted away. She tried the radios in all three too—with the same result as she'd had earlier—there was nothing but hissing static on any of the channels

One at a time she drove the pickups to the roadside and stepped out to let them roll, over the edge and down into what was left of the forest. They disappeared somewhere down a gully, lost in the shimmer raised by disturbed green slime. One of the bodies fell out of the back and rolled up against a tree trunk—she saw that only too clearly, for where it hit the goop it too started to steam and dissolve, deflating like a slow puncture in a tire. She turned away before the process took its inevitable course and looked at the road ahead of her.

There was no other traffic, no sign of another roadblock. She refilled her empty mag with ammo from the backpack and put it with the others in the pouch at her left hip. She lit another smoke, hitched up the backpack till it was comfortable, then headed on down the hill to see if anybody else felt like getting in her way.

She reached the town an hour later. It had all been downhill from the roadblock—easy walking, although the pack had started to chafe despite her best efforts to keep the weight evenly distributed. Her ankles had started to ache too. Obviously she wasn't in as good a shape as she imagined—she put it down to the sickness that had seen her laid up in bed in the first place—she had no idea how long that had been, but she guessed it had been days rather than hours.

She was looking forward to finding somebody else alive, somebody who didn't want to kill her and with whom she might be able to have a conversation. She even had an explanation ready for anyone who asked how she got through the roadblock—but she wasn't going to need it. The town was just as dead as anything else she'd seen on her walk down the valley.

Just as the rain from the storm had melted the trees and her tires, it had also melted the town. The timber houses were all rounded and softened, most of the roofs were collapsed in and the remaining walls sagged in running, almost plastic, curves. Any people that had been on the streets had been melted down as thoroughly as the foliage. Meg walked slowly, navigating her way through steaming piles of slime and blood and goop that might have been people, might have been pets, or even deer—there was so little left it was often difficult to tell.

The stench of rot and decay was almost overpowering. She lit a fresh smoke, and that masked it for a while, but not enough, and by the time she reached the main street, she had to walk with a hand over her mouth.

She walked through another town-square—like the one the night before, there was no sign of life—just a dead dog lying in its own juices. If it was going to be like this all over, she needed to find another ride.

She started to search, looking for a vehicle that had been protected from the melting of the storm's rain and where she could find the keys for the ignition. At first all she found was more melted homes, more dead bodies—some had obviously succumbed to the bleeding sickness, others had been caught in the rain—and others still had all too obviously taken their own lives whether by slicing their wrists or eating a bullet. She thought she was in luck when she came across an ambulance, the lights still flashing, keys in the ignition and engine still running—but like the rest, its tires were shot, in this case almost totally, fused in a lump of melted rubber to the road surface.

She had almost lost hope when she found a newer built property—not of timber, but mostly of red brick. The shingled roof of the main house had fallen in under the assault of the rain. But the garage had a tin roof—and when she went inside she found a black Ford pickup, keys in the ignition, gas in the tank, and tires all as fresh as new.

Five minutes later she was on the road again, heading east out of town.

# JD – 8 Days

*Under the East Wing, The White House*

John sat alone in the PEOC. The bodies—what little were left of them, still lay on the chairs, on the floor, seeping on the table, but he paid them no mind. He stared into a single camera lens, and let the Word flow through him, and out, into the camera, along the wires to be broadcast to everyone who might be listening. He had a laptop in front of him, and he used it to synchronize images with the words—it was a talent he never knew before today that he had—but like the Word, he took whatever was given to him.

"And when he had opened the third seal, I heard the third beast say, come and see. And I beheld, and lo, a black horse; and he that sat on him had a pair of balances in his hand."

John smiled.

"Soon, it will be the time of the weighing—the balancing of the scales. To that end, and to bring the glorious day closer, today we open the third seal. Wonders await us in the days ahead of us—great wonders. But first, there must be a cleansing."

He clicked the mouse, knowing the result would go out over the broadcast. The screen showed mushroom clouds blooming like flowers—

scores, hundreds of them, brighter than suns, higher than mountains—covering whole countries.

Another click—a volcanic eruption, so huge that the whole cone of the mountain was blown apart and black ash piled, higher and higher into the sky. The sea rushed in to fill the spaces and it too exploded, heat meeting cold, red meeting blue and finding antipathy until they too burst into a new explosion even bigger than the first. A cloud—a sea—of ash rose high, arcing like a sheet over oceans and countries alike, blind to national politics, blind to borders, blind to all else but its own, spreading, choking, death grip.

Another click—a silent city—the camera tracked along roads and highways, through parkland and shopping malls, office blocks and suburbia. There was nothing alive—the people were laying in the streets in seeping pools of their own blood, dead, red, wet eyes staring blindly at the roiling, thunderous clouds overhead. Their pets lay beside them, faithful to the last. Birds covered whole swathes of parkland, seeping red into the green. Rats, great throngs of them, choked the sewers with their red wet dead bodies.

"The Lord washed the earth before when man forgot his place in the scheme of things—and once again we have forgotten—forgotten the ways we have been shown yet failed to see, forgotten our path—forgotten the Word."

Another click—a city shook, rattled and rolled in the throes of a massive earthquake—tall buildings tumbled, water mains broke, electricity lines fell to the ground sending blue sparks flying, and people fell—crushed—by buildings and falling masonry.

At first the picture showed no landmarks, just swaying, dancing buildings, terror and panic, death and destruction beyond hope of recovery. One last, lingering, shot, showed the high, instantly recognizable view over Rio—and the statue of Christ the Redeemer falling, tumbling, diving down into a bay churning with debris filled water.

"I am here to bring the truth—those who have eyes, let them see—those who have ears, let them hear."

Another click—a trumpet played a high lone note that rose to almost unbearable heights before it was joined by more, and more again—a thunderous blast in the sky. Lighting forked, crashed, and the screen showed the land being lashed with a thousand whips of brilliant blue and silver. Fires broke out, joined forces, and raged furiously, huge glowing scars across vast swathes of forest that stretched as far as the eye could see in any direction.

"And I heard a voice in the midst of the four beasts say, a measure of wheat for a penny, and three measures of barley for a penny; and see thou hurt not the oil and the wine."

Another click, another image—Africa, and the dead, so thin that they appeared to be little more than skin stretched tight over jutting bones, lay scarcely breathing under a baking sun.

"This is the Revelation which God gave unto me, to show unto his servants things which must shortly come to pass. He sent and signified it by his angel unto his servant John. I have brought this message with me, out of the desert as it was of old. I bear the record of the word of God, and of all things that I see. Blessed are those that hear the words of this prophecy, and those things spoken therein: for the time is at hand."

Even as he spoke, John knew the truth of the words. He felt it in his bones—somewhere, in a desert valley, the beast stirred, waking from its age-long sleep, preparing to rise, preparing for battle.

*The day is coming—the last day.*

John smiled into the camera.

*Let it come—I am ready for it.*

# JD – 7 Days

## New York

Alfie had spent the best part of the last twenty-four hours in the back of an abandoned yellow cab while a storm raged around him, such a storm that he thought there would never be an end to it. Blue lighting lashed and blasted what little remained of the once great buildings, rending them down to rubble and dust which the rain washed away in streams that became rivers and then floods. At one point the cab was also a boat, floating in a river that ran down the road carrying everything before it, and taking Alfie almost a hundred yards before depositing him on what had been a sidewalk and wedging him tight against two other vehicles. Water ran down the windows in sheets. It was so thick it was almost impossible to see out. He could only catch glimpses every now and then when squalls passed though with a brief respite between them. The water drummed on the cab's roof with an incessant roar and every so often the whole cab would lift up several inches only to be banged, hard, to the ground again.

Alfie hunkered down in the back seat, getting himself as comfortable as possible under the circumstances. All he could do was wait it out—he had snacks and drinks, and an occasional view of a spectacular show that seemed to be staged just for him. He hugged the guitar case to him—there wasn't much use in getting it out to play while the storm raged—and he tried not to think about the blue-eyed preacher.

The fact that the man seemed to know his name disturbed Alfie—and he might not know much, but he knew that dead men don't speak, and they don't make veiled threats. But there was nothing he could do, here in the cab in the storm, that would change anything that had happened—he had to put it out of his mind—for his sanity's sake if nothing else. To make progress in any direction at all, he was going to need to know more—about who he was and about how this strange new world worked.

He had been hoping that, with the passage of time, he might regain some memory of the person he had been, even why he'd been in the city when it fell. But nothing had come back to him. All he had was the clothes he'd woken up with, the backpack of supplies he'd picked up in the coffee shop and the guitar. He cradled it like a long lost brother all through the long night that followed.

He managed some patchy bouts of sleep despite the constant crack of lightning, pounding beats of thunder and lash of rain against the cab's roof and windows. But he was far from rested when the storm seemed—all of a sudden—to blow itself out and become thinner, watery light showed in the sky far off to the east.

By the time Alfie had another sandwich and some water, the rain had stopped completely, and although the clouds still boiled angrily overhead, there was no sign of another downpour. Now that the noise had abated, he was all too aware again of the silence that hung over the city. He wound down a window and listened—but the silence was still deep, and seemingly complete. He tried the car radio—there had been nothing but static during the storm, and now, again, there was mostly nothing—save for one man's voice, the same words, over and over again in a loop.

"This is the Revelation which God gave unto me, to show unto his servants things which must shortly come to pass. He sent and signified it by his angel unto his servant John. I have brought this message with me, out of the desert as it was of old. I bear the record of the word of God, and of all things that I see. Blessed are those that hear the words of this prophecy, and those things spoken therein: for the time is at hand."

That name again, John—it meant something, Alfie knew that much. But the voice reminded him far too much of the blue-eyed preacher. He turned it off again quickly—the silence of the dead city was preferable to that memory.

Once he was sure there wasn't going to be any more rain—at least, not any time soon—he got out of the cab onto the road. The storm had been good for one thing—it had washed the ash and dust away almost completely, and when Alfie walked away it was with a firm step on solid ground.

He headed south—the air seemed fresher that way.

The streets were clear—what was left of them, but most of the buildings that had been lining them the night before were simply gone, erased from existence and ground to dust by the power of the lightning storm.

*I'm lucky to be alive.*

He was starting to consider whether luck had anything to do with it—or whether other, much stranger forces might be at work. He walked along the silent streets, remembering the news reports he'd read on the laptop in the coffee shop.

*How can they have been so stupid?*

If he never found anybody, he might never get an answer to that. And the more he walked, the more he thought he might be the only person left in the entire city.

Ten minutes later Alfie found where all the ash and dust had washed away to. He reached the end of the street he'd been walking along since leaving the taxi behind, and could go no further—he stood on what had once been part of that street but was now a shoreline, one that was eroding away fast only yards in front of him. A mighty river—a torrent—roared through, almost as loud as last night's thunder, carrying loose timber, vehicles, rooftops, bodies and billboards along with it, rolling and tumbling off and away to somewhere at the flat eastern horizon. Not only had he come to the end of the street—he'd come to the end of the city, maybe the end of the world.

Alfie was so struck by the view at first that he didn't realize he was not alone in gazing at it. Some thirty yards to his right, a group of half a dozen people sat tightly packed on a ledge under what had been the shore-side section of a tall stone and metal bridge that had at one time led away to the south. The main span of the structures had now been either lost in the initial disaster or washed away by this new flood. There was only a tall stone and concrete stub and a small overhang, which was providing them with shelter. If they'd been out here last night in the storm, they were lucky to have survived.

The nearest figure saw Alfie and waved him over toward them, shouting to be heard above the torrent.

"You need some Joe, brother? We got a stove here."

He knew that Joe meant coffee—and that he liked it—he liked it a lot. That was another thing that was just there, in his head when he needed it. He was now wondering whether he might not be sick—sick in the head, and not just suffering from some temporary amnesia.

It was only when Alfie walked over that he saw the man—and those with him—were all sick in another way—they were all bleeding around the nose and mouth, or they were burned—or some combination of the two that really made little difference to their suffering. Open, weeping sores ran across all exposed skin, and the one who'd shouted him over was losing patches of hair from the thin, close cropped, gray on his scalp and had large, watery boils in clumps on the back of his hands and at his neck just above his collar. The man looked at Alfie, and his smile turned to a frown.

"Why you not sick, man? Everybody's sick and getting sicker. How are you spared?"

Alfie showed them both his empty hands to show he wasn't a threat as he stepped forward.

"I don't know," he said. "I don't know much of anything at all. But I've got food in my pack—I'll share, if I get some coffee?"

The one who'd spoken, despite his boils and obvious sickness, seemed to be the most healthy of the whole group. Three of the others were lying down, and barely raised their heads to have a look at their newcomer, and the other two looked pale and wan—lost somehow—and merely nodded when Alfie looked their way.

But the man who'd called him over shuffled along to make room for Alfie—it seemed he'd been accepted. He shucked off the guitar and backpack and got their story as he handed out sandwiches and cookies—he kept the water for himself as they had a couple of large blue containers packed up between the girders above them.

"Two nights now we been here," the man—Frank—said after they introduced themselves and he'd wolfed down a round of pastrami and pickle. "Thought we was going to get washed away along with everything else. Did you see that storm?"

Alfie nodded, sipping at a cup of strong, almost thick, black coffee that tasted better than anything he'd had since he woke in the subway station.

"I sat it out in a Yellow Cab, back there," he motioned with his thumb toward the street.

"Have you seen anyone else?" Frank asked.

Alfie shook his head. He wasn't ready to talk about the preacher—he wasn't even sure that had been a man at all.

"Is there any sign of help coming?" he asked, and saw the look that passed between the six others.

"Ain't no help coming, lad," Frank said quietly. "Not any time soon—the stupid bastards pushed the big red button and the whole damned world has gone to shit. As far as I know, there might not even be anybody else out there at all—ain't seen nobody but you since yesterday morning when the two Eye-ties passed through. But they were sicker then than we are now—I doubt they lasted the night. Just how did you manage to get passed over?"

That was a question Alfie still couldn't answer—he could only shrug.

"I came to after—down in the 33rd Street station," he said. "Pretty deep down—maybe that's why I'm still here."

Frank chewed on another sandwich for a while before answering.

"Maybe. But some of us here were down deep too—I think that's why we're not dead—yet. I was down in the basement under Bank of America getting some paper for a laser printer when the whole damned building fell on my head—at least that's what it felt like. Billy—he's lying down at the back there—he was down a sewer doing maintenance work, and Martin's a driver on the 7th Avenue line and was down pretty deep himself. But we still got the sickness—all of us. It's in the dust, in the air—we're breathing it all the time—you're breathing it all the time. Damned radioactive ash and dust—the whole city's going to be dead for years after this—centuries. It's real wicked stuff—and you should be just as sick as we are, Alfie, boy."

He coughed at that, bubbles of blood at his lips that he wiped away with a sleeve that was already spotted red.

"You need to see a doctor," Alfie said, and that got him another laugh.

"If you find one, send him over—but don't you get it yet, boy? This shit's terminal—ain't none of us getting out of here alive."

"Ain't nobody ever got out of here alive," one of the lying down men said. "It's the way of the world."

"It's the damned ass end of the world," Frank replied. "That John fella we were all laughing about last week was right after all. I hope he's happy now."

"What John fella?" Alfie said.

"Where you been, boy?" Frank replied. "He's been all over the news for weeks—preaching doom and gloom and end of the world and damnation for the ungodly. He had a straight line to the big guy—or so he said—and seemed to be predicting shit before it happened. Damned spooky—and a big load of BS—or so I thought last week. Now it seems like the bastard was a prophet after all."

"The Revelator," Alfie whispered. Frank nodded.

"So you have heard of him?"

"No—but I know the song." Alfie replied, and patted the guitar. "That's one thing I do know."

"What song's that?" Frank asked.

Alfie didn't get to reply, for the man who'd spoken earlier—the one lying down—started to sing.

"Well who's that writin'?"

"John the Revelator," Alfie answered, singing, and after that there was nothing for it—they insisted—he got out the guitar and sang the song for them.

*"Well who art worthy, thousands cried holy,*
*"Bound for some, Son of our God, "Daughter of*
*Zion, Judah the Lion,*

*"He redeemeth, and bought us with his blood."*

All the while as he was playing, Alfie was listening to the wind, listening for an answering chorus from the city—waiting for the preacher man. But, for now, there were only the echoes under the bridge, and, for a while at least, he was able to lose himself in the joy and the brotherhood that could be found in singing.

Once that first song was done, more was demanded—and there didn't seem to be much of anything else to do but sit and watch the torrent flow. Alfie's fingers and throat remembered, even if he didn't. He sang and played—"Sitting on the Dock of the Bay", "Take me to the river", and "Down to the River to Pray". He was about to launch into a Springsteen song before he thought that maybe all these songs about rivers and waters weren't really appropriate for sick folks who were spending what little time they had left at a riverside. He changed tack—went more upbeat—and gave them "Man of Constant Sorrow" and "Sweet Home, Chicago"— two of them cried at that.

It was only when Alfie stopped at the offer of another cup of Joe that they noticed the man who had started the singing in the first place was lying on his back, staring, dead eyed, at the buckled girders of the ruined bridge above them.

There wasn't much in the way of ceremony to the funeral—they all sang "Down To The River to Pray" again, and they gave the dead man—Alfie realized he didn't even know his name—to the torrent wrapped in a sleeping bag. Frank said some words that meant nothing to Alfie, and for a while nobody felt like talking.

Alfie sat, sipping strong coffee, watching the wreckage of the once great city rush past in the flood. It was hard to be sure but it looked like the water level had dropped slightly since his arrival and the noise had dipped, from thunderous roar to more of a constant rumble. The rushing water was still full of debris though—trucks and pickups tumbled along as if cast aside by a giant, timber and awnings and boats and bodies were all being crushed and mangled, one against the other. He had to close his eyes—it was too much to take in, too much to watch. Strangely he found himself thinking of the preacher again—or more accurately, the kneeling acolytes, and how they had been little but ash, easily washed away in the rain—the same way the river was, on a grander scale, washing away the whole city. He wondered if it might even be more than that.

*Is the whole world being washed away? Have I woken up just to be a spectator at the end?*

Frank spoke beside him, echoing his thought.

"This is the way the world ends—first with a bang—and then with a whimper."

Alfie knew the quote was wrong—but didn't know how he knew, and explaining that was just too much effort to consider, so he kept quiet, and kept his eyes shut as Frank went on.

"I used to come down here, you know—years ago this was—I used to come down here with a few of the boys. Fishing, we told the wives, but really it was an excuse to down some beers and jaw for a while without any womenfolk around—you know, man talk? Chug a few brews, have a few smokes—hell, we even caught a fish once—just the one mind, and it was a poor, feeble gray thing that we threw right back in. Damn, they were good times. I don't suppose any of the rest of the guys made it through this far—but at least I'll be joining them again soon enough. Do you think they have beer in Heaven, Alfie? I hope they have beer in Heaven—won't hardly be worth going otherwise."

Silence fell again. Something clanged, metal against metal, far out in the river, and there was a screech as something tore.

"You should move on, boy," Frank continued after a time. "You should move on right now—just turn around and leave. I ain't sure if this sickness is catching—but I ain't sure it isn't. There's none of us here going to last another night—and you don't need to see us go."

Now Alfie did open his eyes, and waved a hand over the view in front of them.

"There's nothing back in the city for me—and I can't get across this until the water goes down," he said. "Even then, I'm not sure that it's not just going to be more of this wherever I go. Besides—you're the first decent company I've found—I'll just stay and hang out with you for a while—is that okay?"

"Oh—it's fine by me, lad—especially if you've got any more cookies in that backpack—and maybe another song or two in the guitar. But no more songs about water or rivers—I think we've all had enough of those for this lifetime. Deal?"

"Deal," Alfie said.

He picked up the guitar, and sang for his supper.

He sang all day, sending them off easy. Sometimes they sang along, mostly they sat in rapt silence, and the only accompaniment Alfie got then was wet, gurgling, coughs that he tried to sing louder to drown out. He found that he had a wide repertoire of songs in his head—blues, folk, spirituals, pop and show tunes. Alfie liked the blues—they liked the show tunes.

Every couple of hours he helped them wrap another of the group in a bag and send them into the water—they were getting good at singing "Down to the River to Pray" by then. By the time it was getting dark again, only Frank and Alfie were left on the ledge under the bridge. Frank was lying down now—and he had already gotten inside two black bin liners. He hadn't let Alfie help him.

"I want to get ready," he'd said as he struggled with them weakly. "I want to look my best for the Lord." Then he'd laughed, and coughed up blood and Alfie had known then that the end was near.

"What's your favorite song?" Alfie asked.

"Do you know 'Goodnight Irene'?" Frank said. "My old Ma used to sing that to me, back in the days when we lived on the farm. Man, those were good times too. I've had some good times, Alfie—a man can't really ask for much more than that, can he?"

Alfie sang him his song, and Frank cried bloody tears.

"You know, lad," Frank said when it was done, his voice barely a whisper, and too much blood at his lips.

"You might not remember who you are—but I think you were sent to us by Providence—you're a gift, and you've eased our sorrow this day—that's not to be taken lightly in these troubled times. So don't go doing anything stupid like giving up on life—the Lord has a plan for you."

"I don't believe," Alfie said—but Frank didn't hear him—he'd gone, as quickly as that, between one breath and the next.

Alfie did his duty—he sent him into the water—the level was definitely dropping now and there was less debris in it, but he scarcely noticed. He had tears in his eyes as he sang—not about the river, or praying this time—he sang Frank's favorite, hoping to see him again in his dreams. Then he returned to the ledge and sat, cradling the guitar as darkness came round again.

# JD – 7 Days

*Saratoga Springs*

Meg had spent another night in a driver's seat, but this time she did sleep—for almost ten hours straight, worn out from being awake most of the night before, and having walked for miles with the backpack. She gave no thought to the men she'd killed beyond wondering if maybe she should have taken one of the rifles.

Going west out of the melted town—she never knew its name—she'd hit a main highway travelling south, and followed it for several hours, picking her way through abandoned and crashed vehicles before tiredness had finally grabbed her hard. She'd locked herself in, reclined the seat back to almost lying position so that she wouldn't be visible from outside—and was asleep in seconds.

If she dreamed, she didn't remember it, and she woke to a lighter sky under clouds that had lost much of their angry fire and roil. There was still no sign of the sun, but at least it didn't seem like there was another storm brewing. And although she hadn't dreamed, she was hearing songs in her head—a man singing in a clear voice—"Sitting on the Dock of the Bay", "Take Me to the River", and "Down to the River to Pray". She even sang along to that last one, as if it was something she knew—and had always known. But as she woke fully, the songs faded, as if heading off into the distance. She was sorry when they went.

After a sandwich and a smoke, she drove south again.

She saw that the forests on either side here were less affected by the acid rain. There were still little pools of green ooze here and there, but by and large, most of the trees retained their foliage. After another twenty miles or so of driving, she was out of the affected zone completely—she guessed she was at the limit of the big storm's reach.

She came to a town and slowed down, hoping for signs of activity. But there was still no sign of any living people—just more crashed and discarded trucks and cars and, once in a while, a body on the road she had to swerve to avoid. It wasn't the rain that had got these—the now tell-tale signs of wet, sunken forms lying in pools of blood told her that the red plague was more widespread than the storm had been.

Then there was more forest—green and very much alive—but completely devoid of wildlife—no deer crossed her path, not even a squirrel, and she realized that she hadn't seen a live bird since her waking in the house on the hill.

She slowed on the approach to another town—the biggest one she'd come across so far. The sign said "Welcome to Saratoga Springs"—that meant nothing to her. But where there was a larger town, there was a chance of picking up some rations—and smokes. And here she might even meet someone willing to talk to her rather than shoot her.

*A girl can always dream.*

❄ ❄ ❄ ❄ ❄

The early signs didn't give her much hope. The streets were clogged with discarded vehicles, many more than she'd seen in the smaller town to the north earlier. One thing was different though—there were no bodies to be seen anywhere. And when she crested a small hill to look down onto a wider stretch of highway it was to finally see some signs of activity—three large trucks were parked in an otherwise empty large parking lot outside a supermarket, and a small village of tents was set up alongside.

Even from here she saw white suited figures around the trucks and in tent doorways.

*Medical team?*

She considered giving them a wide berth—there would be questions she couldn't answer—and some she didn't want to answer, if they concerned dead rednecks and trucks that had been driven off roadways. She hadn't seen any law enforcement—not any living—but that didn't mean there wasn't some around, and killing rednecks was still murder, even in times like these.

She'd almost made up her mind and was eyeing the road for a route that would let her avoid going near the parking lot when she saw that nobody was moving and that the perspective had tricked her—the white figures were all lying prone on the ground. Their medicine and science hadn't protected them, and the red plague was here too.

The sight of more red death gave Meg pause for thought—maybe she shouldn't be putting herself in harm's way quite so flippantly. But she wasn't sick, and hadn't shown any sign of becoming so despite her encounters with the dead and dying on her journey so far. And she needed supplies—if she wasn't sick, she needed to eat to stay that way.

She put the truck in gear and headed down to the parking lot.

It was immediately obvious that a rescue attempt had been made in the town—and recently at that judging by the state of the bodies she saw around the trucks and tents. And it was just as obvious that the attempt had failed miserably.

She parked up twenty yards away in an empty slot with plenty of room around it, and walked over to check the tented village. She kept a hand near her pistol the whole way over, but she saw that she wouldn't need it. The long tents were makeshift hospital dorms, twin rows of beds, scores of them, all containing dead, wet, bloody bodies. Blood seeped through the cots, clotted in thick puddles underneath, and the stench of rot and decay drove Meg back outside almost immediately in search of clean air.

The lot itself, and the aisles of the tents, was strewn with dead rescuers—all of them white-suited, all wearing masks, some with rubber protective suits and breathing apparatus—none of which had helped them.

There were no scavengers to be seen—half a dozen ravens also lay in bloody piles on the lot, and there was a wet, dead dog at the doorway of the supermarket. Meg decided to get in and out as fast as she could and headed into the store.

There were no dead inside the vast cathedral-like emptiness of the supermarket, and judging by the dampness on the floor and the strong tang of disinfectant, somebody had done a clean up job—for all the good it had done them. The power was off, the teller machines quiet and still, but there was enough dim light coming in for her to find most of what she was after. She took a trolley and, eschewing all the fresh, open, foods as there was no way of knowing whether the red plague taint might lie in them, she filled up with packaged sandwiches, meats, cheeses and dried soups. That, along with sanitary towels, thirty liters of water, twenty-four bottles of beer and two hundred cigarettes—with spare lighters—meant she was fully laden on the way out. Just as she was leaving the store, she realized she'd been singing softly to herself for a while—"Down to the River to Pray" again. Now that she'd stopped wheeling the trolley around, she thought she could hear a singer, echoing around in her head, the same, high, clear man's voice as before, accompanied by an even more distant sound of running water. It faded quickly, and was gone by the time she walked back out to the pickup.

*Maybe I am sick after all—sick in the head.*

She pushed the thought away—the singing was making her feel better, not worse, and she missed it when it was gone. She hoped to hear more of it. As she filled the back of the pickup she was suddenly aware of the silence all around—there wasn't even a distant rumble of thunder now, just a deep quiet—no rustle of leaves, no chirp of birdsong—and no singing in her head. But just as she got into the cab, she heard it—distant and far off—singing. At first she thought it was the same song that she'd heard seconds before—but this was different—this wasn't in her head; it was hymnal, choral—and felt even more familiar to her.

She looked around and finally pinpointed the source as being to the south and west. She got all her shopping squared away then drove slowly in that direction, with the window wound down. It was clear where it was coming from—a tall, stone built church standing proud on a junction. It sounded like there were many people inside, all raising their voices in the old marching hymn.

"*Onward Christian Soldiers, marching as to war,*
    "*With the Cross of Jesus, going on before.*"

Meg knew the song, heard it play in her head—heard herself singing along—a much younger her, someone she should—but couldn't—remember. But the memory was enough to make her stop in front of the church, get out of the truck, and head towards the singing.

The large brass handle on the heavy door felt cold to the touch, but she got a blast of warmer air when she pushed it open and stepped through the doorway. The church was dim inside, but the voices that rose in song filled the space, echoing to the rafters high above.

"*Like a mighty army, moves the Church of God;*
    "*Brothers, we are treading, where the Saints have trod.*"

A tall woman, not much more than Meg's age, stood up at the front, leading the congregation of about forty people in the singing. She wore white robes, long, flowing—and dotted with fresh blood all down the front, with more of it in darker red blotches at the sleeves as if she'd casually been wiping away a bad nosebleed. Blood ran from her eyes, dribbling down her cheeks like cheap mascara in rain, but her voice was strong as she brought the hymn to a rousing end.

"*Onward Christian Soldiers, marching as to war,*
    "*With the Cross of Jesus, going on before.*"

The last note echoed away. The robed woman seemed to notice Meg for the first time, and waved her forward.

"All are welcome here, sister," she said. "And you are just in time—the Word is about to be given."

Now that the singing was finished Meg noticed a distant thump from under the church—they had a generator running, although there was no sign of any electric equipment—the old church wasn't even lit. The only light there was came in was filtered by the high colored windows.

The woman called to her again, more insistently this time.

"Come sister—come and hear the Word—all must hear the Word, before it is too late."

Meg found out why they needed power when a bent, weak youth, bleeding from nose and ears, wheeled a TV set up to the front of the church so that everyone present could see the screen. When he switched it on she expected to see only static, as it had been in the house on the hill and in the police station, but instead the picture wavered, then firmed into focus.

A gray bearded man smiled out at them.

Meg saw the weakened man press a button on a remote—this wasn't live then—but it had to be recent, given the images that played over the next few minutes.

The bearded man spoke.

"Those who have ears, let them hear. Those who have eyes let them see. And when he had opened the third seal, I heard the third beast say, come and see. And I beheld, and lo, a black horse; and he that sat on him had a pair of balances in his hand."

The bearded man smiled.

"Soon, it will be the time of the weighing—the balancing of the scales. To that end, and to bring the glorious day closer, today we open the third seal. Wonders await us in the days ahead of us—great wonders. But first, there must be a cleansing."

The screen showed mushroom clouds blooming like flowers—scores, hundreds of them. The scene shifted—a volcanic eruption, so huge that the whole cone of the mountain was blown apart and black ash piles, higher and higher into the sky. Another scene—a silent city—the camera tracked along roads and highways, through parkland and shopping malls, office blocks and suburbia. There was nothing alive—the people lay in the streets in seeping pools of their own blood, dead, red, wet eyes staring blindly at the roiling, thunderous clouds overhead.

When the man on the screen came back and spoke, the church congregation said the words along with him.

"The lord has washed the earth before when man forgot his place in the scheme of things—and once again we have forgotten—forgotten the ways we have been shown yet failed to see, forgotten our path—forgotten the word."

Another scene—a city shook, rattled and rolled in the throes of a massive earthquake—at first the picture showed no landmarks, just terror and panic, death and destruction beyond hope of recovery. One last, lingering, shot, showed the statue of Christ the Redeemer falling, tumbling, diving down into a bay churning with debris-filled water.

More from the smiling man—more joining along—almost shouting now—from the assembled congregation. Some clapped their hands, some shouted Hallelujah while others seemed to be lost in eye-rolling ecstasy and manic, frantic dancing.

"I am here to bring the truth—those who have eyes, let them see—those who have ears, let them hear."

A trumpet played a high, lone note that rose to almost unbearable heights before it is joined by more, and more again—a thunderous blast in the sky. Lighting forked, crashed, and the screen showed the land being lashed with a thousand whips of brilliant blue and silver.

Everyone in the church was shouting now—some on their knees, some with hands raised high—all of them with fresh blood running from eyes and noses, mouths and ears. Meg tasted it at the back of her throat—hot and coppery and with a sour tang. It tasted like death.

The bearded man on the screen was almost shouting now. "This is the Revelation which God gave unto me, to show unto his servants things which must shortly come to pass. He sent and signified it by his angel unto his servant, John. I bear the record of the word of God, and of all things that I see. Blessed are those that hear the words of this prophecy, and those things spoken therein: for the time is at hand."

The tall robed woman echoed those last words.

"The time is at hand. "

"Hallelujah," the congregation shouted as one.

Then the church fell quiet.

The screen went dark. It seemed the show was over, but the white robed woman had other ideas. She moved to the center of the aisle in front of the TV screen and looked Meg straight in the eye.

"Have you come to repent? Will you join us in the Rapture?"

The woman took a step forward as she spoke, and opened her arms, showing her palms to Meg. They were wet, gleaming and bright red, the blood dripping through her fingers to leave a spatter pattern on the church floor.

"I have nothing to repent," Meg said—and started to check the exits and her immediate available space if she had to move fast. This might be a church, and these might be church-folk—but something was making her nerves sing. She took a pace backward and put a hand on the butt of the Walther. "I just heard the singing and came to investigate."

The white robed woman kept coming. The congregation rose to stand behind her.

"I don't need no trouble," Meg said.

The woman smiled at her. Blood gleamed on her teeth and dribbled from the corner of her mouth.

"There is nothing but peace when you are washed in the blood of the Lamb," she said, and took another step forward. She kept coming, and as Meg backed away, the whole congregation followed her down the aisle and Meg got her first good look at all of them.

They were sicker than she'd thought. Apart from the robed woman at the front who seemed to be their leader, and the weakened man who'd brought in the TV set, the rest of them were in the late stages of the red plague—bleeding profusely at the eyes, mouths and noses. She suspected they might also be bleeding in their intimate places that she couldn't see, for they made moist, wet sounds as they came forward, and left streaks and smears of bloody red on the stone floor behind them.

The white robed woman took another step toward Meg and her eyes filled with blood. More of it bubbled from her mouth as she spoke.

"We told you we'd be waiting for you, Meg," she said, her voice suddenly an octave lower, and much more coarse than it had been. She recognized it—she was already coming to hate it.

"Have you come to repent?" it said.

Meg drew the Walther and racked a round into the chamber. The noise was too sharp, too metallic and sounded harsh in her ears, but her aim didn't waver—she now had the barrel pointed right between the woman's eyes.

"If you know me already, you know what this is and how good I am with it," she replied. "Back off."

"You've only got eight shots," the robed one said and waved a hand over the congregation. "I can afford to lose a few of these if it means we get you. But it needn't come to that. Come to me, girl. Repent your sins, and be washed in the blood of the Lamb."

"I've told you—I have nothing to repent."

When the robed figure spoke again, it was with the voice of the old lady in the hotel room.

"Are you sure about that, dear?"

Then, another voice, the young man that first came down off the pickup on the barricade on the highway, the one she'd shot with so little remorse.

"You put a bullet in my head and left me in a ditch. What do you mean, you've got nothing to repent?"

"Stopping the likes of you isn't a sin," Meg said, taking another step back. The robed figure followed her every pace. "Are you sure about that?" The coarse, deep voice was back again. "How is it that you know so much about sin, when you have only just arrived in this world? And where are you going to go, Meg? You've seen all there is to see—there is nothing left—John has given the word—the follies of mankind have tumbled and gone—Fallen, fallen is Babylon, and its greatness washed away—washed in the blood of the Lamb. Come—let us wash you as we have been washed.

Those who have eyes let them see. Those who have ears, let them hear."

She took another step closer to Meg.

The crowd behind her started to sing again as they too took a step.

"Onward Christian soldiers, marching as to war."

It didn't sound like praise this time—it sounded like sarcasm.

"All you have to do is say the word," the tall robed figure said. Blood ran from her eyes, and more bubbled out of her mouth again as she spoke.

Meg took another step back—she was within five yards of the door, but her opponent had been right about one thing—there were too many of them for her to take down at once—not without some fancy moves.

"Come to daddy," the white robed woman said, and smiled.

Meg put her first shot between the smiling lips—bit of teeth flew, blood poured like a river down the white, and the robed woman fell to her knees even as the congregation marched over the top of her, coming forward fast.

Meg backed off, two more steps—then fired again. Her second shot took out the weakened man—the next strongest of them, if looks were anything to go by. Even before he fell, collapsing into a wet mass of tissue, she'd picked her next targets—two tall men in the center—taking them down blocked the aisle for a second, giving Meg time to gain another few steps back before the rest could follow. Shots four, five and six took out the three closest to her. The remainder of the bloody congregation howled, and stumbled forward faster.

Meg turned and made for the main door, heading at a run for the pickup. As she'd figured, the attackers couldn't match her for speed—some of them weren't even able to make it up the aisle, leaving more long bloody trails behind them as they tried to reach her.

Meg had the pickup's keys in her free hand as she went through the church doors—praying that the remote's battery hadn't run down. It didn't fail her—there was a satisfying beep and clunk from the vehicle as she sped down the gravel drive. She reached the pickup ten yards ahead of her pursuers, turned and used her last two shots to take out the leading attackers—head shots, clean and easy targets—they didn't even try to dodge and weave.

She'd calculated her flight right—but only just—she was far enough ahead now that she was able to throw herself into the truck and lock the doors. That just gave her time to get a new magazine into the Walther before they reached her, a dozen or more of them slobbering on the windows and leaving bloody handprints as they tried to get to her through the glass.

Meg tried to calm herself—her heart raced and blood pumped in her ears. The shot of adrenaline had her jittery, and on edge, but she fought it down, the almost mechanical, rote act of reloading a fresh magazine into the gun and racking a round into the chamber doing much to ground her back in a quieter, calmer place.

Once the gun was loaded, and it was obvious that they weren't going to be able to reach her inside the locked cab, she started the engine. She could just drive away now and have done with it—but that was the problem—she'd always know she'd left them at her back, and worry about them coming after her. She put the pickup in gear, and floored the pedal, taking out two more of them and leaving bloody smears on the road surface in her wake.

But she didn't go far—just thirty yards down the road where she turned side on and opened her window, taking aim.

It was like a fairground shoot—sitting ducks, just lining up. By the time she'd emptied the mag only four were left. She had plenty of time to reload again and take them down. The last one fell right beneath the window, and left a bloody streak of blood down the door of the pickup. A boy—no more than fifteen—looked up at her, and the deep, coarse voice spoke again.

"Repent," it said. "Repent and be washed in the blood of the Lamb."

"Not today," Meg replied, and put a bullet between his eyes. She refilled all her magazines with ammo and made sure they were secure in the pouch at her left hip before she drove away. She checked the rearview mirror, but nothing moved. She drove on, leaving only death behind.

# JD – 7 Days

*The Oval Office*

"My fellow Americans," John said into the camera, and smiled. He sat at the old presidents' desk, tattered remnants of flags at his back, and a view out of a smashed window frame to a smoking waste of a city beyond. "Do not despair in this time of trial and tribulation, for I have come to bring you glad tidings of great joy."

The same setup for broadcasting that he'd used down in the PEOC worked just as well up here in the Oval Office when he got it all connected in place. He had no idea how many people were picking up—if any—but he was sending—the Word was spreading—that was what he'd been tasked with.

"We are one day closer to the Lord," he said. "And as it was foretold, lo, so it has come to pass."

He clicked his mouse and an image went out over the airways—Paris this time, the old city of lights now gone dark and quiet and empty. The Avenue des Champs-Élysées was devoid of traffic and awash with water. Bodies—a pyre higher than the monument itself—burned beside the Arc De Triomphe and the swollen waters of the Seine lapped around the bottom of the base of the Eiffel Tower. The main tall spire of the tower itself was nowhere to be seen, as if shorn off by a blast. The great museum of the Louvre was sunken, drowned and collapsed, the master artworks of the centuries torn and discarded—Mona Lisa smiled as she wafted to and fro in a murky current of dank water. In the city itself, there was no movement—bodies sat slumped in chairs in street-side cafes, oozing sickly fluids to the ground, more of the wet dead lay in the parks, in the alleys, in the streets. A last shot showed Notre Dame Cathedral, listing to one side, in the process of being eroded, inch by inch, ever faster, the old stones were being slowly eked out of the walls and foundations and taken by the swirling river.

"So ends the mighty works of man," John said. "For too long we have been worshipping false idols, living on false hope. Render unto Mammon that which is Mammon's."

Three loud trumpet blasts filled the room and escaped out into the whole city—heard wherever the broadcast was seen, like thunder booming across the sky.

"If he sees the sword coming upon the land and blows the trumpet and warns the people, then if anyone who hears the sound of the trumpet does not take warning, and the sword comes and takes him away, his blood shall be upon his own head. He heard the sound of the trumpet and did not take warning; his blood shall be upon himself."

John clicked the mouse again.

Toronto, the tall towers and spires were all fallen, the great lake was full of the dead, its rippling surface was not blue, but red—blood red.

*Click.* Moscow and Red Square—or what was left of it. The old city was a smoking ruin, the great walls of the palace tumbled. Bent and buckled burned-out tanks fill the parade ground, but even had they been serviceable, there was no one to drive the weapons of war for there was nothing left of the mighty Red army of old but ash and dust and memories of better days.

*Click.* Rome—the Vatican, now as much a ruin as the Colosseum, its great domes and turrets having collapsed to bury the faithful in new stone catacombs. The Trevi Fountain has run dry for the last time. St. Peter's Square is packed, the dead crammed in so tight they have perished standing upright in their tens of thousands and are now all dissolving and decomposing together in a wet, bloody mass of humanity who had gathered to hear the Word and been given it, too late.

*Click.* Dubai—and the silver spires of the tallest buildings in the word, the ultimate monuments to Mammon, were now lying, prone and dead and broken and gray, on the desert sands that are already covering them in long, slow, drifting dunes.

*Click.* Sydney Harbor, the bridge a skeletal ruin, the Opera House's shell like curves collapsed in on themselves and aflame. The waters are clogged with the dead, packed so closely a person could walk across from one side to the other without having to get their feet wet.

*Click.* Tokyo—flattened and burning, the streets clogged with red, wet, dead.

*Click.* Shanghai—dancing, the tall buildings waltzing then falling like drunks on a dance floor as the shake, rattle and roll goes on forever.

*Click.* Volcanoes—erupting, spewing lava down mountain sides to engulf whole cities and piling ash clouds, ever higher, ever thicker into a sky that is already angry and red and glowering.

*Click.* Tsunami—washing everything before it as it funnels up an estuary and a mighty river becomes a raging, boiling, valley of death.

*Click.* The streets of D.C.—mostly burned out ruins, panning in to the partially collapsed White House—quiet.

*Click.* Somewhere in the Bangladesh Delta were the dead—piled high, great burning pyramids of them.

*Click.* Constantinople. The ancient city bridging two cultures, both of which were now as good as dead—burning.

John looked into the camera and smiled again. He felt the power rise up as he spoke the words.

"And when he had opened the fourth seal, I heard the voice of the fourth beast say, come and see. And I looked, and behold a pale horse: and his name that sat on him was Death, and Hell followed with him. And power was given unto them over the fourth part of the earth, to kill with sword, and with hunger, and with death, and with the beasts of the earth."

"The time that was foretold is at hand. A new heaven and a new earth shall rise. But first—we will be judged—and judged harshly—on what has yet to come to pass. The beast, even now, rises, slouches and prepares for the final day that is near at hand. He will call his lords to him, and will master his forces."

And again, John felt the truth of the words. Even now, elsewhere, in that desert valley where his journey had began, the land was cracking, the tumbled building falling into ruin as the pit opened up, deeper, ever deeper, and somewhere—almost impossibly deep, impossibly dark, the long imprisoned beast became fully awake—and began to rise.

"We must meet him—in faith and glory—meet him and put him back down to never more trouble us as we march into New Eden together. Those who have eyes let them see. Those who have ears let them hear. Those who would bear arms for the Lord when the last trumpet sounds—come to me—come to Gehenna—and fight."

# JD – 3 Days

*New Jersey*

Alfie lost track of time. He knew it was the grief—he'd only known Frank and the others for the space of a single day, but that was longer than he'd ever known anyone, as far as he could recollect. Now they were gone, and he missed them—he missed them terribly.

He walked, trudging through a gray wasteland where his songs died in his throat unsung and the guitar stayed silent in the case at his back. There was no space for his music here. Here there was only death—the burned out, never-ending death of all things.

It felt like he'd been walking through it forever.

He remembered sitting under the ruined bridge as the torrent flowed below him—he'd sat there all night, singing "Down to the River to Pray" to his new and newly lost friends somewhere out there in the water. He remembered walking away when the sun came up and it was obvious he would never find a crossing if he didn't move.

And he remembered walking along a blasted and mangled shoreline that used to be a boardwalk, climbing through twisted debris of timber and steel and bits of vehicles and boats. He remembered the bodies he'd uncovered or even just stumbled over, not sure the bundles had even been people—or parts of them—until he was too close to discover otherwise. So many bodies had been strewn to eternity like seed in the wind, either burned or taken by the red sickness—or both.

He remembered his incredulity at finding an intact bridge to cross the river, right at the point where he'd been ready to sit down and give up. He remembered pushing and climbing through a tangle of wrecked and abandoned automobiles, picking his way through more burnt or wet remains of the dead, to get across the torrent that continued to rage and foment far below.

And he remembered meeting a barricade at the far end of the bridge—a forlorn attempt in the recent past by authorities to try to take some control. The dead soldiers lying at his feet as he walked past the barricade were testament to their complete failure.

What he didn't remember was how long he'd been traveling, how many sleeps he'd had, or when he'd last eaten. He knew that his backpack was considerably lighter, having shared with the sick under the bridge, then finishing off what remained while walking. His food was all gone, and all he had left was a bottle of water—half-empty, warm and stale. He'd hoped to be able to walk out of the destruction of the city to find fresher air and something clean to drink, but there was only more ash and ruin and death here too, on the south side of the river. New Jersey it had said on a sign that still stood, hanging lopsided above what had once been a freeway. It no longer looked very new—if it ever had.

He considered—not for the first time—retracing his steps, heading back for the coffee house storage room, where he could survive for weeks, waiting in the hope of rescue. But part of him, befuddled with exhaustion as he was, knew that wasn't an option. It was clear that there was no help coming—not soon enough to save him in any case. Besides, he had to keep heading south—south and west. He didn't know why, but he got a pounding headache every time he tried to move in a different direction or take a different turn. He was being led—and all he knew how to do was follow.

He walked on in a valley of death that seemed to go on forever.

All through his trials and difficulties, he hadn't given any thought at all to discarding the guitar, despite its weight on his back and the tug of the straps on his shoulders. It was the only thing he had to hold on to when tiredness and exhaustion forced him to seek out a spot where he could rest. He'd take it out, start strumming and immediately feel at ease with everything, his troubles washed away, his aches and pains forgotten, for a time, lost in the power of the songs. But here, now, trudging through the left over remains of another city, that too was forgotten, secondary to putting one foot in front of the other and moving forward. He had tried singing to himself, but the songs died before they were even born.

He thought often as he walked about Frank's words—almost his last words—about Alfie having a gift. He certainly knew how to sing and play—it came as easily to him as breathing, and he appeared to know a huge number and variety of songs, each coming to mind as soon as he had need of it. But that didn't help him any—he couldn't remember who'd taught him or how he'd learned. Somehow it felt like something he'd been given rather than earned, and that didn't sit quite right with him.

The one positive thing—the only thing to give thanks for—was that it wasn't raining—hadn't rained since the thunderstorm in the city. It seemed the same thunderstorm had cleared these streets of much of the ash too. But the air felt too hot, too dry, and his throat was once again rough and raw. He tried breathing through his nose, but soon had both nostrils clogged with dry grit that he had to blow free every twenty seconds. Then he started thinking about where the dust and grit had come from—and how much of it might be made up of the burned and flash fried dead. A gag reflex nearly choked him and he had to stop, fighting even to take a breath until he eventually calmed down.

He'd been trying to preserve it, but finally he gave in and swallowed down half of his remaining water. It was too warm, and still tasted tainted—almost as tainted as the air itself. He was just about to start walking again when he realized he'd trudged for the past few miles without looking at his surroundings. The view had changed—there were now buildings—intact buildings—on either side of the road, and a smooth paved surface underfoot. He'd wanted to walk out of the destruction—and it appeared he'd now managed it, without even noticing.

His situation had not, however, greatly improved. If he'd hoped for help, he quickly saw that he was going to be disappointed. The burning—the bomb, or whatever it had been—had not reached the area where he walked—but the red sickness had. He made his way slowly up a street of business premises—banks, credit unions, realtors and insurance agents. The parking areas outside all of them had rows of parked vehicles—and many of those had dead, wet bodies slumped in them, both drivers and passengers. He was coming to realize that the red death was more than just a sickness. It was a wave of destruction that, when it passed, killed many people where they sat. One second they were going about their business in a normal day, the next they were mere lumps of meat, bleeding from the inside out, and losing any dignity they might ever have had in the process. Not everybody went that way—he'd seen that, in the sick under the bridge—but he was starting to think they were exceptions, for everywhere he looked he saw proof of his theory.

He skirted more vehicles in the road—pickups, trucks, sedans and even a school bus—all containing dead, viscous, seeping bodies who appeared to have made no attempt to escape their fate—or had not been given any chance to. Not for the first time, Alfie wondered why he had been spared and wondered whether it had anything to do with the hole in his memory, or the thing that was leading him on to some unknown destination.

He considered investigating inside one of the business premises. Surely one of them would have water at least? But wandering around strange buildings in the gloom did not appeal to him in the slightest—the silence and solitude was getting to him, and Alfie admitted to himself that he was getting more than a little spooked. He stuck to the road and kept walking, hoping to find easy—and well lit—access to what he needed.

A mile or so later he got exactly what he wanted. He came to a junction and saw a food truck sitting on the corner—a glorified hot dog and burger stand at most, with a wet, red, dead man at the wheel. The back door entry was closed but not locked, although it took a hefty tug for Alfie to open it, and the old door gave out a screech that sounded far too loud in the silent street. He stood there, his heart in his mouth for several seconds, waiting to see if he'd drawn any unwanted attention—but nobody came.

Once inside the truck, Alfie found—alongside already moldering hot dogs and a batch of fries congealing in cold oil—a small fridge full of soda cans and bottled water. The fridge wasn't all that cool—but cool enough that the water tasted sweet and clean when he chugged half a liter down in a couple of gulps. There was also an under counter cupboard filled with loaves—also moldering—and packs of chips and snacks which looked undamaged. He stuffed his rucksack with water and tortilla chips, filling it as solid as he could manage. He took another bottle of water and two packs of snacks in his hand as he went back outside, hoping to eat them in moderately cleaner air that didn't smell like meat that had gone off.

He stepped down out of the truck—and came face to face with someone trying to get in. Alfie gave out a startled yelp and almost fell on his butt. The newcomer was just as surprised to see Alfie and stepped back, hands up as if to protect himself.

"Don't hurt me none, mister. I ain't got nothing worth taking."

It was an older white man with long straggly hair and a wispy beard, both thin and gray. He wore a denim jacket that looked as old as he was, and a pair of jeans made up almost solely with frayed patches. The trainers on his feet were worn right down to paper-thin soles, his T-shirt had stains that showed all of his recent meals—and many older ones—and he only had three good teeth left in his mouth. But he didn't look sick, and now that he was smiling he was the happiest person Alfie had seen since his awakening. He patted Alfie on the arm, as if trying to convince himself that he wasn't dreaming, then he grinned widely again.

"My Lord, son, am I glad to see you. I thought everybody had all gone on without me again and left me all on my lonesome."

Alfie saw that the newcomer had a shopping trolley at his back—it looked to be mostly filled with booze. The man saw him looking.

"I paid a visit to the liquor store down the road," he said.

"The door was open—it ain't stealing if the door was open, is it? Besides, there weren't nobody there to take money, even if I had any to give them."

There was a gleam in the man's eyes that Alfie didn't quite recognize, but suspected might be madness. But if the old man was mad, he was very happy with it.

"Damn, but I really am glad to see you," he said again. "It's not right for a man to be talking to himself all the time, but I can't stand quiet for too long or I start to hear them talking to me."

Alfie thought that now wasn't the right time to ask who "they" might be—but he wasn't given time for a question in any case.

"Do you mind?" the man said, motioning for Alfie to step aside. "If I'm going to be having a guest and doing some drinking, we'll need some munchies."

Alfie stepped down out of the truck and let the man make half a dozen journeys to and from the shopping cart. By the time he was finished the cart was piled high with all variety of kinds of chips and salted snacks, all sitting precariously on top. Alfie noted wryly that the old man hadn't bothered with any of the water or soft drinks that were left in the fridge—he'd obviously got all the liquids he needed from the liquor store.

Once the old man got everything arranged in the cart to make sure nothing would fall out when he rolled it away, he turned back to speak to Alfie.

"You heading anywhere you need to be right now?" the man asked. "Only, I been drinking alone for a few days now and that ain't right—man needs some company when he's drinking. Will you join me?"

He looked like an excited puppy that was waiting for a ball to be thrown—there was no way Alfie could refuse and not feel bad about it. Besides, he could do with some company of his own. He nodded, and the man smiled again—the clouds might still cover the sky, but there was plenty of sunshine in that grin and Alfie suddenly felt like a weight had been lifted from him.

"The name's Dawson—Tom Dawson," the older man said and put out a hand.

Alfie had to put down his water and snacks to return the shake.

"Alfie Collinson. Pleased to meet you."

"Pleasedtameetcha right back," Dawson said, and cackled while pumping Alfie's arm as if he was aiming to draw water. Alfie looked him over—his first impression had been right—the man didn't look or sound sick, there was no sign of the red plague, or of the burns he'd been seeing on everyone else. He did look like he hadn't washed in a week.

*I'm probably no oil painting myself. At least we're both alive, and have managed to meet up. Maybe my own survival isn't so unique after all.*

"Come on then," Dawson said. "I weren't expecting no houseguests, so you'll have to excuse the mess."

He followed Dawson as they headed off down the street; the only sound was an insistent squeak from the slightly lopsided shopping trolley.

Dawson led them to an old VW camper van—it was painted in an acid, lime green that must have looked almost fluorescent in sunlight in its day, and pretty cool with it. But that day was some years in the past—the old van had obviously put in many tough miles on the road. The paint- work was dinged and scratched, the frame looked to be hanging low on the rear axle, and everything below three feet from the ground was caked in dried mud under what appeared to be a much more recent layer of dust and ash. It looked in pretty poor shape. Dawson saw him looking.

"She's not mine," the man said. "I'm kinda looking after her for a friend—although I don't think he's coming back anytime soon. And don't let her looks fool you none. She's old but she's got a good heart—and a couple of hundred thou' miles on her already. I reckon she's good for a hundred more if I'm spared along with her. Come into my parlor."

Alfie stepped up into the van. Despite Dawson's warning, he was surprised to find that everything was neat and tidy, all squared away properly inside.

"I thought you said it was messy?"

Dawson moved an unwashed plate, knife and fork from the small counter and put it in a tiny sink.

"This is messy—for me. And my old Sarge would have my guts for gaiters if I slacked off," Dawson said.

"You were in the military?"

"Three tours in the Gulf," Dawson replied. "That's where this shit all started—I been telling folks that for years. But nobody listens to old vets that drink more than is good for them—and they still won't be listening now. I don't even get to say 'I told you so.'"

If Alfie's confusion showed, Dawson didn't notice—he went back outside, and was now intent on unloading the trolley through the back doors and into the far rear of the van. There was what should've been a sleeping area in the back but it was mostly taken up by the man's stash. There was a lot of booze—and packs of snacks—in there already; Dawson had been squirreling stuff away, but it was in neat ranks and it didn't take him long to get the trolley's contents added to the rest. He shut the door—the clang rang all around the inside of the van—then he came back round to the side door.

"So where you headed with that guitar, Alfie lad?" Dawson asked when he climbed up inside.

"South and West," Alfie said. "Although I don't rightly know why."

"I think I might be able to help you with that," Dawson replied. "But first things first—can I get you a drink?"

He waved a full bottle of JD towards Alfie, but Alfie took a beer—he didn't know much about booze, but somehow he knew that drinking hard liquor on top of how he felt right now wasn't a good idea.

*Even the beer might be pushing it. I feel like I could sleep for a week.*

Dawson showed no such reluctance. He carefully poured himself three fingers of JD in a tall glass, and pushed the bottle out of his reach after he'd closed it.

"Damned fine sippin' juice," he said, and clinked the glass against Alfie's beer bottle.

The beer was warm and too full of fizz, but right then it was about the sweetest thing Alfie had ever tasted. He resisted the urge to chug it all down in one, limiting himself to a small sip at a time to make it last.

"South and west, you say?" Dawson said after a minute. "And I say, you've heard the call, Alfie—you've heard the call the same as I have."

"What call is that?" Alfie asked.

Dawson's reply almost made Alfie spit beer back at him across the camper. He sang.

"Who's that callin'? John the Revelator."

Alfie was ready to run—his memory of the old Preacher back in the city still big in his mind—but Dawson was just looking at him, a big grin on his face.

"How do you know about that?" Alfie said.

"I seen him—on the TV just before everything went to shit. Hey—don't let his old fire and brimstone spiel spook you—that fella John's just another snake oil salesman—ain't nothing to be afeard of there. Trust me—I've been dead already—I know."

"What do you know?"

Dawson took a slug of JD that would have floored Alfie before answering.

"I was dead afore—I told you that—back in the Gulf. Big Iraqi shell just about blew my ass all to bits—all my pals too—and I was away for a long while—right peaceful it was too, just like swimming in the ocean on a warm day. I didn't want to come back but the docs insisted—and when I did, my pals didn't come with me. I just got sent back here for more drinking on my own. I thought that was why I got passed by this time round—because I was dead already. But here you are, Alfie, boy—how about you? Were you dead afore?"

It had come out of him as if he wanted to say it all before he could stop himself, and after he was done, he needed another drink. Alfie sipped at his beer—he didn't have an answer—not anything he could understand in any case—but he found himself talking anyway.

And in the same manner as Dawson had, it all came out in a rush. He didn't talk about his memory loss—he didn't know how to do that without having to explain it—and he didn't have an explanation. But he did talk—about the subway, the Preacher, the song, the storm, the dying men under the bridge and the long walk—following something—or somebody's call.

Dawson nodded, as if he understood.

"You've been called, that's clear enough. I don't see the attraction myself, but a man's got to go where the calling takes him, same as it ever was."

He poured himself another JD and passed Alfie another beer.

"I can take you down the road a way, if you'd like?" Dawson said. "The old gal isn't much of a mover to tell the truth, but it sure beats walking around in that shit out there."

That was something Alfie could definitely agree with.

"I'd be glad of the company," he said.

Dawson grinned so widely it looked like the top of his head might roll off.

"Me too, lad—me too. There's one condition though." "Name it."

"We go in the morning—I'm too loaded to drive anywhere today anyway—and I want to hear some of the old songs—will you play some of the old songs for me."

Alfie got the guitar out of the case, and Dawson whistled.

"Hell, I don't know a lot about them, but I know that's a mighty fine gal of your own you got there."

Alfie nodded.

"I don't remember much of anything, but I'm sure she's been with me for a long, long time."

"Then here's to a long time more with our gals for both of us," Dawson said, then clinked Alfie's glass again and downed the JD as smoothly as if it was lemonade on a hot day.

They sat there in the middle of the death of the world. Alfie played "Smokestack Lightning", "The Sky is Crying" and "It Hurts Me Too" to start with. Dawson sang when he knew the words—mostly in the choruses—and not that well, but with enough gusto to make up for his shortcomings in range. Then Alfie moved on to "That's All Right, Mama", "I Walk the Line" and "Peace in the Valley". Dawson cried a bit then. They both drank too much and ate too many salty chips, and it was the best time Alfie ever remembered having.

# JD – 3 Days

*Albany and Points South*

Meg had spent the last three days in Albany looking for someone—anyone—who could tell her what was going on—someone who wasn't sick. All she found was more wet, red death. And unlike in Saratoga Springs, there hadn't been any attempts here at cleaning up the streets—the bodies lay everywhere—on sidewalks, slumped over tables in cafes and bars, and behind the wheels of crashed and mangled vehicles. When the red sickness came, it came fast.

She wondered why the church congregation had been given more time to suffer. One conclusion she reached was that they'd been waiting just for Meg to arrive. Meg didn't know much of anything, but she didn't think the universe worked that way—it didn't exist purely to screw with her head. Then, on her first afternoon in the city, she'd found a house that reminded her strangely of the place where she'd woken up, and she started to wonder if she'd have to revise that opinion.

She'd been keeping an eye open for somewhere that might be safe from another downpour like the storm on the forest road, and spotted a sturdy property with a new tin roof that had been fitted on both the house and accompanying garage. Although this property was in a street near what had been a busy city center rather than hidden away up a quiet hillside track, and was built of brick rather than timber, the owners were—or had been—of a similar mind to Meg's parents. They weren't home—the garage was empty—but their basement was a hoard of supplies, both food and water, plenty of gas, a heavy duty generator, and more than enough weaponry to start a small war.

Meg felt almost at home.

Despite the feeling, she was jittery for a good half hour after entering the house—it felt too good to be true, too easy, as if she was being led by a hand that knew what she wanted—what she needed. But once she'd ascertained that the house was secure—deadlocks on all doors and windows, and double thickness glass throughout—the owners hadn't been messing around—she started to relax.

She slept in the big master bedroom at nights, searched the city for anyone else left alive by day, and even managed to cook herself some hot meals, washed down with beer—another thing the house owners had hoarded in abundance. There was nothing broadcasting on the TV or radio—just more of the dancing white static—but she had plenty to keep her occupied. She found a large collection of films in the box below the TV set, and watched a series of big dumb action movies before the wanton destruction on screen reminded her all too clearly of what had happened just outside the window. She switched to the other half of the collection—something that called itself "classics"—mostly black and white, mainly comedies. She discovered a liking for anarchic slapstick—a bunch called the Marx Brothers kept her entertained for hours.

As she watched the movies roll, she was also discovering just how large the gap in her memory was. Obviously famous people were referenced that she had never heard of and world events were discussed that she knew nothing about. She was particularly distressed to discover there had been at least two World Wars in the past.

*Did I just survive the third? Or is it still going on?*

She had no way of answering that question. She knew just enough to keep herself alive—as if that strange, guiding hand she'd imagined had decided that was all she needed to know.

She put it to the back of her mind. She was alive—plenty of other folks hadn't been allowed that privilege. She intended to make the most of it.

When she slept, it was in a huge, comfortable bed that seemed to swallow her up, and she was gone, back to the black, for up to eleven-hour stretches at a time. By the end of the third night at the property, she was completely rested. She was also starting to think she might be best served hunkering down right here and seeing things out. She had supplies to last for months, after all, and when she needed gas for the generator, all she had to do was go out and get some—there wasn't anyone else using any.

*If I was led here, then maybe this is where I was meant to be all along.*

But on the fourth morning, just as she set out for another patrol of the dead city, the radio in the pickup sprang to life. She was pretty sure it hadn't even been switched on, but she was beginning to get used to weird shit happening around her. She was surprised, not scared. It was a man's voice, not the high clear one she'd heard before, but deeper. An older man was the impression she got.

*"Well Moses to Moses, watchin' the flock*
*"Saw the bush where they had to stop."*

She turned a corner—the sound faded, but when she went along a long curve, it got stronger again when she was facing south.

*"God told Moses, 'Pull off your shoes,'*
*"Out of the flock, well you I choose."*

She turned slightly away—the sound came and went, but strengthened every time she pointed the pickup south.

*"Tell me what's John writin'? Ask the Revelator.*
*"What's John writin'? Ask the Revelator.*
*"What's John writin'? Ask the Revelator.*

*"A book of the seven seals."*

She was being led again—and every time she turned away from pointing south, a headache, like a vise around her temple, gripped her hard until she went back to the right direction.

*Okay—okay—I get the message.*

She went immediately back to the house, packed her own backpack and as much food and drink as she thought she'd need for a week into the pickup—including a couple of gas canisters from the garage—and headed back out—not into the city, but south onto the freeway.

Every so often the radio would kick in—and now she knew for sure—she was definitely being led, led toward the singing. She didn't know why—but she meant to find out.

> *"What's John writin'? Ask the Revelator. "A book*
> *of the seven seals."*

❖ ❖ ❖ ❖ ❖

She had to take it slowly at first—whatever wanted her to go south wasn't taking into account the tangled wreckage on the roads out of the city. It was only when she got onto the four- lane highway that she was able to push the needle much above thirty. Even then she had to stop several times and get out to drive other vehicles out of her path. Twice she had to drag the drivers—what was left of them—out of their seats—and then find something to use as a cover to avoid sitting in their discarded body fluids.

The further south she went the more obvious it became that the disaster was widespread—probably countrywide—maybe even worldwide. There was only the dead—there were no more rescue teams, no more church congregations waiting for the end, no more of anybody except her.

Every now and then she'd hit a clearer stretch of road and think that maybe—hopefully—she was coming out of it. But the going was slow again to the north of Newburgh. Once more she had to pick her way through increasingly dense traffic, discarded, broken down or crashed, and she tried—but wasn't always successful—to avoid the wet puddles of clothes and decaying flesh that were almost as numerous as the vehicles.

She went through the town of Newburgh quickly—the air felt thick there, and brought a tingling, buzzing, sensation in her head that she didn't like at all. Some of the bodies she passed in the streets weren't bloody and liquid like the red plague victims, or melted by rain from an acid storm, but were pale, with weeping, red sores that looked like burns, and with their hair peeling off their scalps in clumps. The buzzing intensified when she looked at them, like a warning going off in her head—she trusted her instincts, kept the windows rolled up just in case, and drove through as fast as she could manage.

After a couple of hours she needed a rest—her hands ached where she'd been grabbing the wheel too tight, and she had a tension headache that a cigarette or two couldn't cure. The radio was kicking in louder and clearer now too—every ten minutes even when she was sure that she'd definitely switched it off, still the same man's voice.

> *"God told Moses, 'Pull off your shoes', "Out of the*
> *flock, well you I choose."*

She was trying to edge past an accident that had involved at least a dozen vehicles all piled in a tortured mangle of glass and metal, chrome and flesh, and when the singing started up again she'd had enough. She pulled to the side of the road on the crest of a hill, switched off the engine and got out, intending to look out over the view while having a smoke. The cigarette stayed unlit in her fingers when she looked up and over the railing.

It had been a great city once—she'd seen a road sign to New York some miles past and guessed that was it. Likewise, she'd seen images of New York in several of the action movies she'd watched in Albany—but there was nothing in this blasted landscape ahead of her that she could recognize either from memory or from the movies.

There were no tall towers of stone or glass, and no throngs of people going about their business—no statues welcoming the dispossessed and the needy to a new land. It looked like a giant hand had come out of the sky and flattened the place to the ground—after it had been burned first. Patches of tumbled ruins were scattered around in the rubble and ash, but for the most part all she could see from her high view was a gray, barren desert of dust and death. In the distance, far off at the horizon, a darker line marked where sky met sea, but there was no color anywhere, just washed out hues of gray and black. She thought the sight of the dead lying untended in the road was the worst thing she'd seen—but she'd been wrong. This had been a great, vibrant, multitudinous city, one of the shining monuments to modern civilization, if the movies were to be believed. Now it was all gone, with no one—not even Meg—to remember its former glory.

She climbed back into the driver's seat, closed the door and had her smoke. She didn't look out of the window again. Five minutes later she drove off—heading south.

She'd thought herself to be emotionally uninvolved—some strange by-product of her memory loss that prevented her from grieving, even to the extent of being untouched by the death of people who had obviously been her parents. But the sight of the dead, silent city had hit her hard, and she felt hot tears at the corners of her eyes that she wiped away lest they obscure her view of the road. She tried the radio again, hoping for music to soothe her as it had the night of the storm, but there was still only hissing static—until the auto- tuner picked up a channel on the AM band, crackling and fuzzy, but somehow familiar. A man's voice read, calmly and steadily.

"I looked, and there before me was a white cloud, and seated on the cloud was one like a son of man with a crown of gold on his head and a sharp sickle in his hand. Then another angel came out of the temple and called in a loud voice to him who was sitting on the cloud, 'Take your sickle and reap, because the time to reap has come, for the harvest of the earth is ripe.' So he that was seated on the cloud swung his sickle over the earth, and the earth was harvested.'

The voice wasn't in any way comforting—it reminded her too much of the song she'd been hearing. Although she couldn't see his face, she thought that this too must be the same man, the one she'd seen on the recording in the church—this must be the prophet—John—the Revelator.

She thought back to the face she'd seen, trying to fix his image in her mind. This was her target, her focus from now until it was done. If he was the perpetrator of all of this death and destruction, then she intended to meet him, face to face, and ask him why. Then she was going to kill him. Kill him and burn him to the ground and trample on his ashes as thoroughly as New York had been trampled.

She kept driving south—her tears had dried now, and the louder the voice came on the radio, the faster she drove towards it. She was taking more risks now, pushing other vehicles out of the way rather than trying to go round them, driving over the top of wreckage that might cause her to have a puncture, and going too fast through gaps that were too small. The pickup was getting dinged, bodywork screamed as she squeezed past other vehicles, and she lost her passenger side wing mirror. She didn't care—after all, there were discarded vehicles all around her—and taking care of somebody else's truck was the least of her problems right now.

She was making better time, which was the most important thing.

Then, somewhere just north of Morriston the radio stopped talking at her and started talking to her.

It wasn't the Revelator—she'd definitely come to recognize the man's voice. But she also recognized the coarse, gravelly tones that came over the airwaves after a brief spell of quiet. It was barely a whisper to begin with, and she'd last heard it back in the church in Saratoga Springs.

"Hello, dear," it said. "I bet you thought you'd rid yourself of us?"

At first she put it down to stress and emotions finally getting the better of her—it was just the dead, trying to be heard. But the voice came again almost immediately, stronger and louder.

"Why are you running, Meg?" it said. "You've seen all there is to see. What did you think of the city? New York, New York—so good they bombed it twice."

The last bit was in a sing-song voice, but she didn't know the song—just the sentiment.

"That place in Albany was nice though," the voice said. "It looked like you were cozy and snug there. Why would you want to leave all that behind? We got there just too late to join the party, but we could all have been happy there, don't you think, Meg? Why don't we all go back and try? Eat, drink and be merry, for tomorrow, we die."

The voice echoed thoughts that Meg had still been having for herself—thoughts of hunkering down somewhere quiet—somewhere safe—riding things out until the cavalry showed up. But she knew now, given what she'd seen on the road, that was a coward's way out—and the call of the Revelator was stronger than her fear. She meant to have a reckoning—and that meant she needed to keep moving, keep heading south. For now at least.

"You have nothing to offer me," Meg said, feeling almost embarrassed to catch herself talking to a disembodied voice on the radio, and wondering if the thing at the other end could hear her hesitation, however slight.

The gravelly voice cackled. When she heard it, Meg thought of the old woman back in the hotel room rather than the much younger one in the church.

"We know offering you the world looks like a pretty poor deal at the moment," it said. "But things will not always be this way. The day is coming—the day that was foretold when the world turns. A new Heaven and a new Earth—that is what is promised. And you, little Meg from the farm, you get to choose where you want to be—a fresh start with all the opportunities that represents, or stay right here, right now, locked into the same old same old, from here to Eternity."

"Let me guess," Meg said. "I'm really, really special—I'm not like all the other girls. I've been put here for a reason—chosen for a higher purpose. It's just that I don't remember it, and you're here to show me the error of my ways?"

"Now you're getting there," the voice said.

"Fuck that," Meg replied. She slowed the pickup, making sure she wouldn't hit anything if her concentration wavered, then tore the radio out of the dashboard, having to put her weight into it. Something sparked and hissed, but it came away cleanly enough—and it made a satisfying thud on the road when she tossed it out the window.

The phone in her breast pocket started to play a tune to her—she'd forgotten it was even there—she had carried it all the way from the house on the hill. She knew who it would be before she even flipped the phone open, but she had to check—just in case it wasn't.

"That wasn't very polite, now was it, Meg?" the gravelly voice said.

"You want polite? Fuck you," she shouted. "And the horse you rode in on."

She threw the phone out the window and saw it bounce and shatter into pieces on the road behind her. She waited, wondering if the voice would come even when there was no radio, no phone—but everything stayed quiet and there was only the rumble of the engine—for now. She'd lost the song—it had been her compass, the thing that had been leading her so far. But she knew the tang of it, could feel it, like a magnet in her head drawing her on—south, always south.

It was getting on in the afternoon by the time she approached Princeton. She'd intended to keep driving as long as it took to reach her destination, but she had no idea how far that might be, and even pushing and shoving her way through the discarded traffic was taking time—and concentration—she didn't want to spare.

She sang to herself—at first, she hardly noticed she was doing it—"Smokestack Lightning", "The Sky is Crying" and "It Hurts Me Too" to start with. It was as if someone else was there with her, in her head, keeping her occupied, mellowing her out. It sounded—felt—like the same voice she'd heard before—the one that had been going down to the river to pray. And there was even an accompanying guitar. She sang along at the top of her voice through "That's All Right, Mama", "I Walk the Line" and "Peace in the Valley" and immediately felt better.

She still needed a rest—but the thought of heading into another dead town didn't appeal to her, and she was pretty much self sufficient with what she had stowed away in the truck. Sure, the possibility of a soft bed and comfort was enticing—but the voice on the radio had known that, and tried to trick her with it. She couldn't leave herself open to that kind of temptation. She spent the next twenty minutes looking for somewhere off the road where she could park. Despite not having seen anyone else on the move, she would still feel more secure knowing she was safe from being rear-ended.

She finally found what she was looking for and pulled the pickup over into a mostly empty parking area outside a service station and store.

She killed the engine, and lit up a smoke. And at the same time, her brain stopped thinking about driving, and started to dwell on what she was doing.

She hadn't done much thinking at all on her situation, not even in the three nights she'd spent in Albany. She had nothing to compare it with, no point of reference that would tell her this wasn't normal. All she knew was that she'd woken up in the damp bed in the house on the hill, and that she'd gotten from there to here by not letting her guard down—by surviving, by facing up to whatever came at her.

*I'll keep doing that then.*

The smoke went a long way to relaxing her, and after she washed down a sandwich and a packet of chips with a bottle of water she felt more like herself. She settled down in the seat and closed her eyes, intending only a quick nap before getting back on the road.

When she woke it was full dark outside the windows.

Her first thought after noticing that night had fallen was that she urgently needed to pee. She turned on the headlights of the pickup and they lit up an empty stretch of the forecourt in front of the service station. She measured the distance, and thought of her options—she could go beside the truck—it wouldn't be the first time. But they'd have a washroom over there—maybe hot water, definitely soap, and possibly towels. But they'd also be in near total darkness—the risk involved just for a few seconds of possible comfort wasn't worth it.

She stepped out of the truck and did her business beside the door, cleaning up with paper tissues and water, intending to be on her way again right away—but as she turned the key in the ignition, she spotted she was getting low on gas. The station's pumps would be useless without power—but she'd come prepared—there was gas and a funnel in the back of the pickup, courtesy of the hoard of the house owners in Albany.

She got out the pickup and closed the door, leaving the lights on—they were the only bright patches in a sea of total darkness and they helped—some, just not a lot—to allow her to find what she wanted. She found the gas and the funnel quickly enough, then took several long seconds to locate the cap in a darker patch of shadow behind the cab. She twisted it open. The ratcheting noise echoed far too loud across the parking lot, and she suddenly felt exposed.

She kept an eye open, looking around into the shadows, as the gas gurgled from container to funnel to tank. She put all the spare gas she had into the pickup—it took both of the twenty-liter containers she'd brought with her and still wasn't full—then threw the empty containers into the back. She turned to go back to the driver's side.

Somebody blocked her way—a dark shape silhouetted against the headlights behind. Meg's hand instinctively went for the Walther.

"I don't want any trouble," she said.

"Oh, this will be no trouble at all," a gravelly voice replied. She'd been so intent on the figure in front of her, she didn't spot movement in the shadows at her back until it was too late. A pair of strong arms reached round from behind her and pinned her arms to her side, stopping her from reaching the Walther. The shadowy figure in front of her came forward. At first, she thought it was going to be the tall-robed woman from the church, risen from the dead to taunt her. Instead it was a tall, thin, black man wearing the black suit and dog collar of a preacher, with a wide brimmed hat pulled forward to leave his face in shadow—she didn't have to see to know that his eyes would be bleeding.

"You should have stayed in Albany, Meg. It was nice there," he said. Something gurgled, wet deep in his throat and he moved slowly, carefully—as if he was afraid that bits of him might fall off if he did anything too sudden.

"There's nothing you can do to hurt me," Meg said. She struggled, looking to see if there was any wiggle room in the hold on her, but the grip was too tight.

The man laughed and took a step toward her—it sounded like a wet slap when his foot hit the ground—if it hadn't been so dark, Meg reckoned she'd see the bloody footprints he was leaving behind him.

"Why would we ever hurt you, Meg? You're special, remember? We just want you to join us—come to our side and be part of the flock. Let us wash you in the blood of the Lamb—be washed and be saved."

The man moved forward again, almost close enough to touch. The hands around Meg were still gripping her strongly—but there were other parts of her that weren't held down. She felt hot wet breath at the back of her neck as the grip tightened, chose her moment and whipped her head back hard into the face of her assailant. She got the result she'd hoped for—nose bones crunched—far more easily, and softer than she might have expected—and the hands at her side fell away.

"It's not going to be that easy," the man in the hat said, and stepped up toward her, his hands raised. Meg had just enough room to kick out, catching him with the point of her toes, right in the groin. He didn't buckle, didn't even grunt in pain, but her foot seemed to go in too far for a normal kick, and the man staggered, bow-legged as she rolled away. She didn't try to draw the pistol yet—it was too dark here with no clear targets, just darker shadows, so she rolled again before standing and, in five paces, was in a better position, five yards in front of the headlights. They came straight after her—four of them, dark silhouettes against the lights.

They never stood a chance. The Walther cracked, three times, and three bodies fell.

The tall preacher was the last to go down. He waddled into view with a hand held up to her. The other was at his groin, trying, vainly, to hold his innards in place—he already had a long trail of exposed gut hanging below him, trailing like a red, wet tail on the ground.

"Receive the blood of the Lamb or be damned for eternity," he shouted, in that rough, gravelly voice she kept hearing. His eyes flared red, fiery embers in the night.

She fired—two in the chest—and the preacher fell on his knees in front of the pickup then toppled to one side with a wet thud. When she stepped over to make sure he was dead, he looked up at her and smiled. Red coals burned in his deep black eye sockets.

"Behold, the Lord High Executioner. Aren't you tired of dealing in blood and death yet, Meg?"

"I'm not the one bleeding," Meg replied.

"But you could be, if you'd only join us—we can promise you rest— quiet, peaceful rest for all of eternity. Surely that is better than this?"

He coughed again as he spoke—more blood came up, and he seemed to sink further into himself. Something gave way, moist spattering on the ground below him—but he still wasn't done—not quite.

"Did you ever wonder, these past few days, where you learned to move and shoot like that? Your daddy taught you well, Meg. He'd be disappointed in you right now. He'd want you to be one of us."

"You know nothing about me," Meg said, and raised the Walther.

"Oh, the things we could tell you." He coughed, and this time pints of thin watery blood came up and ran down his vest. His next words were barely a whisper. "We've had our eye on you since you were born, little Meg. We know all there is to know. All you have to do is ask—allow yourself to be washed in the blood of the Lamb, and ask."

"I've seen too much blood already, preacher," she replied, and put a bullet between the red eyes, putting him down for good. But she stood there for long seconds to make sure, watching the red embers dim and fade, until there was only the blackness left.

# JD – 3 Days

*The White House*

John waited patiently. His duty was almost done—he had spread the Word and it was heard.

*What will be, will be.*

His first acolyte arrived with the darkening of the sky as another night drew on. It was a woman in her fifties, caked in a piebald pattern of ash and dirt, her dress tattered, her knees scraped and her make up running over her face giving her the appearance of a manic clown. She looked tired, and wan, as if she had not slept or eaten for a while, and her steps were stumbling, exhausted. But she smiled broadly as John met her by the dry fountain on the lawn and took her by the hand.

"Praise be," she said. "You are real after all. I have found you."

"No," John said, clasping her to him in a hug. "You have found yourself. Welcome sister. We are the Alpha and Omega, the first and the last, and together we shall work wonders."

John felt the power rise in him again as he spoke. He didn't need the monitors and cameras and microphones now—it was all worthless since the electricity had failed completely. Now he only had the Word, but the

Word was enough.

"And when we opened the fifth seal, I saw under the altar the souls of them that were slain for the word of God, and for the testimony which they held. And they cried with a loud voice, saying, 'How long, O Lord, holy and true, dost thou not judge and avenge our blood on them that dwell on the earth?'"

As he spoke, he knew—judgement was coming. Indeed, it had already come for many of those who denied the Word. And those remaining who had ears to hear would hear—and those who had eyes to see would see what John saw. What the Word now showed them—the evidence that was cried out for, as it was spoken, so it had been done.

The great cities of the world lay in ruin—New York, Chicago, London, Paris, Berlin, Moscow, Sydney, Tokyo, Rio, Toronto, Cairo, Rome, Athens—all gone forever—some bombed, some burned, some flooded, some taken by the red death, others just gone, swallowed by the earth to be digested and remolded. The works of man had all fallen quiet. Silence lay across the planet and the dead lay unburied, mute and lost.

"And the horseman carried with him the key to the gates of life and death. And the gate was locked and death came forth in its blackness and spread across the face of the earth. And where it passed the sons of Adam fell before it, and the cities lay quiet and the noise of the works of man was heard of no more."

He felt the power of the Lord wash over him, and shared his vision so that all who listened could see it—Jerusalem, the old city a tumbled ruin of blackened dust and ash, the holy places blasted and barren. Bodies lay burned to cinders at the Wailing Wall. The stones of the church of the Holy Sepulchre were strewn to the four winds, and a terrible silence hung over everything.

Another sight—Mecca, a smoking crater in the desert.

Another—Lhassa, the ancient city and its monasteries were tumbled and fallen and scattered over the mountainsides.

Another—Jesus, Christ the Redeemer in a pile of broken stone under a swirling mass of the bodies of the dead in the water.

Another—Paris again, Notre Dame again, and the great cathedral fell with a roar and a last peal of the bells into the swollen, raging, waters of the Seine.

"Fallen, fallen is Babylon; and all the images of her gods are shattered on the ground. She has become a dwelling for demons and a haunt for every impure spirit, a haunt for every unclean bird, a haunt for every unclean and detestable animal."

Another vision of the beast, a shadowy thing. Only half- seen, but immense, huge almost beyond comprehension, clawed its way up out of a smoking, sulfurous pit. A throng stood on the rim, rank after rank of pale figures, thousands—millions—of them all bleeding from red eyes.

"If anyone worships the beast and its image, and receives its mark on his forehead or hand, he too will drink the wine of God's anger, poured undiluted into the cup of His wrath. And he will be tormented in fire and brimstone in the presence of the holy angels and of the Lamb."

He shared another vision—this one of a Grand Duke of Hell, Murmus, a huge demon with fiery eyes, was assembling a host for his master. He stood on a flat, gray, landscape scourged of everything but dust and ash, and his followers soared above his raised hands. They were black, and filled the skies like a huge flock of gigantic crows, their wings spread wide, flapping in the wind with the sound of a hundred, a thousand, a million kites soaring.

"Do you hear it? A sound of tumult on the mountains, Like that of many people! A sound of the uproar of kingdoms, of nations gathered together! The fight will be joined. The Lord of hosts is mustering his army for the last great battle."

A last vision he showed them was of himself, of John, the Revelator, towering high, way up over the White House that sat like a doll's house between his feet. He loomed up over the ruins of Washington, his arms outstretched in welcome.

"The final day is nigh. Those who have eyes to see let them see. Those who have ears let them hear. Those who would bear arms for the Lord when the last trumpet sounds—come to me—come to Gehenna—and fight."

# JD – 2 Days

*Philadelphia - Alfie*

It was almost noon when the VW Camper drove into what was left of Philadelphia. They'd made good time along almost empty highways, and Dawson seemed none the worse for wear for having drunk the best part of a bottle of JD the night before. He'd even cooked them both a huge breakfast of ham, hash browns, sausage and baked beans on the small camping stove in the back of the camper. It had Alfie thinking about going back to sleep all over again, just to get away from a heavy brick that had settled in the pit of his stomach.

But after a quick wash, and a shot of coffee so black and strong he felt it kick-start his heart and buzz in his head, Alfie sat up front in the passenger seat and Dawson kept up a running commentary as he drove.

"You ever been to Philly, Alfie, lad? It's a wonderful city. And it's a great place for old vets like me too—they know how to treat you right here. The VA always has time for me—a bed and a coffee is all I ask most times—they won't give you a drink though. If they did I'd never leave the place. But I've made a lot of friends here over the years. It's not home— not like Gainsford—but it's got a bit of my heart—it'll always have that."

Dawson seemed blind to the fact that the streets were empty apart from the fallen, rotting victims of the red death. Although to tell the truth, there was little of them left now. Decomposition seemed to be accelerating as if someone—or something—was cleaning house fast, and there was little inside the scattered bundles of clothing but dust and dried blood. They passed a figure—whether it had been a man or woman it was impossible to tell, but they had died clinging to a roadside streetlight. A breeze got up, just enough to stir the dust in the road. It was more than enough to bring about the dead figure's final dissolution—it fell out of the remains of its clothes and was scattered, mere shadows in the wind, gone before its jacket hit the ground.

And it wasn't just the bodies that were going fast—the trees at the roadside were melting, dripping globs of brownish-green, smoking, ooze onto the sidewalks and verges. Any grass they saw had gone brown and dry, also crumbling into dust that was swirling in the air all around them as the breeze got stronger.

"And the old Heaven and the old Earth will be washed away," Dawson said softly. Alfie guessed it was another of those religious things he either had never known, or didn't remember.

Then Dawson surprised him.

"So—you didn't answer—have you been to Philly before, Alfie?"

The truth came out before he could stop it.

"I don't remember. I don't remember much of anything at all."

"What do you mean, you don't remember?"

"Just what I said—my memory only goes back a few days—to when I woke up in the subway. I told you about that bit already, remember? Beyond that, there's just blackness."

Dawson didn't seem surprised in the slightest.

"You got a touch of retrograde amnesia—at least that's what they said when I got it in the desert. But it comes back, lad; it always comes back—whether you want it to or not."

"You think so? You think I'll remember everything?"

"Maybe not everything, but enough. Maybe even enough for you to want to forget again.

There's a lot I wish I could forget again, lad. The booze helps, but it's not enough. It's never enough. Maybe you're better off the way you are now." Alfie saw the pain in the older man's eyes and remembered what Frank had said to him, under the bridge. If he did have a gift, he couldn't think of a man more in need of receiving it right now.

He got out of the seat and climbed through to the back of the van, got out the guitar, and started to sing "After You've Gone", then switched smoothly into "Accentuate the Positive" and finally back to the blues with "It Hurts Me Too". That got Dawson's eyes wet again, but when Alfie put the guitar away and climbed back up front to join him, the older man had a wide grin on his face, and he clapped Alfie, one-handed, on the shoulder.

"I didn't know that I needed that, Alfie," he said. "But, my Lord, it's done me the world of good—so thank you."

He turned back to watch the road—the grin stayed though, despite the increasing carnage they saw all around them.

The wind rose another notch as they approached the city center.

❊ ❊ ❊ ❊ ❊

As they reached the more tightly packed areas, they noticed that the buildings were crumbling around them. The streets and towers and office blocks weren't burned—they hadn't been bombed or flooded—they were just falling apart, as if time had accelerated and the timber, mortar, chrome, glass and brickwork was all succumbing to the effects of advanced age. The rising wind was only speeding matters along further, tossing pebbles and dirt and bits of glass into whirling, dancing vortices that Dawson was having trouble avoiding.

"It's like somebody put a stake in the planet's heart," Dawson said softly.

Again, Alfie didn't get the allusion, but he understood the intent of it well enough. It appeared that he'd woken and been brought into the world just as everything else was dying. Suddenly he felt infinitely sad.

*A witness to the end of all things—is that all I am to be?*

The wind picked up another notch, rocking the old van from side to side and spattering fine dust and debris against the windshield. The steeple of the old stone church on the corner ahead of them crumbled at the base, rocked twice, then tumbled in a roar of stone and rubble to the road, sending more dust dancing in the air. Just beyond that, Alfie saw a tall modern block sway violently, then fall in on itself as if explosives had been set off around its base. The van shuddered as the roadway shook underfoot—not an earthquake, just the combined seismic shaking of so many structures all falling at once. Dawson had to swerve violently to avoid an area of wall coming down from a three-story building to their left.

"I think we should get out of the open for a bit, Alfie lad," Dawson said almost casually. "I know a place where we can lay up real quiet and wait things out."

Alfie felt the draw, felt the calling, of the Revelator—but that was still some way to the south of them—closer than before, but far enough that it felt risky to make the attempt in the old Camper through what looked to be fast becoming a dangerous situation. Besides, he'd already traveled much more than twice as far today as he might have managed alone on foot and he had discovered he needed—enjoyed—the companionship. He nodded, then realized Dawson was concentrating on the road, and spoke up.

"Sounds like a plan to me. Can you find your way?"

Dawson grinned and gave Alfie a thumb's up.

"I might be screwed up in the head, but my sense of direction has always worked just fine. It's just a couple of blocks ahead of us. We should be there in five minutes."

It took ten, due to having to weave around discarded vehicles on the roads, battle against a wind that was turning into a gale, and avoid the tumble of rock and glass and torn steel girders that were now coming down from the buildings on either side of them. Several times Alfie thought they might get crushed completely under the falling rubble, but Dawson handled the old van like a racing car, braking and accelerating at just the right times to keep them safe. Finally, Dawson turned, wheels screeching, into a wide alley then down a steep ramp into an underground car park beneath a tall office block.

Everything fell quiet—there was only a distant rumble to tell of the chaos going on above them.

"Won't the building come down on top of us?" Alfie said, suddenly claustrophobic at the thought of being trapped again, down in a dark place—one from which he might not escape this time.

Dawson smiled.

"Not down here. We'll be okay down here, Alfie, lad. This bay is cut deep into the bedrock—that keeps it nice and cool in the summer, which is how I came to know about it—we took to sleeping down here, back in the day when I was on the streets. There used to be a crotchety old night watchman who was always trying to move us on back then, but I figure he's got better things to do today."

Dawson drove them down two levels. Dim light filtered down from somewhere above, just about enough to see by as they parked, reversing in against a wall to give them a view out over the wide—and empty—expanse of the bay. They were the only occupants to be parked on the whole level.

"Guess nobody came to work today," Dawson said, and chortled.

He switched on the overhead light in the camper. It flickered, dimmed—Alfie held his breath—then it steadily brightened. Dawson saw Alfie look up.

"Don't worry—we've got a big old battery in this baby. It's built to be used on camping trips in the wilds where there's no source of power, so we got juice for a long, long while as long as we don't run the heater or air-con, and it don't look like we're going to need either here for a while. So settle down and relax—it looks like we're safe here, so what say we kick back and let the world go fish for a few hours?"

Alfie was still thinking about the building above them and how rapid the deterioration would have to be before everything up above was gone completely.

*Then what will I do? How will I get south if there are no roads to travel—if there's no south there to be reached?*

Dawson seemed to read his mind.

"Ain't nothing we can do now except keep on keeping on, Alfie, lad," he said. "Trust me—I've been doing it for many years. The good thing about it is that it's not hard if you don't allow it to be. Now, how about a drink and a song?"

They sat there in the back of the van for several hours, Alfie picking at the guitar, occasionally breaking into songs that they both sang along, Dawson sipping at JD. Alfie made a bottle of beer last—the lure of the liquor wasn't as strong as the lure of the voice telling him to head south, and he thought he'd better keep a clear head, in case an opportunity arose that needed to be taken fast.

All the while they were accompanied by distant rumblings and rushing noises, and the ever increasing whistle of the wind—it sounded like a gale had ramped up out in the city. At one point the van lurched several inches to one side, Alfie let out a surprised yelp, and Dawson laughed.

"Don't worry, Alfie—bedrock, remember—it'll take a full- scale earthquake to get us down here."

*That's what I'm worried about*, Alfie thought, but didn't say. Dawson seemed able to see the best in any given situation—that in itself was a gift almost as welcome as Alfie's own abilities with the guitar and song. But the darkness of the parking bay reminded him far too much of his awakening in the ruins of the subway, and now that he was here, alive, he had no desire to return to the black emptiness from which he'd been born.

He clutched the guitar tighter, strummed twice, then, without any conscious thought, he was playing the song again—the Revelator's song. It seemed Dawson knew that one too, for he sang along, at the top of his voice.

> *"Well who's that writin'? John the Revelator,*
> *"Who's that writin'? John the Revelator, "Who's*
> *that writin'? John the Revelator,*
>
> *"A book of the seven seals."*

After they were done and the final chord rang out, Alfie spoke up.

"Do you know any more about this John—this 'snake-oil salesman' as you called him?"

Dawson swigged on his JD, thinking before he spoke.

"Only that he says he's a prophet—a messenger from the big man up in the sky spreading the word about the end of all things. I've heard it all before—there was a guy in the F.O.B. in the Gulf who spouted much the same stuff. Didn't help him any—he got his top half and his bottom half separated by a mortar. That was the end of his prophesizing—and he didn't see it coming."

"And this book? The book of the seven seals?"

Dawson shrugged.

"It's from the Bible—that's about all I know—a book that's a record of all there ever was, all there will be. A damnable big book, it'll have to be, to fit all that in. Each seal, as it's opened unleashes some other bit of crap on us poor schmucks until they're all open and we're all dead, then we get judged for our sins and fucked over, all over again. Same as it ever was."

"Then why am I hearing the call from the south? Why would some-body—anybody—want me to have anything to do with it? I don't believe. I can't believe in something I know absolutely nothing about."

Dawson shrugged.

"Maybe it's a matter of faith," Dawson said, then finished off his glass of JD. "But I'm not the one you should be asking, Alfie. I don't know any of that stuff, lad—I learned in the Gulf to just keep my head down until all the shit goes away."

*I'd love to have the luxury—but I'm not sure that's an option this time.*

It now sounded like a full-blown hurricane was raging above them, and there was almost no light at all coming down to where they were parked. That didn't help Alfie's anxiety levels. Dawson seemed completely uncon-cerned, although he did notice Alfie's glances out the window.

"Ain't nothing to be worried about, lad," he said after another rumble shook the van again. "The time to worry is when them big Iraqi shells fly all around you, and one of them's got your name on it and it blows you and your pals to hell and back."

"To hell and back—that sounds like something the Revelator would say."

Dawson nodded.

"I heard tell that he was a vet himself—walked out of the desert a few months back leaving a bunch of dead troopers in the sand and getting a case of the Holy Joes in his head. I've been there—I kinda understand where he's coming from."

"But you don't believe a word of it?"

"Ain't no Hell, lad—none except the one we make for ourselves. If you refuse to let it in, it can't get to you."

Alfie remembered the blue-eyed Preacher in the ruins of the city— he had sure felt like something that had come straight from hell. But again, he kept quiet—Dawson was in too good a mood for him to spoil it with his own worries.

Dawson cooked again—baloney and beans, and again it tasted just fine. After that, Dawson drank some more—the JD didn't seem to be affecting him any. Alfie nursed another beer, and played and sang—happier tunes this time—"Blue Moon of Kentucky", "That's All Right, Mama" and "Sittin' On Top of The World". Dawson bellowed along and the old Camper van rocked and rolled.

It wasn't until Alfie put the guitar down to take a sip of beer and looked out the front window that he realized there was someone—or something—out there in the parking bay watching them.

# JD – 2 Days

*Philadelphia - Meg*

Meg drove all night after the incident in the service station parking lot—she'd spent enough time sleeping—it was time to get south, get to whoever or whatever was drawing her there, and have that reckoning.

The going was even slower in the dark though, and she still had to push and shove her way along the highway through a mangle of crashes and discarded vehicles. It didn't help that she was annoyed with herself for letting them ambush her quite so easily in the dark, and for taking time to talk to the dying preacher—she should have just put him down straight away—she knew better than that—she'd been taught better than that.

Part of her knew that the preacher had been right on one thing. She'd learned her moves from her father—and he'd been a man who'd looked forward to times like these—times when a man would be beholding to none, answerable to none. Times when the Lord would wipe the Earth and start again. She wondered why he hadn't been spared to see it.

❊ ❊ ❊ ❊ ❊

She'd arrived on the outskirts of Philadelphia with the dawn and another splitting headache from peering ahead in the dark for too many miles and too many hours. She found a relatively empty bit of highway on a high turnpike, pulled over onto the shoulder, and stopped for a rest as dim light washed across the sky from the east.

She drank almost a full bottle of water, chewed, not really tasting it, a slightly stale sandwich, and had a smoke. She was zoned out, not really looking at the view at all, until a splash of color caught her eye in the trees just below her high position. It was green—green and dripping from the trees, and she was instantly reminded of the acid storm in the forest and almost drove on immediately. But there was no rain here—at least not now, and the road surface was dry—her tires were safe.

The trees weren't doing so well.

Green ooze—melted leaves and branches—dripped in thick globs and turned to hiss and steam on the ground. From where Meg sat, high up, she saw a long bank of grass run away to her left—grass that was still green in parts, but was mostly a burnt brown color that looked dried out and dusty. In the time it took her to finish the smoke all the green went out of the swathe, and the burnt debris were scattered in a light wind.

Her progress south was halted to a snail's pace—traffic was packed tight on the turnpike and after several hours of frustration—and an added ratchet of pain in her headache—she gave up and took the first available exit, one that led down into the city itself.

Bodies littered the streets here. Although they were obviously victims of the red plague, they weren't wet and bloody like the ones she'd been seeing previously. These were little more than dried out husks, going as brown as the grass—and as dry. She saw one body collapse into itself when it was hit by little more than a light breeze. There was more of the green goop down here in the city too—dripping from shrubbery and copses, steaming where it landed. She had the window down for a time, but the acrid stench soon became too much even when she tried to mask it with a smoke, so she shut herself in and had the air-con blowers going on full. It almost masked the stench, but she knew it was there, and drove as fast as she could in the crowded streets, hoping to reach clearer, fresher air.

Every few blocks she had to make decisions when she came to streets that were completely blocked with no way through. She tried to keep heading south as much as possible, but after a while she lost track of how many turns she'd made. She couldn't find any signs to indicate how she was doing, and the light was now diffused across the whole of the dome of swirling cloud overhead, so she couldn't get her bearings.

*I could be driving in circles for all I know. I need a map.*

If she'd been smarter, she could have picked one up much earlier, but now that she had thought of it, she started looking for anywhere she might be able to find one. And her luck was in—two streets later she spotted a chain bookstore. She parked outside, locked the pickup, and headed in with her hand on the Walther.

The shop sat in darkness but the maps were in a rotating display unit just by the tills so she didn't have to step into the darker shadows at the rear. She found a Philly street map right on the top row, and had taken it out of the rack when something shifted at the back of the shop, as if someone had moved something heavy across the floor. A voice, deep and gravelly came out of the darkness.

"What's the matter, Meg? Don't you want to play with us no more?"

She couldn't move—stuck to the spot with a childlike fear of the thing in the dark—it had caught her unaware despite her promise to herself not to get ambushed—she wasn't as good as she thought she was. And that terrified her.

Something else shifted, and the voice came again.

"Come into the dark, Meg. Come into the dark where we can see you."

She took a step—not to the door, but toward the rear of the shop, then another.

The gravelly voice laughed. "Come to daddy."

Meg was ready to go to it, to go to the dark—then she heard the guitar in her head again, and a voice singing, clear and true—a song she knew as soon as it started. "Accentuate the Positive" allowed her to stop moving forward, to stop messing with Mr. In Between.

"What's the matter, Meg? Cat got your tongue?"

Meg didn't waste time replying, nor in considering where the singing might be coming from—she gripped the map in one hand, the butt of the Walther in the other, and headed back out toward the light.

The voice called out again from the back of the shop as she reached the doorway.

"Your chances are running out, Meg. If you're not washed in the blood of the Lamb when the time comes, there will be no redemption, no new Heaven and new Earth for you—just more of the same old shit, from here to eternity. Is that what you want, Meg? Is that what you really want?"

She ignored the voice, unlocked the pickup, got into the driver's seat and drove away. She kept an eye on the rear view mirror until she hit the next junction, but nothing came out of the shop to follow her. The singing in her head had stopped too—but it had done its job—she was free—for now.

❄ ❄ ❄ ❄ ❄

She waited another two blocks before stopping in the middle of a junction to read the map. It took a minute or so after that to control the shakes in her hands—she'd been close—seconds away—from giving up and letting the thing in the dark have her. Now it wasn't fear that was making her tremble—it was anger, at her own weakness and frailty. If it hadn't been for the song coming right when it did, she'd be gone and bleeding the red death by now.

But she couldn't afford the luxury of spending any time thinking about it—the call from the south was getting louder again, the tugging more insistent in her head.

*Times a' wasting, Meg. Get your ass in gear.*

She unfolded the map then looked out the window to check the street signs.

They told her that she had stopped at the junction of North Broad Street and Callowayhill Street. If she kept straight on, she'd go right through the town center—but she could see from where she had stopped that the road was clogged with heavy traffic if she went any further that way. She decided to head left, toward the river, where she saw that she could join the Delaware Expressway and head South and West all the way out of the city.

She still felt the call in her head, pulling her on. And looking at the map, she got a feeling where it was leading her every time she looked at a certain place name—Washington—a place she only knew of from the action movies she'd watched back in the house in Albany.

The more she thought about it, the more she knew her hunch was right—she finally had a goal to aim for. She traced the route with her finger—a straight road from the river expressway all the way southwest. With luck she could be there by sundown.

She drove off, took a left, and headed for the river.

❊ ❊ ❊ ❊ ❊

She was headed the wrong way down a one-way street. There was no one on the move but her, and she had no trouble for the first couple of blocks. But even as she got her first sight of the river ahead of her, a wind got up seemingly out of nowhere and rocked the pickup on its suspension. A three-story building on her right swayed, and bricks tumbled and fell around her, two bouncing off the hood and leaving deep dents, and one hitting the roof above her with a bang like a gunshot.

She floored the accelerator as the wall of the building crumbled and collapsed. Something hit the back of the pickup and half-turned the vehicle so fast that she had to fight the wheel to keep control, then she was free—but only for a second. More debris fell—behind and in front of her. A tall office block collapsed completely, filling the road only fifty yards ahead with steel and glass and rubble that she wasn't going to be able to pass. She threw the wheel right just in time to avoid a chunk of debris that would have flattened the truck like a bug, then swung, doing sixty, down a too narrow alleyway as more rubble and brick fell around her and her view filled with dust.

The truck bounced over bricks and debris on the road and the wheel bucked in her hands. There was a crash—too close for comfort, and the wind went up a notch again, dashing pebbles and dirt against the windshield.

*I need to get out of this.*

She thought she wasn't going to make it, that she'd be trapped in a canyon of buildings as they toppled onto her, but she was saved when she saw an on-ramp, an exit to the expressway, straight ahead. She wasn't stupid enough to head onto the expressway itself—not in a wind like this one was threatening to be. But she was able, after putting her foot hard down on the floor, to get out of the alley, speed at full pelt across a junction, over what had been a grass verge and pull up, tight, under one of the concrete foundations of the ramp. She took her time parking, despite the blowing debris and roaring chaos, to make sure to get into a spot where the structure would act as a windbreak and provide her with maximum shelter.

She switched off the engine. It looked like she wasn't going anywhere for a while.

The storm kept rising and rising. All she could see out the windshield was a swirling vortex of dirt and ash. The wind howled and raged, but she was sheltered from the worst of it by the column of reinforced concrete just inches outside the driver's side door. It got darker, although she knew it couldn't be much past midday, and darker still as the storm ratcheted up. Every so often the ground would tremble and shake and in her mind's eye she saw the great towers and steeples of the town collapsing into more debris to be thrown into the air. But after ten minutes where the pickup only rocked slightly on its suspension, she realized she had indeed parked in relative safety.

Now all she could do was wait for the storm to blow itself out—and hope that it would.

# JD – 2 Days

*Philadelphia - Alfie*

A pair of burning, red eyes—too far apart and too high off the ground to belong to anything human—looked back at Alfie from out in the parking bay. He was glad the Camper's headlights were turned off—he didn't think he wanted to see the thing those burning eyes belonged to.

He didn't have to see it to know it was here for him—he felt it in his head, the same way he felt the pull and call of the Revelator to draw him south. This didn't feel like the man Dawson called a 'snake oil salesman'—this felt more like the one-eyed, blue-eyed, Preacher in the ashes of the blasted city.

He remembered the Preacher's words. "We can tell you all you need to know—all you have forgotten—all you have to do is take my hand."

He'd said then that the Preacher had nothing that Alfie needed, but that wasn't true—Alfie wanted to know what he had been, and why he was here. He was getting tired of watching the world crash and burn. He needed to know there was a purpose—a design—maybe even a designer. Dawson had told him it might be a matter of faith. Alfie didn't have any, but he might be prepared to consider it if he was only given enough facts with which to work.

The thing outside wasn't offering anything at the moment. It wasn't even moving, just standing out there in the darkness, eyes burning, watching the Camper van—watching Alfie. He tried to keep calm—he didn't want to spook Dawson, who was sitting in the back, that same wide grin on his face, sipping down the liquor. But the older man knew something was off as soon as Alfie turned toward him.

"What's the matter, Alfie, lad? The dark got you spooked? Hell, this ain't even real dark at all. Real dark is when everything goes away—everything gets shut down except your own little light, shining." He tapped himself on the side of the head. "It shines way down, so far down you never think you'll climb up out of it, and the darkness crawls and creeps, gnawing away, trying to put your light out for good—telling you it'll be for the best. And yet something keeps you just keeping on—something keeps the lights on and shining. But the darkness is always there too, pushing against your shine, waiting for it to falter."

"That happened to you?"

"Not happened—happens," Dawson said. "Every damn night when I close my eyes and sometimes during the day too—why do you think I drink? It's seductive, that dark, Alfie. Don't let it in—or it will eat your light right up."

That was the most Dawson had said in one spell since they'd met; it seemed to have agitated him some. But he calmed again after taking a sip of the JD. He saluted Alfie with the glass.

"Slow and steady, Alfie, lad—that's the way to keep the light shining."

Alfie sat opposite the man and picked up the guitar again. He still felt the red-eyed stare, fixed on him from out there in the dark, but just holding the guitar helped, and picking a tune helped even more—it made his light shine brighter, like Dawson's smile.

"I need to take a leak," Dawson said a while later. "Be right back."

Alfie tried to keep panic out of his voice. He felt safe as long as they stayed locked inside the van. He knew that was probably only a false sense of security, but the thing had stayed out there thus far—opening the door felt like tempting fate.

"Don't you have a portable thing in here?"

"Yeah—but I prefer going outside—keeps the smells down." Dawson winked and grinned. "Don't worry, lad—ain't nothing but the dark out there—and my light's shining bright tonight."

"Don't," Alfie said. "Please don't."

"Hell, boy—you're as spooked as a jittery squirrel. What's got into you? Look—I'll do it from here if you're so worried." Dawson slid open the Camper van door. The noise of the storm had abated but the wind still whistled loud around the bay. It sounded like a scream. A voice spoke out of it, deep and gravelly.

"Come on out, Alfred," it said. "We told you we'd see you down the line away—come on out and be washed in the blood of the Lamb."

"There's nothing you have that I want," Alfie replied.

The voice laughed. It sounded old—old and cruel.

"We both know that's not true—not now. There is much we can tell you, if you'll only listen. Who do you think taught you your songs? Would you like to know of your mother, Alfie? Would you like to know how she died—or whether she survived—whether she is out there somewhere even now looking for her little Alfred? Would you like that, Alfie? We will only offer one more time, before the end. And you will come to regret it if you make the wrong choice—that we can promise you."

Alfie kept quiet—the thing seemed to know what he'd been thinking. He tried to empty his mind of everything and focus on a song in his head, a simple thing that he could bring to mind immediately.

The voice outside chuckled.

"We are not so easy to dispel," it said.

"Friend of yours, Alfie?" Dawson said. He'd unzipped himself and was taking a leak out of the open door of the van as if he didn't have a care in the world. He gave a wiggle, pulled up his zip, then reached above the door. Alfie hadn't spotted it before, but there was a pump-action shotgun clipped in a fitting that came down easily into Dawson's hands as if it belonged there.

"This boy's my guest," Dawson shouted into the darkness, pumping a cartridge into the weapon. "If any harm comes to him, you'll have to deal with me and my loud friend here."

The voice came again.

"Such as you cannot defy me. I am Murmus, a Grand Duke of Hell," it said.

"Pleased to meet you," Dawson replied. "I'm Tom Dawson from Gainsford. Now fuck off."

He raised the weapon.

The gravelly voice laughed out in the dark.

"I am not here for you, old man."

"You've been here for me every night," Dawson replied. "I recognize your voice—so don't go pretending that I don't. You're the dark—the creeping dark that wants to put my shining out. Well, come on then—let's have at it once and for all. Let's see what you've got."

Dawson turned to Alfie.

"Give us a song, Alfie, lad," Dawson said. "You'll know the right one, I think."

Dawson turned back to the door, standing with the weapon raised, a broad grin on his face. And he was right—Alfie did know just the right song—the one that been in there for the past few minutes. He picked the first four bars, then launched into it. Dawson came in right on the beat to join him. He couldn't really hold the tune, but he made up for it in volume.

"This little light of mine, I'm gonna let it shine."

The darkness outside the door surged and swirled and something big came forward—Alfie felt the rush of it, like an oncoming train.

The overhead light in the Camper van brightened, then blazed.

"Let it shine, let it shine, let it shine."

Alfie's world lit up, a lightning bolt of brilliance, as Dawson pulled the trigger.

"I told you already," he shouted above the song. "Fuck off." The blast from the shotgun was deafening inside the Camper van, and kept the Gibson ringing for seconds after Alfie stopped playing. The sounds echoed and died.

The parking bay fell dark—dark, and quiet.

"I guess he fucked off," Dawson said, and smiled.

# JD – 2 Days

*Philadelphia - Meg*

Meg thought the storm would never end. The pickup rocked and rolled. Sand, gravel and some bigger pebbles rattled against the bodywork and the windshield—one stone hit so hard as to leave a six-inch crack in the glass, and she guessed the black glossy paint job was taking another bashing—one from which it would never recover. But the wind never reached her inside the cab. She was warm, almost cozy. She had food, water and smokes a-plenty, and nowhere else to be right now. She could wait.

She tried to empty her mind, go with the flow, but her thoughts kept returning to the voice that had come from out of the darkness in the bookstore.

*"Your chances are running out, Meg. If you're not washed in the blood of the Lamb when the time comes, there will be no redemption, no new heaven and new earth—just more of the same, from here to eternity. Is that what you want, Meg? Is that what you really want?"*

In truth, she didn't know what she wanted, or even why she was here, woken into this strange, blasted place. Neither did she know the origin of the guitar playing singer who seemed to be arriving to bail her out just when she needed him—she was wondering if that was someone she'd known before, in the dark place from where she'd woken—a friend maybe?

But she still had no way of knowing. All she knew was that she was being called south—and she was getting close. Once this storm blew over she hoped to get a lot closer.

She sat and smoked and the storm kept raging. As she lit a new cigarette from the butt of the last one, a memory came to her unexpectedly. A man—her father she guessed—sat in a rocker on the porch of the house in the hills, handing her a smoke.

"No need to worry about these getting you, gal—the Rapture's coming soon, just you wait and see."

"What's the Rapture, dad?" she heard herself—her younger, shriller self—ask.

"That's when the good Lord takes us that's been good and true up to sit at his side while the rest of this festering ball of shit and pus goes to hell where it belongs."

She remembered something else too now. Dad had been angry—he'd been angry a lot, almost wishing that the world would die in fire and holy rage. But if this was the Rapture, he hadn't taken part in it—and it didn't feel very rapturous at all to her. At least the memory was something new—it gave her hope that there were more details yet to come back to her. Maybe she'd even get an explanation as to why she'd been spared—and what was expected of her now that she was here.

She sat there for several hours, reclining back in the seat, her feet up on the dash watching the dance and swirl of debris outside. She listened to it drum frantic rhythms against the pickup. The wind rose and fell and rose and fell—it too was almost rhythmical at times, and, fancifully, or so she thought at first, she started to hear words in it—the recurring song again. She sang along, tapping against the dashboard with her feet in time.

> *"Tell me what's John writin'? Ask the Revelator,*
> *"What's John writin'? Ask the Revelator,*

"*What's John writin'? Ask the Revelator,*

"*A book of the seven seals.*"

It was only when she stopped that she realized the song was continuing without her, whispered in the wind itself, beat out in the drumming of debris against the truck—running round, over and over, in a loop inside her head.

"*Ask the Revelator, "Ask the Revelator.*"

She felt the pull from the south again, the desire—more of a need—to be on the move, a sense that she did not have as much time as she thought, and that matters might be coming to a head.

*And I need to be there.*

Hours passed. Several times she heard louder crashes and rumbles even above the wind and assumed it must be buildings coming down, but it was almost pitch black outside now and she saw nothing expect swirling dust. At one point she tried the headlights, but that only made the gloom slightly less black, so she switched them off, conserving her battery in case she was here for a long stay.

Finally, almost imperceptibly, the wind dropped and the lashing of debris against the truck diminished to little more than a tickle, then a fine brush, then stopped completely.

Now, when she switched on the headlights, she saw a field of strewn rubble and dirt ahead of her.

She rolled down the window, listening. It was still windy, but it was a clean, whistling breeze with no debris in it—and no sign of the recurrence of the song. She opened the door and got out, hoping to stretch her legs while checking for any damage to the pickup.

A voice spoke from the shadows to her left, deep, gravelly and horribly familiar.

"Well look who it is. It's Meg. Little Meg. Fancy meeting you here. You're not going to run away again now, are you?"

She turned, expecting to see another priest or preacher, or maybe a drunken redneck—but the red, fiery eyes that stared back at her from out of the shadows were too wide apart, too far off the ground, for this to be a person. She instinctively put a hand on the butt of the Walther. But now she wasn't thinking it was a person at all—now she was thinking something bigger—bear maybe—and she knew she didn't have the firepower to put something like that down—not quickly enough to stop it from getting to her.

She steeled herself, waiting for an attack, but none came. The red eyes flashed and the thing—whatever it might be—laughed.

"You've got spunk girl, we'll give you that. But why do you keep fighting? Look around you—fallen, fallen is Babylon, and all the images of her gods are shattered on the ground. Come—join us—be washed in the blood of the Lamb and rejoice, for the time that was foretold has come to pass. Walk with us, into the world that awaits—a world replete with possibilities and endless joys for those with the will to grasp them in their hands."

"My idea of joy and yours seem to be a bit different," Meg said, sidling back towards the driver's door of the pickup. She was gauging distances, wondering if she had time to jump in, start the engine and drive away, knowing that she had to try or she might, this time, succumb to the draw of this strangely seductive voice.

"We know you, Meg," it said. "We know you have considered it— back in the shop there, we felt your need for companionship—for someone to tell you who you were, and where you are going. We can do that for you—just come to us, come to the blood."

"Like the preacher at the rest stop? Like the priestess in the church? Like the rednecks—and the old woman above the bar? Did they come to the blood? Were they washed too?"

The thing laughed again, and the red eyes flared, like bellows applied to hot coals.

"All are welcome in the blood, for we are Legion. We will not ask again, Meg—this is now a one-time, last chance offer for the saving of your eternal soul from damnation. The day is coming, and all must choose a side. Join us—come into the blood—or be forever damned, from here to eternity."

Meg drew the Walther.

"Don't take this the wrong way," she said. "But if the choice is between spending eternity with the likes of you and returning to the darkness of sleep, I know which one I'm choosing."

"Who said anything about allowing you to sleep?" the voice replied. The shadows around the fiery eyes darkened and swirled, took on solidity, heft and depth. There was a roar—not the wind this time, and the black came for her, rushing all at one as if she stood in front of a speeding truck, hypnotized in its headlights.

She raised the Walther and fired, three rapid shots between the thing's eyes and moved, rolling aside in the rubble, already knowing it was too little, too late.

Time slowed—the blackness kept coming at her, swelling and growing, red eyes blazing.

"Come to daddy, you little bitch," it roared.

But there was something else now, another song—one she hadn't heard until now. The sweet, clear voice sang again. It might have only been in her head before, but this time it seemed to ring out, all across the blasted landscape, accompanied by a guitar that rang—almost tolled—like the peals of an old church bell.

"This little light of mine, I'm gonna let it shine."

The headlights of the pickup blazed, as if floodlights had just been turned on, and the encroaching blackness seemed to quiver and quail. The voice in her ear kept singing. Meg joined in on the beat.

"Let it shine, let it shine, let it shine."

She fired again, and at the same time heard a boom and felt everything quiver, like a bomb had gone off. The black thing wailed, a scream louder than any wind had been throughout that long night, then it fell apart into dust and shadows. The red eyes fading, dimming, were the last things to go, leaving everything quiet and almost still save for a breeze that blew the last of the black dust away.

The headlights dimmed to their normal brightness, and the sound in her ear—a last ringing chord from the guitar, faded and left her alone in the quiet dark.

# JD – 2 Days

*The White House*

John heard the last ringing note of the guitar and smiled as he looked out over the crowd that had grown on his lawn. To him it was a bell, being sounded to call the faithful to arms, and another sign that the time was close now. Scores had answered the call, just shy of a hundred so far, and he was hopeful of more on the way.

He clapped his hands together as he spoke—he didn't have to shout—he knew that the Word was being carried to all that had ears to hear. The acolytes came and stood in ranks in front of him. Some were ashen and pale, some bloodied and broken, and their clothes would never have passed muster and scrutiny at church in days before this one—but all were clear-eyed and smiling, awaiting the Word. "My fellow Americans," he said. Some laughed—most cheered. "The great day of His wrath is coming; and who shall be able to stand?"

They cheered, and John knew that the sound was being heard—not by many, for there were not many left to hear.

But the Word did not care about numbers—it only needed to be heard.

"Fallen, fallen, is Babylon," he said, and the images rolled out from him to join the spreading Word.

The massive edifice of Edinburgh Castle—what little was left of it—tumbled and fell into a crater full of lava that surrounded the old rock and encompassed most of what was left of the old city. Tall buildings, centuries old, teetered on the brink of the inferno before crashing down like dominoes. The old closes of the Royal Mile were stripped away from low to high, foot by foot—taken by the lava and melted, reformed, ready to be cast anew.

The towering pyramids of Giza plateau, now no more than piles of broken stone, were washed and worn away as a torrent of water raged around them. The Sphinx, still inscrutable, looked on until the torrent lapped at her paws. She smiled, just once, before the great head dipped and fell, and the last remnant of another once great civilization was washed away by the tide of history.

In Beijing—the old temples and great libraries were being consumed in flame just as rapidly as the mountainous piles of the dead on the city's outskirts.

In Niagara ,dry dust was the only thing that fell down the face of the falls.

The Amazon rainforest was burning.

Siberia, the tundra, was a bubbling lake of green, smoking, goop in which herds—vast, innumerable herds—of caribou bucked, kicked and died.

The plains of Africa were lifeless, dry, barren and dead.

John looked over the acolytes and smiled.

"We are nearly there, brothers and sisters. The time of strife is nearly at an end. The land is being cleansed in readiness for the final battle, for the beast is almost risen."

There was another vision—something climbed up over the rim of a pit on a desert valley floor, something vast and angry, billowing black smoke that obscured the bulk of it as it came.

"We few, we happy few, stand here as witnesses at the end of all things. The world will turn, the world will change, but we have the Word, and we have the strength, and we have the will.

"We will prevail."

The crowd cheered and John smiled.

It was almost time.

# JD – 1 Day

## On the Road - Alfie

They didn't sleep. Dawson and Alfie sat up all night, drinking coffee and singing songs, all the while waiting for any return of their visitor from before.

"So—that's what a Grand Duke of Hell looks like?" Dawson said as he brewed the coffee. "I was expecting something a bit more spectacular, to be honest."

Alfie laughed at that.

"Are you scared of nothing, man?" he asked.

Dawson grinned widely.

"Not since the Gulf, no—not really. Being lost in the dark all alone with no pals—maybe that. But here, now, with my newest pal and his guitar and the song and our little lights shining bright? No—Alfie, lad—a theatrical villain with a deep voice and red eyes just needs to fuck off—like I told him to."

Alfie had started feeling the tug to head south almost as soon as the thing—demon—whatever it had been, had gone. But Dawson had drunk too much

JD to get behind the wheel—and besides, traveling in the dark held no appeal at all.

So the night passed and they waited, and Dawson kept away from the bottle, although Alfie saw the temptation almost get the better of his new friend several times. The songs seemed to help keep the urge for booze away, so Alfie obliged, and the old Gibson rang pure and true as ever as Alfie sang, testing the extent of his repertoire. Dawson asked for songs, and Alfie tried to play them. He had a blank when it came to much of what Dawson called "Rhinestone Country", and no knowledge at all of some modern rock and pop that the man mentioned, but other stuff—"old-timey stuff " Dawson called it, seemed to be his forte. Not for the first time, Alfie wondered where—and when—he'd learned it all.

The night passed slowly. After a while thin light started to seep in from somewhere above again. But the parking lot stayed quiet—quieter even than earlier, for the wind had now dropped to a mere whisper.

Dawson rustled up some breakfast. While he was doing that, Alfie had a quick wash and used the portable chemical toilet—he wasn't ready yet to step outside. The food was plentiful and tasty—beans again, with wiener sausages and hash browns—then they were ready to go.

"So where are we headed?" Dawson said as he got behind the wheel. "You still got a hankering to go south?"

"That I do. But there could be trouble ahead. You don't have to take me any further, Tom," Alfie said. "You've been more than good enough to me already."

"I think I'll come with you down the road a bit yet, lad," Dawson replied and smiled again. "Besides—where else am I going to go?"

They drove slowly up out of the subterranean lot—Alfie wasn't sure what he expected to see, as the storm had been a bad one and the city had been crumbling. He hoped they wouldn't be blocked in and would have to dig—he'd done enough digging himself out of the ground. They turned round the last corner, up the last ramp—and emerged into the first sunshine he'd seen since his awakening.

It was only thin, watery, light, but after the darkness below it was enough to make Alfie blink and shield his eyes until they had adjusted. It was several seconds before he was able to look out of the city and several seconds more before he could believe what he saw.

The city was gone—no trace of it was left except for the entrance to the parking garage at their back, and as they drove out, the whole darkness of the tunnel behind them collapsed in on itself with a soft, muffled, thud and a small puff of dust.

The Camper van sat on a flat, gray plain of ash and dust that stretched away from them into the distance. The dark clouds still hung, swirling and roiling angrily above, but here and there they were breaking up, and thin breaks in the cover allowed wide swathes of light that looked almost solid, beaming down from the sky to the ground. Dawson and Alfie looked at each other and Dawson smiled.

"Things are looking up. At least nothing's falling on us now," he said. "That's a start."

In the distance, across the field of gray and over a mile away, a turnpike looked to be still standing—a high stretch of road that might take them across or around this new landscape—if they could reach it. Alfie pointed it out to Dawson.

"Can we get over there onto the road?"

Dawson grinned.

"We can try."

He pushed the pedal, softly, and the van headed onto the field of ash. It was bumpy, like driving over rough gravel and pebbles, and the suspension creaked and squealed in alarm at some of the dips and troughs, but as long as they kept the speed low they were able to make progress.

"Don't worry, Alfie," Dawson said. "I've taken this old gal across ice lakes and deserts alike and she ain't failed me yet."

Alfie didn't mention his thoughts—he wasn't thinking about the integrity of the van at all—he was thinking about basics—gas, food and water, and where they might find them in this strange new place. Dawson didn't appear to be thinking about any of that—he was smiling like a kid setting out for a day of play as they drove over the gray plain.

It was slow going. They bounced over the sea of ash.

"Just like those guys on the moon, eh, Alfie?" Dawson said. "There are men on the moon?" Alfie replied, astonished at the idea.

"Not now—but there were—when I was a boy. I watched it with my old grandma and…"

The story kept Alfie's mind off the view outside for a good five minutes, and when he next looked up, they were almost halfway toward the roadway, and inching closer.

Dawson didn't want to push it in case there were even deeper hidden dips and hollows in their path, and the dust itself was thicker in some places than others. A couple of times the back wheels spun trying to get traction before catching.

Dawson laughed again at that.

"Don't you go worrying none, Alfie, lad," he said. "I ain't gonna make you get out and push."

After that it was just a slow—a very slow—drive the rest of the way over to the elevated Freeway. As they approached it, they saw that the high roadway ahead was clear of traffic—and clear of any sign of damage or dissolution. Dawson grew serious, his grin fading.

"You know, Alfie, I've been thinking."

"Don't strain yourself, old man," Alfie replied, and the grin came back, but only for a second.

"But I have been thinking, ever since that so-called Duke of Hell bastard last night." Dawson replied. "I've been thinking that this has all been too easy—too cozy. You survive the big one in New York, you find me right when you need me—I'm right thankful for that though. Then we find a nice empty garage for the night right when we need one, that big demon thing fucks right off when we tell it to. And now there's this—a shiny clear road, somehow untouched when everything else has gone to shit—a road that's going right where you want it to go."

"It hasn't felt that easy," Alfie replied, remembering the dead city, the Preacher, and the poor dead and dying folks under the ruined bridge. But on thinking about it, things had been a lot more comfortable for him since meeting Dawson—and the demon thing had gone away without putting up any kind of a fight at all. He started to see Dawson's point.

"I think you're meant to be somewhere, Alfie," Dawson said softly. "And I think I'm meant to help you get there—me, and somebody else."

"Who else is there?" Alfie said, waving his hand to indicate the wide, empty expanse of gray.

Dawson pointed—not out the way, but up, and it took Alfie a few seconds to catch his meaning.

"God? I thought you didn't believe?"

"I never said that. I said I don't believe in folks that try to make me believe. A snake oil salesman is still a snake oil salesman, whether he says he's got God on his side or not. But trust me, Alfie—I feel it in my bones—we're following a plan here. We might not see it yet—but we will—or at least you will—before the end."

Once again Alfie waved out the window at the flat gray plain.

"I thought this was the end."

"Nah," Dawson replied, and his grin came back full force. "This is the beginning of the end—or the end of the beginning—something like that. We've got a ways down the road to go together yet you and I, so come on—fetch the guitar and give me a song. One more for the road."

As they hit the ramp up to the freeway, Alfie launched into "Going Up the Country" and they were both singing at the top of their voices, driving in sunshine high above the flat gray plain.

# JD – 1 Day

*On the Road - Meg*

Meg was ten miles ahead of the Camper heading down the same freeway, going south. She hadn't slept; she was on edge all the time waiting for the red-eyed thing to try another attack. But it never came, and slowly but surely the storm had abated completely, leaving her parked under what appeared to be the only structure still standing in a flat, featureless gray plain. When she inched the pickup slowly, carefully, out from under the bridge, she saw the full extent of what had happened. The old city was gone as if it had never been, wiped clean from the face of the earth, leaving only ash and dust in its place.

Overhead, dark clouds still rolled across the sky, but there was no more wind, no thunder and lightning, and there were breaks in the cloud cover where sunlight speared down to the ground, like great floodlights, searching, always searching.

Suddenly Meg had felt exposed, open to attack. She'd driven off from under the bridge and turned to see that the turnpike was still intact, unaffected by the storm that had laid waste to the city. More than that, there were no discarded or crashed vehicles on it all as far as she could see. It looked—smelled—of a trap—but the thing in her head was still dragging her south—and the road went that way. She drove up onto it and she had the whole four lanes to herself as she slowly pushed the needle up, thirty, forty, fifty, sixty.

Something in the south still called to her, demanding her to hurry—and the faster she got to it, the better she'd feel.

She lit up a smoke, trying to empty her mind of everything but the road ahead.

The red-eyed thing in the storm had spooked her again—but so too had that distant but clear singing, and the ringing of the guitar. It hadn't sounded like the coarse, gravelly, voice she'd come to associate with the thing that was following her—this sounded more pure, more right. She felt that if she could only hear more of it everything would be well and all her worries could fall away.

*Maybe that's what's calling me south—maybe that's the voice that's waiting for me.*

But part of her knew better. There was a reason she carried the Walther—a reason she was proficient with it, and a reason she'd been woken from whatever deep dark she'd fallen into. And it was a reason she needed to understand.

She pushed the needle up again—seventy and still rising. The view to either side of the freeway didn't change—there was nothing as far as she could see but the gray plain of ash—towns, cars, trees, grass, people—all rendered down, ashes to ashes, dust to dust. The beams of sunlight came down from the clouds, like a flashlight being shone from above, but they only lit up more of the same—more of the gray.

The needle was pushing eighty now, and the pull in her head leading her south was getting stronger with every mile. Then she heard it, a voice—no, two voices—and a guitar, singing a chugging blues she vaguely remembered. But she knew the voice well enough, and knew already the sound of that guitar, as clear as the tolling of a bell. And this time it definitely wasn't coming from south—it was coming from somewhere behind her on the road. The call from the south urged her on, but the singing and guitar playing was stronger from the north. And it was definitely getting closer, heading down the same empty highway behind her. She slowed, pulled into the roadside, and stopped just past a four-way junction.

She wanted to meet that guitar player—maybe he would have an answer for her.

# JD – 1 Day

## *On the Road - Alfie*

The freeway was completely empty for as far ahead as they could see. Alfie kept playing and singing, Dawson kept bellowing along, and they went that way for more than twenty miles, the old van rocking and rolling along with them. The sun kept shining through breaks in the cloud, and despite the vast expanses of gray emptiness on either side, Alfie felt surprisingly well—he felt alive, really alive, probably for the first time since he'd crawled out of the dirt in the subway station.

His good mood wasn't to last though—he saw Dawson repeatedly check his wing mirrors, then push the old van to go faster—fifty, almost sixty now, and everything had started rattling and groaning.

"What's the matter?" Alfie asked.

"I don't like the look of them clouds behind us," Dawson replied. "I think there might be another storm coming, and I'm hoping to outrun it. You say you don't believe, Alfie, lad—but a prayer wouldn't go amiss right about now."

Alfie looked in the mirror on the passenger side. It was dark back there—a couple of miles back, but getting closer. It looked like a blacker mass on the road—only that it was roiling and seething as it came, lightning cracking inside it, and the distant rumble of its passage could clearly be heard even above the rattling and clanging of the old Camper van. And whatever the black mass might be, it was definitely catching them.

"Can we go any faster?"

Dawson indicated at the speedometer. It read somewhere around sixty-seven.

"I got my foot hard on the floor as it is," he said. "And she's not gone this fast for ten years and more."

The old van was definitely complaining—groaning and rattling with every turn of the wheels. The groaning was quickly joined by a screeching, grinding noise from the rear.

"Back shaft's going to go," Dawson said. "Hang on, Alfie lad—it could be a bumpy ride."

Alfie looked in the mirror. The blackness was closer now—much closer. It would be on them in a matter of minutes.

"Give us a song then, Alfie, lad," Dawson said, as if they were just out for a pleasant drive in the country. "I think—I hope—you know the one we need."

# JD – 1 Day

*On the Road - Meg*

Meg heard them coming before she saw them.

The song rang loud and clear in her head, the guitar picking sweetly along, the clear voice, full of confidence, filling her with something that reminded her of the front porch of the house in the hills, of hot summer days and ice cream and a mother who smiled.

"This little light of mine, I'm gonna let it shine."

An old battered VW Camper van crested a hill to the north of the junction and bounced, hard. Behind it—right behind it—a black, rolling cloud rode at its tail, sparking off blue lightning, tumbling and rolling angrily as if the van was prey—and it was hungry.

Meg thought about driving to their aid—but they were going to reach her before she had much chance to move. The singing voice and guitar rang out clear.

"Let it shine, let it shine, let it shine."

The VW seemed to be lit up, as if a sunbeam was directly on top of it and keeping pace with it as it rushed towards the intersection—it made Meg feel like cheering.

But disaster struck, only a hundred yards or so from where she stood. The back axle of the van collapsed and the rear end swung round, hard, fishtailing one way then the other, sending showers of sparks across the road. The van bounced, bounced again, then tumbled over completely, sending it rolling two, three times, before it came to a screeching halt in the middle of the intersection. The dark cloud pounced on it, like a hawk on a mouse, and the van was engulfed in a storm of swirling black smoke and sparkling blue lightning.

Meg didn't think—she got out of the pickup and had the Walther in her hand before the door clunked shut behind her.

She fired, twice, taking care to aim away from where she'd seen the van come to a halt.

"Get away from there! Leave them alone!"

# JD – 1 Day

## *On the Road - Alfie*

Alfie heard the shots. At first he thought it was Dawson, but the man was right here beside him, still in the van. They were lying on their side, hanging half out of their seatbelts—which had been the only thing that saved them in the tumble. Amazingly, the guitar lay seemingly untouched against the nearest bit of wall Alfie could see, just to the right of where the windshield had been—an area that was now a rolling mass of black smoke and cracking lightning. Somewhere out there, two fiery, red eyes stared back at him.

A voice called out—a woman's voice.

"Get away from there! Leave them alone!"

The blackness swirled and coalesced. Alfie was aware that Dawson was trying to disentangle himself from the driver's seat above him, but Alfie couldn't take his gaze from the blackness—and what it was becoming. The shape took form quickly, as if solidifying the smoke and lightning into a tangible solidity—a nine-foot tall figure of darkness, feathery shadows like great wings flapping behind it, red eyes blazing as it turned its attention to the woman's voice.

"Meg, Meg, Meg—I hadn't expected to see you until later," the gravelly voice of the demon—Murmus, if he was to be believed—said.

Two more shots rang out—Alfie saw them hit, raising flickers of white fire at the demon's breast. Murmus stopped, as if surprised, then moved forward again.

By this time Dawson had disentangled himself from his seat and was climbing out the windshield, the shotgun in his hand.

"Wait!" Alfie shouted, trying, and failing, to reach his belt buckle.

"Nobody messes with my ride," Dawson said and rolled out onto the road. He turned as he stood.

"Give us a song then, Alfie," he said, and smiled. "I think you know the one we need."

# JD – 1 Day

*On the Road - Meg*

The demon brushed off the two new shots she'd put into it—she'd seen the white flame so she knew she'd hit it—but this time the Walther didn't dispel it like it had during the storm. This time the demon kept coming towards her.

She saw past the smoky dark figure that a man had rolled out of the van and was raising a shotgun—but he couldn't shoot—she was in his line of fire—if he missed the demon, Meg would be hit.

She started to sidle to one side to change the angle. The demon laughed.

"Last chance saloon, Meg," it said. The voice had deepened even further now that it was corporeal. "Join us—be washed in the blood of the Lamb, while there is still time. The world has turned—it is up to us to turn with it."

She kept moving sideward, and raised the Walther to aim between the red blazing eyes. At the same time, she saw the man from the van raise the shotgun.

"You have nothing I want," she said.

"You're not thinking clearly, Meg," the demon replied. A long, red, flaming sword appeared in its right hand. "I don't just have you here now—I have your little friends."

It turned away from her toward the man with the shotgun. "No!" Meg shouted, and fired two more shots at the back of its head. Again she raised two tiny flickers of white flame, but the demon kept moving away from her.

# JD – 1 Day

*On the Road - Alfie*

Alfie rolled out of the tumbled van just as Murmus turned his attention on Dawson. He pulled the guitar out with him—amazingly, it was still whole. He saw the woman fire two more shots, but they appeared to have no effect.

Dawson raised the shotgun and the demon raised a sword that had flames running up and down the length of it. The sword came down at the same time as the gun went off. Alfie's hand gripped the guitar, and a single dissonant chord rang out. The sound of it seemed to divert the stroke of the sword. Instead of cleaving Dawson in half it caught him a glancing blow on the left arm, sending him spinning and rolling away, trying to put out sudden flames that had taken hold of his jacket at the left shoulder.

Dawson cocked the shotgun again as he rose.

"The song, Alfie!" he shouted. "Any time now would be good."

Alfie wasn't sure he was going to be able to play—the fiery eyes of the demon locked their gaze with his and almost struck him immobile. The muscle memory of his fingers saved him—they tripped into the tune without him needing any conscious thought, and as soon as the notes came, Alfie found his voice.

"This little light of mine, I'm gonna let it shine."

The demon laughed.

"I am Murmus, Grand Duke of Hell. You seek to banish me with a song?"

Dawson spoke above Alfie's singing. He stepped forward, raised his arms high and put the barrel of the gun in the demon's face.

"No—I seek to dispel you with this."

"Let it shine, let it shine, let it shine," Alfie sang.

Dawson pulled the trigger.

# JD – 1 Day

*On the Road—Meg*

At the same moment, Meg put her last two shots into the back of the demon's head.

It came apart in a flash of golden light so bright that she saw it behind her eyelids for long seconds afterwards, and it took longer still for her sight to return to normal. She reloaded the Walther with another mag—she didn't need eyes for that—and she heard the unmistakable sound of the pump-action getting racked. But when her eyesight cleared, she was standing on a clear, sun-drenched roadway with a smiling man and a youth cradling a guitar—there was no sign of the demon—and when the younger one spoke, she knew his voice straight away, could hear the song in it.

"You're not sick," he said.

"Neither are you," Meg replied. She walked over toward them. She knew she should feel wary, but that was the last thing she felt—it felt like meeting old friends after a long absence, and when the older man pulled her into a warm hug she felt tears spring in the corners of her eyes.

It felt like coming home.

# JD – 1 Day

*The White House Lawn*

It was time.

The opposing forces were gathered, trumpets had been blown and all that had the ears to hear had heard, all that has eyes to see had seen. Everything that had been foretold had come to pass—everything that had happened since he walked out of the desert valley with the angel's touch on his brow had led to here—now.

John raised his hands high and the crowd on the lawn went quiet.

"The Spirit of the angel of the Lord is upon me. He has anointed me to bring good news to the afflicted. He has sent me to bind up the brokenhearted, to proclaim liberty to captives and freedom to prisoners, to comfort all who mourn, to proclaim the day of his righteous vengeance and judgment."

"Praise be," the crowd shouted as one. John stilled them again.

"And behold—we open the sixth seal, and, lo, there comes a great earthquake; and the sun shall turn black as sackcloth of hair, and the moon shall become as blood."

As if in tune with the words, what had been a bright afternoon turned dark. More clouds arose and grew as if out of nowhere, darkening, boiling, filling the whole dome of the sky from horizon to horizon even as the orb of the sun dimmed, and faded, and turned, from yellow, to orange, to red, to black.

The earth shook—rubble fell from the already weakened walls of the house at John's back, and several of the crowd members standing in front of him were thrown off their feet. He knew this was nothing compared to the movement of land now taking place all across the planet.

On the far side of the globe, the few people left alive looked up to the night sky, looked up at a blood moon, painting the landscape in a red, bloody glow, even as the ground was swept aside below them.

The Great Rift Valley in Africa widened—and widened further. At its northernmost end the Indian Ocean breached a last, thin thread of land and crashed through even as the continent tore itself further and further apart.

India crashed repeatedly into the Himalayan mastiff and Everest grew miles higher into the dark clouds, a height that no man would ever climb.

"And the stars of the heavens fall unto the earth, even as a fig tree casteth her untimely figs, when she is shaken of a mighty wind."

John saw it in his head, knew the truth of it—the blood moon screamed silently in the starry void as it is torn apart. Rock crashed into rock, the satellites crumbled and fell in on themselves. The pieces were being drawn, inexorably pulled down into the gravity well, deeper and deeper until they crashed to earth like fiery fruit. They struck—on land, on sea, on the fractured and fracturing ice shelves of the South

Revelator

Pole—blasting fiery hell from the heavens as they came.

The ancient city of Athens had stood proud until now, almost miraculously surviving all the upheaval of the countries around it, but it couldn't survive one last thunderbolt from the skies. The Acropolis and all ancient places were pounded into dust, leaving only a smoking crater to show for centuries of waiting.

A chunk of the moon almost a hundred yards wide crashed headlong into the North Sea. A wave two hundred feet high fell over the remains of the Low Countries. The Netherlands and Belgium ceased to exist and half of England was submerged in less than an hour. There was no one there alive to see it.

"And the heavens depart as a scroll when it is rolled together; and every mountain and island are moved out of their places."

The Hawaiian chain of volcanoes all blew at once, and as the great Pacific plates moved, so did the waters above them. The last small remnants of the U.S. Navy were swamped in waves over a hundred meters and more that circled the ocean like vultures looking for carrion to feed on.

"And the kings of the earth, and the great men, and the rich men, and the chief captains, and the mighty men, and every bondman, and every free man, hide themselves in the dens and in the rocks of the mountains. And they say to the mountains and rocks, 'Fall on us, and hide us from the face of him that sitteth on the throne, and from the wrath of the Lamb.'"

The Russian Premier and his staff sat in their bunker deep, way deep, below the Kremlin. They had already survived an air strike directly above them that had leveled the old Palace—and most of Moscow. They had survived the plague by shooting and expelling anyone who so much as sniffled or had a nosebleed. They had watched as the world collapsed, and congratulated themselves that Mother Russia—or some part of it at least—would emerge to take over when the cataclysms above blew themselves out. They hunkered down for a long stay—and they never saw the asteroid coming that dug their whole complex out of the ground and blew them and their schemes and their dreams apart like confetti in the wind.

John smiled, his grin widening.

"For the great day of his wrath is come; and who shall be able to stand?"

# PART THREE

## JUDGEMENT DAY

# Alfie

The sky darkened again while Dawson was still trying to salvage what he could from the wreck of the VW van. The clouds bubbled up, dark and menacing. Over the space of a matter of minutes the sun dimmed, and faded, and turned, from yellow, to orange, to red, to black, with only a tracery of crimson veins running through it to show that its heart still burned inside. All the brightness of earlier was gone, leaving them in a gloomy twilight world where the predominant color was the flat gray of the ash-covered landscape.

The newcomer—Meg—hadn't said much apart from introducing herself, but she seemed genuinely pleased to have met fellow travelers on the road. There was something else too—something Alfie felt rather than knew. It was a tugging, like the one he felt from the South, but softer, somehow sweeter, and he found himself looking her way even when he should be trying to help Dawson in rummaging through the strewn and tumbled wreckage inside the van. He could scarcely keep his eyes off her, and if he glanced toward her, he usually found her looking at him, and wearing the same expression he imagined he wore himself.

*Perhaps we knew each other—in that hole in my memory—in the dark? Were we friends?*

He resolved he'd ask her—if he ever got the chance.

The clouds overhead scudded ever faster across the sky, and grew darker still, heavier—angrier. Way over on the northern horizon, the sky flickered as lightning whipped the ground, again and again. Distant drum rolls of thunder echoed around them, getting closer.

"We need to get moving," Meg and Alfie said at almost exactly the same time, and they smiled at each other before Alfie forced himself to look away and back at the van. Dawson was still inside, and they heard the noise of pans and cutlery and bottles being tossed around.

"Have you found everything you need?" Alfie shouted. The older man crawled out of the broken windshield, pushing Alfie's guitar case in front of him. It was even more battered than before, but the Gibson still fit snugly inside as Alfie put it away. It gave a soft ring, as if it was disappointed, then fell quiet.

Dawson stood. He had an old battered gym bag over his shoulders, a full bottle of JD in one hand and the sawn-off in the other. He patted at his pocket.

"Sorry I took so long—I needed some ammo. Liquor, guns and clean underwear," he said with a beaming smile. "Everything a growing boy needs."

He motioned toward the black pickup.

"Can we catch a ride, please, ma'am?" he said, and Meg gave Dawson a smile that Alfie wished she'd given to him instead. The guitar rang in the case—a warning this time.

*Keep your mind on the road, Alfie, lad.*

He heard it in his head as if Dawson had spoken it.

"It looks like we're all going the same way," Meg said. "And it might be a long wait for a bus."

All three of them headed for the pickup. Dawson got into the tight passenger seat in the back of the cab.

"I can stretch out in here, no problem," he said, and held up the shotgun. "And I can watch our back if we need it."

Alfie got into the front passenger side, and when Meg stepped up into the driver's seat, he was aware of how close they were—he felt it, like a heat spreading through him. He stuck the guitar on the floor between his legs, and it rang again.

*Eyes front, Alfie lad.*

"Where were you heading?" Alfie asked, but knew the answer even before she spoke.

"South," Meg replied. "There's somebody there that wants to see me."

The storm still raged to their north—he could see the flashes and the dark dancing clouds if he turned around. It seemed to be getting closer, but unlike the last time, it did not appear to be rushing towards them at a great speed—it would be a good while yet before they had to think about dodging it.

They had plenty of other things to worry about though. The flat plain of gray on either side of them was being rent asunder by forces from below. It cracked, wide fissures and crevasses opening and closing with alarming regularity, as if the ground itself was breathing, sending out wisps of noxious plumes with each exhale, the stench of which soon forced them to wind up the windows.

Something impossibly bright hissed and crackled across the sky, a yellow gold fireball that rushed to the ground far to their west. Seconds later there was a boom louder than any thunderclap and the pickup rocked on its suspension as the whole length of the road bounced, bucked and swayed. Meg spun the wheel, left, right then back again, struggling to keep control—they were lucky there was no other traffic around, for the truck swerved wildly from one side to the other across the lanes.

Alfie had visions of the surface opening up below them and swallowing them whole, but finally, after what seemed like an age, everything stabilized, and they were back, driving on a smooth road again.

"You handled that well," Dawson said from the back, speaking to Meg.

"I don't know how," she replied. "I guess I've got my dad to thank for that too. When I woke up last week I wasn't even sure I knew how to drive at all. I didn't know much about anything apart from the fact I'd been sick."

That's when it clicked.

"You don't remember your past, do you?" Alfie said. "You're like me and I'm like you—that's why we're both being called south."

After that there was nothing for it but for him to tell his story.

He spoke as they drove above what was now an ever shifting plain of dust, ash and vast chasms belching clouds of smoke and shooting flames high in the air. Somehow—miraculously—the road remained solid and untouched below and in front of them. Alfie was starting to think it wasn't a coincidence.

He told Meg of his wakening, and spoke of the subway, the preacher, of the death of the sick and his walk out of the dead city. He told her how he and Dawson had met, and of their road trip to Philadelphia, then of the encounter with Murmus in the parking garage.

She stopped him there.

"I heard you," she said. "More than once too. I've heard you singing. I think you might have saved me from it—Murmus—whatever the hell it was."

Dawson spoke from the backseat.

"Is, not was—we just sent it away, we didn't defeat it completely. It'll be back. Your demons always come back."

❋ ❋ ❋ ❋ ❋

Meg told them her story—of waking alone and sick, of meeting the wet, red thing in the motel, then the rednecks on the road and how the demon had tried to trap her, in the church, at the service station, in the bookstore and under the expressway. Alfie hadn't been aware of doing it, but at some point he put a hand over hers on the wheel, and when she spoke again of his singing he felt her squeeze, warm and tight.

"There's something that doesn't want you two going south," Dawson said.

Alfie nodded, and tapped the side of his head.

"And there's also something else that really does want us there. I think its part of all of this." He waved his hand at the view outside, and at the clear, empty road travelling through chaos.

"We're on a mission from God," Dawson said. It sounded like a quote from something—Alfie didn't get the allusion, but he got the meaning.

"This little light of mine, I'm gonna let it shine," he sang softly. The guitar rang in time inside its case, and suddenly the air in the truck felt fresher, the gloom seemed to lift, and all three of them were smiling.

# John

John felt the power rise up in him again. He spoke the words, as they had been spoken to him, the Word given to him with the touch by the angel in the desert.

"And the Lord sent a horseman, a pale rider, and his name was Death. And his skin shone silver and his hair spread behind him in a great cape. But his eyes were like pits of blackness in the depths of space, and no smile touched his features. And the horseman carried with him the key to the gates of life and death. And the gate was unlocked and death came forth in its blackness and spread across the face of the earth. And where it passed the sons of Adam fell before it, and the cities lay quiet and the noise of the works of the Adamities was heard no more."

He—and all who heard his words—saw the pictures that came to mind with the giving—the vast cities of man—some blasted, some burned, some full of the wet plague dead, and others no more than gray, empty plains. All quiet—all dead.

"And there came a second rider, and his name was Darkness. And he threw a great cape over the burning orb of the sun. And the heat went out of it then, and when the cape was lifted there was only the sky and the stars."

The sun pulsed and beat, as if a throbbing heart lay inside it, red veins, glowing briefly in the black, but getting dimmer and dimmer as the beat slowed and finally stalled, leaving only the darkness of the void.

"There was a chorus in the heavens as of the chant of a great throng, and the Lord called for his first made to come forth. And the earth trembled and shook, and the works of the Adamities fell into its cracks and crevices. And there was a great churning and crackling on the face of the earth, and a wind arose, a wind that scoured and cleansed wherever it passed. And when the wind fell all traces of the Adamities had gone."

Now there was only a gray emptiness, lashed with storms and blasted by fiery debris from the stars. Hills—even great mountains—were flattened and laid low, the seas boiled and seethed, volcanoes rumbled and belched and great cracks ran the length of continents across the face of the earth. Moans and screams rose up from below as the land reshaped itself into new forms, but there was little life anywhere, only blasted rock.

"And there came a third horseman, who was called Repentance, and he carried a flaming sword. And his likeness was also as of an angel. And he called from under the ground the old adversary, the great serpent. And the serpent came, in fire and in thunder."

John looked out over the crowd gathered in front of him. And in the ground, something stirred, ready to be born again.

John raised his hands high.

"I am Repentance. And I have come for this last task—I come to break the seventh seal and to call the beast up to answer for his crimes—as it was written, so shall it be done."

He opened his hands wide. A book took solid form in the air—a huge thick leather-bound volume, whose pages flew and fluttered open then closed and open again as he spoke the Word.

"And when they were standing before the Lord the great ledger was brought forth, in which all their deeds were etched forever in the fabric of time. And each was judged, and each repented of the deeds of life."

He looked out over his flock—there were only a hundred or so here—but he felt the rest—all of them, everyone who had ever walked the earth, gathered to receive the word, gathered to be judged, to repent, or to forever suffer.

"Do you repent!" he shouted.

A multitude of hosts answered eagerly. They would be judged in return. An equal, if not greater multitude did not answer at all—and they did not need judgement, for their fate was already sealed.

The screaming started.

John smiled.

# Meg

It felt like she'd known the two of them forever, although it had only been two hours since they met at the crossroads. Maybe it was because they were the only people she'd met since her wakening that she could talk to properly without the demon making its presence felt. Or maybe—and she thought this more and more likely as time went on—maybe Dawson had been right earlier—they were on a mission, they were a team, with a bond that was meant to be. She didn't know anything about any God—but she knew friends when she found them, and that was enough for her.

There was something even more than that—and she knew Alfie felt it too—a tugging, warm feeling between them, heat and joy and pure emotion, every time they looked at each other. It confused her greatly—but in a way it was comforting, although she had to keep her eyes on the road to maintain her concentration.

*Did we know each other in the time before?*

There was no way for either of them to tell. All she knew was that everything was better now—much better—and she looked forward to whatever was waiting for them in the south, not with her previous apprehension but with something new.

It felt like hope.

Dawson leaned over from the backseat.

"How much further?" he asked. He smelled, of guns and booze—and again Meg had a flash memory of her father standing at her back as she aimed a BB gun at a row of tin cans.

She—and Alfie beside her—answered at almost the same time.

"About a hundred miles."

Dawson grinned widely.

"Two for the price of one. Bargain. Come on, Alfie, lad—give us a tune then. If we've got a hundred more miles of this shit to get through, I'm either gonna need some JD or some cheering up."

Meg leaned sideways to give Alfie room to open the guitar case. Alfie got the instrument into his hands, hit a major chord, and it felt as if everything in the truck had lit up again. Meg turned to Dawson—she'd remembered her dad again—after teaching her to shoot he'd sat on the porch with a jug of moonshine, and she and mom had needed to drag his sorry ass to bed when the sun went down.

"There'll be no drinking, mister—not in my rig. Not until the job's done," she said with a smile, and got a salute in return.

"Yes, sir—ma'am," he replied, and grinned again. Meg hadn't met many men that she knew of, but she was willing to bet she hadn't met another who took so much joy in life.

Alfie started to pick out a tune, eight bars of it before he sang—sweet and high and pure.

*"We are climbing, Jacob's ladder," "We are*
*climbing, Jacob's ladder,"*

❄ ❄ ❄ ❄ ❄

Dawson joined in—and so did Meg. She hadn't thought she knew the song, but the words seemed to come into her head right when she needed them and all worry poured out of her, emptied her out as the song filled her with light—and something she didn't know she needed until she had it. It filled her with joy.

*"We are climbing, Jacob's ladder,"*
*"We are brothers, sisters and all."*

They sped down the road, a shining bullet of light in the midst of darkness.

Alfie sang for an hour and more—old chugging blues, mournful spirituals, show tunes, pop and protest songs—Meg was able to sing along to all of them.

"How do you know all of these?" Alfie asked.

"I don't know," Meg replied. "How do you know them?" "I've been thinking about that—I think my mother might have taught me most of them—and I think I was a street—or subway—performer. I think that's why I was down there that day."

Meg nodded—it sound feasible, as far as her experience went—which wasn't very far. But the fact that they both seemed to know all the same songs was another indication of the bond that had so very quickly grown—was still growing—between them.

Alfie was just about to start another song when Dawson spoke from the back seat.

"You might want to put a step on it, Meg," he said. "I think we're going to get company again."

Meg checked her mirror. It was dark back there—almost too dark to make out much detail. But Dawson was right—they weren't the only movement on the road any more. What she was seeing was still a mile or so back, but it was definitely closing—and there was more than one of them. A dozen or so black shapes—not so much driving along the roadway as flying just above it, with huge wings extended. At this distance it looked like a flock of black crows. But they were far too big for that.

And there was something else. As the black shapes flew over the road, the whole structure fell away below them, finally succumbing to the ravages of chaos like everything else on the gray plain, falling into ashes and dust. It was as if the last of the old reality was unraveling in their wake as they passed over.

Meg put her foot down—not all the way—not yet—and the pick-up gained speed, the needle going up—sixty to seventy and still creeping higher. The things behind them kept coming on—kept catching up to them. And beneath them, the road kept crumbling.

"What is it?" Alfie said. Meg saw him try to turn round—he couldn't check the wing mirror on that side—she'd lost it on the road a while back.

"More damned demons is my guess," Dawson replied, and racked the pump-action. "Let them come—we already sent that big one away—we can cope with these. Another song, Alfie, lad—and keep them coming—we know that works. And if it doesn't, I'll just tell them to fuck off."

Alfie sang again, but to Meg it didn't sound quite as high and clear—Alfie's worry was coming through in his playing—worry, and more than a trace of fear.

She nudged the needle up again—seventy-five, heading for eighty.

The black crows kept coming.

The road kept crumbling.


Meg reckoned they were within twenty miles of their destination in the south—but it was obvious now they weren't going to get there before they were caught by the blackness at their back. She'd already pushed the truck up over a hundred, and although the road was clear and wide ahead, the pickup bounced and rattled so much she didn't want to risk going much faster.

But the road was falling away fast now behind them—the black things—they could see now that they were demons, not crows—red-eyed, blank-faced, howling and screeching like banshees—were just a hundred yards back. And they were still closing.

Dawson leaned forward toward Alfie.

"Shuffle over lad, and open your window—let's see if I can even the numbers. And give me the song—you know the one I mean."

Alfie leaned to his left and Meg felt his body next to hers. Again she felt the heat, the tug and the pull of emotion, and it only grew stronger as Alfie picked a tune and sang.

"This little light of mine, I'm gonna let it shine."

All three of them joined in, and the light in the truck glowed—almost golden.

Dawson leaned out of the window, picked a target and fired. The bang was loud enough to obliterate everything else for a second and leave Meg's ears ringing. She checked her mirror. One of the demons fell away, fluttering, one wing torn almost completely from its body, screeching as it spiraled down to be lost in the tumbling rubble as the road collapsed away.

Dawson let out a shout of triumph and racked the pump- action to get another cartridge in the chamber. At the same moment blackness swooped out of the attackers, a single demon, heading straight for him. Meg had her eyes on the road so she didn't see what happened too clearly. She heard Dawson let off another shot, saw a black shadowy form fall away on the road just behind them. And she saw the shotgun bounce along the roadway, obviously torn from the man's grasp—it joined the falling demon in the debris and rubble as the road collapsed—only fifty yards behind them now.

Dawson pulled himself back inside and fell into the back seat. Meg saw blood at his shoulder when she chanced a turn around to check—a lot of blood

"Alfie—he's hurt."

"Don't mind me," Dawson replied, and she heard the pain in his voice. "Just keep driving. Maybe they'll get tired."

He laughed, and blood bubbled at his lips.

*This isn't good.*

She managed to coax another two miles out of their flight by flooring the pedal. The highway dipped down toward the gray plain just ahead, and she put her foot down harder, trying to gain an extra few yards to reach the spot where the road was closest to the ground below.

Ten yards behind them the demons wailed—their howls were loud enough to drown the sound of the engine—and the roar and tumble as the road fell away below them.

"I'm going to stop down there," she shouted. "When the road gives, we're going to fall. I don't know how far, or how rough it's going to be, so hold tight. If it comes to the worst, we're going to have to bail out of here, so get ready. And Alfie…"

He looked over at her.

"Keep singing," she said.

As soon as they reached the bottom of the dip she hit the brakes. They screeched to a halt, just seconds before the blackness descended on them and the roadway started to crumble away under the back tires.

"Hold on," Meg shouted.

The back end fell first, so that they tipped and Meg looked out, not at road, but at a dark, thunderous sky. Then the rest of the vehicle started to slide, slowly at first, but quickly gaining momentum. The view out of the window filled with swooping, dancing demons that swirled around them anticipating their doom.

The fall seemed to take forever, but in the event was shorter than she'd been worrying about—only ten feet or so. Even then, the landing wasn't a soft one—they hit with a crash, back end first. Something crumpled, and Meg had a second of worry about being crushed as easily as a beer can in a strong hand. They bounced, twice, then their weight in the cab brought the front end down, so that they bounced again. The front suspension couldn't take the strain and gave in with a crash and a grind of tearing metal.

There was only a second or two of total silence before the demons screeched in triumph and swooped down from above, sensing easy prey.

Meg tried the ignition, hoping to be able to get started and maybe even limping along despite the suspension problem—but the engine—and the truck's electrical systems—were dead. They weren't going to be driving anywhere.

The demons fell on them, tearing at wipers and wing- mirror—the bull-bar was torn away—Meg saw it fly, impossibly far through the air before landing in a puff of dust way out on the plain. The demons' attack got more frenzied when they realized they couldn't get into the cab—they ripped off anything that could be ripped. They got into the back of the pickup and started to pull and tear apart the gear Meg had stowed there.

Two of them pounded at the windshield—it was already cracked in several places by the fall—cracks that were getting longer by the second. Everything was a flurry of black feathers, scratching talons, high pitched screeching and fiery, red blazing eyes.

Meg reached down and drew the Walther. She looked over at Alfie. He seemed to be unhurt by the fall and was cradling the guitar.

"Give us a song, Alfie, lad," she said in perfect imitation of Dawson. "I think you know the one."

He smiled, she smiled back, and he plucked at the strings and started to sing.

"This little light of mine, I'm gonna let it shine,"

Dawson joined in—weakly to start with, then stronger as Meg too joined the chorus.

"Let it shine, let it shine, let it shine."

She opened the truck door, stepped out, and started shooting.

# Alfie

*If Dawson was right about them being on a mission from God, then Meg must be some kind of kick-ass angel,* thought Alfie as he watched her move and flit among the demons.

She seemed untouched by any of them despite their efforts to get to her, taking them down quickly, almost casually—each one precisely shot between the eyes before she moved on the next. She was always on the move, never giving them a standing target, rolling when one came too close only to rise before it could soar away and shooting it, almost point blank in the head, sending it down to join the others. The muzzle of her handgun flared, golden light blazed like the lost sun, and her voice rang and echoed around them as she sang along with Alfie.

"This little light of mine, I'm gonna let it shine."

She got six of them before the remainder backed off, soared up and away and continued off along the roadway headed south. What was left of the highway crumbled away below the departing shadows. The falling debris rumbled like distant thunder that faded with the last of the screeches as the demons disappeared from view in the gloom.

Their easy path south was now gone, leaving them in the middle of a flat, gray featureless wasteland.

Alfie saw Meg reload another magazine in her pistol—she did that with the same economy of movement and efficiency she'd shown during the shooting—whatever she'd been before he doubted very much that she'd been a subway performer. He had to force himself to drag his eyes away from her when Dawson groaned in the back.

"I'm in need of some help here, Alfie, lad," the man moaned, and when Alfie turned he was dismayed to see that Dawson's shirt was caked red all down his left-hand side. Dawson had it peeled away at the shoulder, inspecting a deep gash that gaped down to where white bone showed. Blood pulsed and flowed—too much, far too much of it.

Between them, Meg and Alfie managed to get the man out of the back seat—he screamed, twice, at the pain, but finally they were able to lower him to the ground.

"See if you can find my backpack," Meg said. "It's a tall blue one, with a tent attached at the bottom buckle. It was in the back and they've probably thrown the stuff far and wide—but I had a medical kit in it—bandages and needles and antiseptic creams and the like. See if you can find that—I'll try to get his bleeding stopped. And if you find a box of ammo—that'll be good too. But get the medical kit first."

For the next five minutes Alfie searched the strewn belongings that had been torn and thrown from the back of the truck. He felt naked and vulnerable without the guitar, but he'd left it in the driver's seat of the pickup—it was only going to get in the way of the search. All the same, he sang to himself as he searched the ash for anything that might be useful.

"Let it shine, let it shine, let it shine."

He had one eye on the ground and the other on the sky, expecting a fresh attack at any minute, but none came. There was no flutter of black wings, no wild screeching, just distant rumbles of thunder and the call—the tug and pull of the thing that wanted them to go south. Alfie pushed it away—he had a friend to attend to first.

Just when he thought the backpack and its contents had been thrown to the winds never to be seen again, he found it, lying some twenty yards from the truck, half buried in fresh rubble. He rummaged through it—becoming slightly embarrassed when he found Meg's underwear—then finally found the small blue zip bag containing the medical gear.

He took it and the backpack back over to where Meg was working on Dawson. She too was singing under her breath.

"This little light of mine, I'm gonna let it shine."

Dawson was sitting up, the bottle of JD in his good hand and a smile on his face as he saw had Alfie returned.

"Ah—the wandering minstrel is back."

Without thinking, Alfie replied in song.

"A thing of shreds and patches, of ballads, songs and snatches, and dreamy lullaby."

Dawson laughed out loud.

"Get out of my head, Alfie—I sang that one at school—long time passed—back afore you were even thought of."

The distraction seemed to have taken his mind off the pain though, so Alfie considered it a job well done.

Mag took the kit from him.

"Ammo?" she asked. Alfie shook his head, and Meg didn't seem to waste any time thinking about it. She already had her hands in the kit bag, deciding what she needed.

"It's bad," she said when she looked back at Alfie, "But with what I have here now, we should be able to get the bleeding stopped and get him patched up. He's not going to be going anywhere for a while though—and he's certainly not going to be walking."

She went back to work, as efficient with the stitching, sewing and bandaging as she'd been with the pistol earlier.

*Definitely not a subway performer.*

It took the best part of half an hour to get Dawson stitched up and bandaged, and by then he was a good way down the bottle of JD—if he was in any pain, it wasn't slowing down his drinking.

Meg checked out the pickup—and Alfie could tell by her expression there was no hope of ever getting it moving again. He took the guitar out of the driver's seat and found the case, replacing the instrument gently in its faux-velvet padded coffin. If he was going to be walking again, he at least wanted the Gibson to be safe—he didn't know how, but he knew he'd need it before the end.

Meg saw him sling the guitar across his back.

"You feel it too, don't you?" she said.

He didn't have to ask—he knew exactly what she meant. The urge—the need, to get moving south was getting stronger by the minute.

Dawson started to rise from where he'd been sitting against one of the pickup's front wheels. He looked deathly white and drawn, almost like a victim of the red plague—if it hadn't been for the ever-present grin.

"I don't suppose you found my sawn-off back there?" he said to Alfie. "It might come in handy."

"You can't be walking with that wound," Meg said. "You shouldn't even be getting up."

"Who died and made you my mother?" Dawson replied, still smiling. He grimaced then took another swig of JD. "Besides—you two are going south—and I'll be damned if I'll let you leave me here on my own with this mess."

"We don't have to go," Alfie said, but he heard the lie in the words even as he said them.

"Of course you do—that's what all of this shit is all about—that's why these fucking demon things are trying to slow you down. You gotta be somewhere, Alfie lad—and so does Meg here. And I've got enough invested in you now to want to see it through to the end. So let's stop jawing about it and get it done. What have we got and what do we need?"

They started walking ten minutes later. Alfie and Meg both carried backpacks, Alfie also had the guitar, and Dawson had his, half-empty, bottle of JD. Meg had eventually found enough ammo to fill her spare magazines and they had enough water and food for a couple of days, three at the most, but Alfie didn't think they'd need anywhere near that much. Wherever it was they were heading, it was only fifteen miles to the south now.

The going was tough. The ash was soft and easy to plow through, but there were patches of underlying stone and rubble that they had to pick their way across carefully. It was darker now too, an all-pervasive red-tinged gloom that wasn't quite as dim as full night, but was steadily heading that way. At least they were spared any more demon attacks—if they'd even really been attacks at all.

He remembered Dawson's earlier words.

"So you really think these demons are just trying to slow us down?" he asked.

Dawson smiled—it wasn't the full blast effect though, his pain was all too clearly etched on his face.

"As I said before—it's been far too easy for you—both of you—so far." He held up a hand as Alfie started to protest. "I know—I know—crashing the van and rolling it over, then falling off a collapsing road isn't exactly a piece of cake—and that talon I took in the shoulder reminds me at every step that's it's not all shits and giggles. But they could have killed us several times over by now if they wanted to—you know that—you both know that, right?"

Alfie and Meg looked at each other, and nodded at the same time as Dawson continued.

"Now either they don't want you dead—I'm not too sure of that so don't quote me—or you're protected in some way that stops them from killing you. I kinda like that idea better. And the longer I hang with you two, the longer I get to stay around myself. So whatever it is you're doing—don't stop."

"I've not been doing much except heading south and singing," Alfie admitted.

This time he did get the full effect grin from Dawson.

"Then give us a song, Alfie. If we're following the Yellow Brick Road, we need to have a song."

He didn't take the guitar out of the case—but as soon as he started singing and the other two joined in, he felt the light and joy pour through him, and once again, they headed south, climbing Jacob's ladder.

Alfie's songs sustained them for the first few hours, during which they only covered five miles. There was a limit to what they—and the JD—could do to sustain Dawson. His legs threaten to buckle, and Alfie only just managed to catch him as he stumbled. With Meg's help they lowered him to a sitting position on the ash. Dawson moved to take another swig of JD, but Meg swiped it from his hand, and gave him a bottle of water instead, and two candy bars.

"Water and sugars—it's still the same stuff—just better walking fuel."

"Thanks, mom," Dawson said, grinned and then grimaced as pain hit him again. "How far now?" he asked.

Alfie turned to face south, and felt it, like a shout in his head, calling for him to hurry.

"Less than ten," he said. "Another couple of hours."

He saw the look Meg gave him over the top of Dawson's head—it was going to take longer than that. Looking at Dawson's drawn, pale features, and the red patches showing through the new bandages, it might be going to take a lot longer. He didn't say anything though. However it went from here, they were in this together, all three of them, until whatever end would come.

And when it came, Alfie vowed, he would be singing.


They gave Dawson half an hour of rest, but by then the call from the south was becoming a bellow in Alfie's head, demanding to be obeyed. It lessened as they started to walk, and lessened further when Meg took his right hand in her left. Dawson's steps had become less assured. He was stumbling more often now, and mumbling to himself, talking to the pain, trying to force it away.

Alfie sang—happy songs, bouncy tunes, and that seemed to help as they stumped their way across the ash.

As the sky darkened further they saw a light in the sky ahead of them—golden, gleaming, like a beacon calling them forward.

They headed for it as fast as Dawson could manage.

# John

John shut the great book with a slam that sent a thunderclap running around the gathered acolytes on what remained of the once-perfect lawn of the White House. The book drifted apart into shadows and dust as if it had never been there at all, and the crowd sighed. He raised his hands again, and spoke—softly, but his words carried to everyone who wished to hear.

"The Lord promises us a new beginning, a New Eden and a New Jerusalem. But first, there is one who must be conquered—one who cannot be allowed to take this journey with us. The Seventh Seal is open. The beast shall arise and the battle will be fought. Who will stand with me against him?"

As he knew they would, the crowd cried out with one voice in assent.

He gave the Word again, as he had heard it from the demon.

"And I saw the seven angels which stood before God; and to them were given seven trumpets. And another angel came and stood at the altar, having a golden censer; and there was given unto him much incense, that he should offer it with the prayers of all saints upon the golden altar that was before the throne."

Seven trumpets blared. Seven tall candlesticks appeared on the ground at John's feet, and the smoke from them was sweet—musk and lavender wafted across the lawn.

"And the smoke of the incense, which came with the prayers of the saints, ascended up before God out of the angel's hand. And the angel took the censer, and filled it with fire of the altar, and cast it into the earth: and there were voices, and thundering, and lightning."

John threw a hand out, as if casting something aside. The earth shook and screamed, lightning crashed all around them, and thunder drummed, a crashing beat of doom across the skies.

"And the seven angels which had the seven trumpets prepared themselves to sound.

And I heard a great voice out of the temple saying to the seven angels. Go your ways, and pour out the vials of the wrath of God upon the earth."

John cast out his other hand. The earth heaved, as if tugged hard from below, and bucked as if they rode on top of a huge, wild, beast. At the edges of the lawn the land rose up like the rim of a plate, then higher until they appeared to be sitting at the bottom of a long, dusty, valley.

John stood, at the door of a tumbled, ruined building beside a dead tree, with dark night overhead and a rumbling, trembling in the ground at his feet.

It felt like home.

He smiled.

The time was very near now.

# Meg

Dawson was nearly spent. The light in the sky to the south was close—a golden dome that shouted in her head, urging her on, emphasizing the need for hurry, for action. She knew Alfie felt it too, for he tugged at her hand like a dog on a leash when she slowed to allow Dawson to keep up with them.

They only had a mile or so to go now, but he wasn't going to make it without another stop to rest, and the thing in her head was telling her there was no time—no rest—no rest ever again unless she moved her ass right now.

Dawson seemed to sense their urgency, and tried to put on a spurt of speed, but he tripped, stumbled, fell forward, and Meg was too late to catch him. He hit the ground hard—the ash was too thin at that spot to cushion him much and he rolled, taking most of his weight on the injured shoulder. His screams echoed all across the plain and the bandages turned red and started to seep blood at the edges.

Dawson sat up, but didn't attempt to stand.

"Guess I'm going to be missing the show after all," he said, and tried to smile. His face had lost all color, white now, with his eyes sunk in deep dark shadows.

"Come on, get up," Alfie said. "We're nearly there."

Dawson did manage a grin this time.

"Save me a seat with a good view—I'll be along in a bit," he said. "You two go on ahead—you'll miss the start if you don't hurry."

"I'm not leaving you here," Alfie replied. Meg felt his hand tighten in hers for a second, a goodbye squeeze, then he left her side to kneel down by Dawson. "I'm just not leaving you here."

Dawson smiled, and patted Alfie on the shoulder with his good hand.

"You can come back and get me when you're done. I'll be right here, Alfie, lad—where am I going to go? Run along—quickly now. Whatever you've got, it's contagious—I can feel it too," he tapped at the side of his head. "In here—calling to me, shouting at me. Get going—while you still can."

"Get up, old man," Alfie shouted.

"I couldn't if I tried," Dawson said sadly. "This time, I'm done. Take your lass, head on over and see what's what, and sing me a song. Promise me, Alfie, that'll you'll sing—one last song for old Corporal Dawson."

Alfie had tears in his eyes as he stood.

"Anything I sing, from here to however long we've got left, it's for you, my friend—just for you."

Dawson had tears of his own as he looked up.

"Then all's well with the world."

Meg took the bottle of JD from her backpack and handed it down to the sitting man. More blood—too much of it—was seeping from the bandages. She could get in there—he could stem the flow and stitch him up again—but they were out of time—and she saw in his eyes that they both knew it.

"Be careful with that bottle," she said, looking Dawson in the eye. "Drinking it all at once might kill you."

Dawson smiled back up at her and nodded as he took the JD from her—he'd got the message.

"Thank you kindly, ma'am," he said. "Now get—before I go all mushy on you."

Meg took Alfie by the hand.

"I'll be back for you," Alfie said. "That's another promise." Dawson raised the bottle in salute, and Meg turned, taking

Alfie with her, setting her eyes on the golden dome ahead.

They didn't look back.

Alfie sang, softly, almost mournfully.

"This little light of mine, I'm gonna let it shine." The tugging in her head was insistent now.

*Hurry.*

Hand in hand, they ran as fast as they could dare. Alfie sang as well as he was able, and Mag felt his heat and light come through his palm, into hers, and all through her so that she felt like light herself.

As they approached what they thought had been a dome they saw it was a valley ahead, the golden light shining up out of it to illuminate the low clouds above. They'd reached their destination—but between it and them stood rank after rank of tall, black, winged figures, their fiery red eyes fixed on hers.

One was even taller than the rest, a black figure she knew, even before he spoke. The demon duke, Murmus, stood in front of his army, directly between them and their goal.

The demon spoke first, that same gravelly, deep voice she had come to hate.

"Did you expect to just walk in? After all the chances I gave you to take a different path?"

"I expect you to stand aside," Meg said, and drew the Walther. Alfie let go of her hand and swung the guitar case off his back. The Gibson rang loudly as it was set free—it seemed to glow, soft and golden, as if lit from inside with warmth. Alfie strummed a chord and the air between them and the demon wavered like a heat haze.

Murmus laughed.

"Your parlor tricks are of little use now, here at the end of all things."

"Right back at you," Meg replied and, as Alfie started to sing louder, she raised the Walther and, raising her voice to join the song she fired, four beats to the bar.

"This little light of mine, I'm gonna let it shine."

The muzzle flare was golden yellow, flaring so bright she saw it behind her eyes for seconds afterwards. Flames rose on the demon's body where she hit—five in the chest, three in the face. Murmus staggered. His great wings fluttered and scattered shadowy feathers in the air that were only ash and dust before they hit the ground. The red eyes dimmed to little more than deep-set embers that flared and dimmed in time with the singing.

"Let it shine, let it shine, let it shine."

Meg reloaded, slamming a new mag into the pistol. But even the short seconds the act took were too much time—Murmus stood up straight again and the red eyes glowed, as strong as ever as he raised himself to his full height. A fiery sword grew out of his right hand.

Meg raised the Walther again, and Alfie kept singing, but the demon seemed unmoved and came forward, the sword raised. Meg fired, four shots for the four beats.

"This little light of mine."

Another line of flaming holes appeared in the demon's chest—but this time they quickly filled in until all trace of golden flame was gone and only blackness was left. The sword came up for a killing blow—just as another voice—a bellow, joined theirs from behind them.

"I'm gonna let it shine."

Dawson ran past them before they could even think of stopping him, and threw himself in a running jump, inside the swinging sword, to slam the bottle of JD against the demon's face. Meg saw her chance and fired, three more shots right at the red eyes.

"Let it shine, let it shine, let it shine."

Where the bullets hit, golden flame rose as it met the spilled alcohol and took alight in an inferno that exploded around the demon's head. Murmus screamed, a high, screeching wail louder than any thunder, and tried to escape, to take flight. But Dawson had his arms locked around the demon's neck, his legs clasped at its chest. Even while he too burned, Dawson screamed into the fire that was all that was left of Murmus' face.

"I'm gonna let it shine."

The demon fell—to its knees, then in on itself, collapsing into dust and ash. Dawson dropped to the ground just as the last of it, the great black wings, went up with a whoosh then fell apart into charred black cinders that were quickly dispersed in the breeze.

Alfie was first to move—he ran to Dawson, ignoring the hot ash and cinders that were strewn all around, and knelt at the man's side. Meg reloaded the Walther again, keeping one eye on the ranks of silent demons as she went to join Alfie.

She was just in time to see Dawson look up at both of them, and grin widely out of a burn-ravaged face.

"You two look after each other—do you hear me? Thanks for the songs. See you down the road a way," he said—and died.

# Alfie

Alfie couldn't bring himself to stand away from Dawson's body. Hot tears ran down his cheeks and filled his eyes so that everything became a watery blur. He was vaguely aware that Meg stood above him, but everything seemed to be happening far away—and not important. He held Dawson's hand, trying to will the song into him, trying to feed him with the light.

"Let it shine, let it shine, let it shine."

Dawson's grin didn't fade—but his light didn't shine.

Meg pulled at Alfie's shoulder.

"Come on—we've got to move."

"We shouldn't have left him alone," Alfie said.

"We had no choice," Meg replied. "He was a soldier—he understood. And he died a soldier's death—we did that much for him at least. Now move your ass, Alfie, otherwise we'll be going straight to join him."

Alfie stood, and as he did so his hand went round the neck of the guitar and a chord rang out. Heat and light poured into him. He left the battered guitar case on the ground beside his friend.

"Look after this until I get back, old man," he said softly and, tears still running down his cheeks, he turned—facing south.

The dark ranks of demons hadn't moved since the fall of their leader. They stood—ten rows or more, arranged all around the valley rim. The ones between them and the golden light beyond were all facing toward Alfie and Meg, an array of fiery red eyes glowing like coals in the blackness of their faces.

Alfie remembered the shimmering in the air when he'd played a chord—was it only minutes before? It felt like hours. He strummed another—G major seventh—and it happened again—the air in front of them shimmered, and he felt heat and light rush through him.

Meg moved up to his side. He didn't have to hold her hand to feel the warmth and joy flow between and through them. The tug in his head shouted again—loud imperatives.

*Hurry!*

*Now!*

He picked his way into a tune, eight bars, then they both started singing as they walked forward. The ranks of demons parted in front of them, the song traveling like a great wave ahead toward the valley rim.

Alfie and Meg kept climbing Jacob's ladder, and it was as if Dawson was there too, singing along beside them.

"We are brothers, sisters and all."


It only took them minutes to make their way through the dark throng and reach the rim. They looked down into a dusty, dry valley. A crowd of about a hundred strong was gathered around a single tumbled white building beside a large dead tree. The golden light seemed to rise up from the ground itself, but it felt cold to Alfie—it didn't have the feel of the warm emotion that flowed through him when he sang, or when he looked at Meg. This felt more solitary, more distant, although no less powerful.

A figure stood in the doorway of the tumbled building, and even from here Alfie knew who it must be.

*Who's that writing?*

The guitar rang once in answer, then fell silent again. He slung it across his back as they went over the lip of the valley rim and started to descend. Alfie felt Meg take his hand in hers, and once again the light, the pure, surging joy of it, filled him and swept through him.

The dark ranks of the demons lined the rim, red eyes gleaming as Alfie and Meg went down into the golden light.

They followed what appeared to be an animal trail down a dry, rocky track to the valley floor and made their way across toward the tumbled, white house. They met no resistance—the crowd parted to let them through. Alfie saw that none of those gathered with the Revelator in the valley were sick—many were bruised and battered, and some were bleeding—but just from minor wounds, not from the red death. They all had something else in common too—they all had wide-eyed stares, stares of wonderment, and grins almost as wide as the one Dawson had worn at his death.

The Revelator did not seem surprised at their arrival as he welcomed them at the door of the white building.

"Ah—Orpheus and Eurydice, I presume? And have you ventured into the wrong story?"

He laughed as if he'd made a joke, but Alfie didn't understand it at all. He did understand what he saw in the Revelator's eyes though—and it wasn't a wide-eyed stare of wonderment. He saw dancing, flitting darkness and he knew, beyond a shadow of a doubt, that the man they'd been brought all this way to meet was completely, irrevocably insane.

# Meg

Meg recognized the man in the doorway immediately—John, the Revelator—she'd seen his image back in the church in Saratoga Springs, seen how the congregation had hung on his every word. The gathering here in this valley appeared to be cut from the same cloth—and the man seemed ever bit as wrong to her as the robed woman who had pretended to serve him.

*We came all that way for this?*

The Revelator lifted up his hands to speak, and an expectant silence fell over the valley before he spoke, his voice soft, but carrying so that everyone heard the Word.

"Then I saw an angel coming down from heaven with the key to the Abyss, holding in his hand a great chain. He seized the dragon, the ancient serpent, the devil and Satan, and bound him for a thousand and a thousand and a thousand years. And he threw him into the Abyss, shut it, and sealed it over him, so that he could not deceive the nations until the years were complete. For God did not spare the angels when they sinned, but cast them into hell, delivering them in chains to be held in gloomy darkness until they too would meet their judgment."

The Revelator looked at Alfie and Meg and smiled.

"And now that glorious day has finally come around again.

He will rise—rise and be judged."

The ground below their feet trembled and shook, and they had to stand back as it sunk away—a small depression at first, quickly becoming a hole. The congregation had to retreat to the valley edges as dirt fell away, the hole widened, and within seconds they were standing on the edge of a black pit that seemed to go down into endless dark. Something shifted down there—something huge—something monstrous.

It started to climb.


The Revelator spoke again.

"And I saw a beast coming out of the dark. It had ten horns and seven heads, with ten crowns on its horns, and on each head a blasphemous name."

Meg saw the fervor—the mania—dance in the man's eyes as the thing in the pit crawled up towards them. She caught glimpses of it as it shifted in the darkness—there was a scaly claw, the size of a house, and an eye, red and burning, as big as a truck. It had a mouth—many mouths—gaping maws filled with steel-trap teeth that clanked together and squealed—it sounded like hunger—ages old, ravenous, hunger.

She looked back and saw that the Revelator was grinning—a smile as wide as any of Dawson's, but with none of the joy or humor in it.

*He wants this to happen.*

She shouted in his face.

"Why are we here—why did you call us?"

He kept smiling, and he didn't reply, didn't take his eyes off the thing coming up the pit wall.

"He did not call you—I did," a voice said in the doorway of the house.

An angel stood there, bent over to avoid the lintel, white wings folded behind him and giving the impression of a hunch. Golden eyes shone from a face as smooth as old ivory, the white broken only by the darker area of bruising and dried blood around a wound in his head. He looked almost too frail to be standing, and had to hold onto the doorjamb for support, but Meg knew right away that he had spoken the truth.

He had the song in him, she heard it ring, heard Alfie's guitar chime in response—and she felt the light and heat and love pour off him in waves. The angel stumbled, and Meg moved instinctively forward, lending him her shoulder. As she knew he would, Alfie had done the same on the other side, and together they half-carried the wounded being to the edge of the pit.

The beast in the deep, as if seeing them for the first time, roared a great wail that sent more dirt tumbling down into the dark. The climbing became more frantic.

John, the Revelator, cried out, in the throes of ecstatic joy, and his congregation cried out with him in reply. The sound made Meg look around at the gathered crowd—just in time to see all of them jerk and spasm in a strange parody of a dance. When their heads came up, they looked back at her from red, fiery eyes.

Up on the valley rim, the black winged ranks started to descend to greet the coming of their master.

"Why did you call us here?" Alfie said, echoing Meg's previous question

The angel smiled wanly. When he spoke, it was with Dawson's voice.

"For a song, of course. Give us a song, Alfie, lad. You know the one."

The noise from the pit below them was deafening now—the beast, huge and hungry—thousands upon thousands upon thousands of years of hunger—rushed upward, and the congregation of demons in the valley screeched and wailed and howled in anticipation.

John raised his hands again, and intoned.

"And I saw the dead, small and great, stand before God; and the books were opened. Another book was opened, which is the book of life. The dead were judged out of those things which were written in the books, according to their works."

The angel sighed deeply.

"I had thought that he would be able to keep the Word in him, that he had the strength for the task—but I fear it has unhinged him and he cannot hold the glory. And now, the time is here—and we can do nothing but stand."

He turned to Meg.

"Will you stand with me?"

The scrambling, bellowing, raging thing in the pit was close now—she heard it, felt it in the ground at her feet, smelled it in the hot stench that was rising with it. Meg thought of all that had happened since her wakening, the good, and the bad—and all the good parts of it were associated with the light and heat and—what he had called glory – she now felt with Alfie at her side.

She nodded, and drew the Walther. The angel smiled and turned to Alfie. "Let there be song," he said.

And there was song.

# Alfie

John, the Revelator, raised his hands high again as the noise from the pit reached a thunderous crescendo. The air was full of black, swooping, screeching demons, the valley floor rocked and quaked with the violence of the beast's coming, and John's former acolytes sang and danced in a chorus of discordant, raucous wailing that grated on Alfie's nerves like nails on a chalkboard.

"Let there be song," the angel said, but it wasn't the angel's voice that Alfie heard, it was Dawson's again, clear and loud as if his friend was standing at his shoulder.

"Give us a song, Alfie, lad. You know the one."

John shouted, his voice carrying above the cacophony. "Here is wisdom. Let him that hath understanding count the number of the beast: for it is the number of a man. And his number is six hundred threescore and six."

Alfie unslung the guitar from his back and picked out the first eight bars, feeling the heat and the light and the glory of it fill him up and wash out and through him.

The beast crawled out of the pit, just as Alfie started to sing.

"This little light of mine, I'm gonna let it shine."

# Meg

*"Let it shine, let it shine, let it shine."*

Meg sang along as the first head of the beast rose up out of the pit. It was a scaly, wedge shaped thing, green and smelling of rot and decay, with a wet, red tongue as long as Meg was tall—a tongue that bled steaming drops of blood to the ground where they hissed like boiling oil. An eye, a burning coal set in a rim of golden fire, stared and she felt it, a tug and tease in her brain—they might have gotten rid of Murmus, but this was more of the same thing, just bigger. She raised the Walther.

The Revelator called out.

"And the serpent came, in fire and in thunder. And there on the dust under the stars they fought, as ages passed, under the sight of the Lord."

She fired. A bolt of golden flame passed from her, and the beast's eye exploded, flame running over the eye socket, burning and raging, an inferno that engulfed the whole head as if fell back into the pit.

The Revelator was still shouting.

"Great was the battle, and great was the blood spilled. And the serpent sprouted many heads, and each was struck from its body by the force of the sword of Repentance."

Two more heads rose up out of the pit, and Meg moved to avoid one as it lunged at her, rolled to one side, and fired. Soon, there was nothing but moving and firing, the sweet sound of Alfie's guitar, and the singing, her voice joined with his, and the golden heat and light and joy and glory as she smote the beast and sent its heads down into fire, four shots to the bar.

*"Let it shine, let it shine, let it shine."*

# Alfie

Everything was movement and noise. Alfie saw Meg tumble and roll and shoot and reload, golden flame lashing in gouts at the beast, sending great wedge-shaped heads blazing back into the pit as fast as they came up. There was a roaring down there now, and heat, blasting like a furnace from below. When Meg sent another head down, it fell away wailing, and there was a crashing sound in the deep, followed by great gouts of high flame that shot up to the sky. He realized she wasn't just setting fire to the heads—the flames were being sent down to hit the body of the beast, and it too was burning, trapped now in an ever more fiery pit.

Alfie kept singing.

"This little light of mine, I'm gonna let it shine."

Meg sang as she rolled and tumbled and fired, and more heads fell, more fires, more heat sprang up out of the pit. Flames caught and grabbed at the soaring black wings of the demons above in the sky and the fire took them too, phoenixes into the flames to be returned to the ash.

Then Meg stopped singing.

"Last mag!" she shouted, as three huge heads loomed above her.

Alfie's fingers faltered and hit a sour chord, and the song got lost in his throat.

All around them, the horde of black demons swooped and roared—their triumph was near.

Alfie felt a hand on his shoulder, felt warmth spread. He turned to face the angel.

It had Dawson's face.

"Give us another song, Alfie, lad," it said. "You know the one."

Alfie's fingers started before he'd even thought about it, and his voice, stronger then ever raised high and clear over the din.

"We are climbing, Jacob's Ladder."

Meg came in on the beat.

"We are climbing, Jacob's Ladder."

The Revelator joined in and they sang together.

"We are climbing, Jacob's Ladder."

The angel grinned, and started to sing. Meg fired. Glory filled the valley.

"We are brothers, sisters and all."

# Meg

She only had four shots left—and five heads to deal with. But as soon as the angel started to sing, she forgot to worry about it.

"We are climbing, higher and higher," Alfie sang.

The angel took wing, filling the whole valley with light, and a long, golden sword sprang up in his right hand as he swooped down into the pit. Two more heads came up, lunging towards him. Meg took them out.

"We are climbing, higher and higher."

The flaming sword struck and smote the beast. More flames flared upward into the sky—more black demons, burning in golden fire, fell into the pit, added to the conflagration there, and were consumed. The beast raged. A talon raked across the angel's torso, opening a wide wound from which light blazed like a new sun. The angel's sword flashed, faster and faster still, and the beast started to fall back, the fire taking it.

The beast cried out a call for help. Its armies of fiery-eyed beasts—the winged from above and the former acolytes of the Revelator from the valley, all leapt as one into the pit to try to sustain it, but the fire was too great and they were consumed in the inferno.

The angel was weakening now, the sword strokes less powerful and the light fading where it showed at the huge wound. The beast below roared, and with one last defiant lunge a mouth gaped wide, steel-trap teeth ready to chew down.

"We are climbing, higher and higher," the glory sang.

Meg put her last two shots down the beast's throat, and it fell away, screaming, to be lost and burned away in the bottom of the pit.

"We are brothers, sisters and all."

# Alfie

He brought the song to a halt, and all of them finished on the same beat. The angel fell, a wounded bird, crashing into the dry dirt at Alfie's feet. He slung the guitar over his back so that he could bend to its aid.

Dawson's grin smiled up at him.

"Thanks for the songs. See you down the road a way," he said—and died.

The light in the wound across its chest and belly brightened, and then got brighter still. Alfie felt Meg's hand reach for his and took it.

The warmth and the heat and the light and the glory washed over and through them, and there was a blast of thunder so strong it knocked him to the ground and down into a deep dark blackness that felt strangely familiar.

Waking up this time wasn't so difficult. He felt Meg tugging at his hand, found his footing and stood, blinking as his eyes adjusted to the light.

They were in the bottom of a dry valley, alongside a tumbled, white house beside a glorious tall apple tree in full leaf and laden with heavy fruit. Overhead white fluffy clouds drifted slowly across the bluest of blue skies and a warm, golden sun beat heat down on the whole scene.

There was no pit and no sign of the angel—but they hadn't come to this place alone.

"And I saw a new heaven and a new earth: for the first heaven and the first earth were passed away, and there was no more sea."

The Revelator stood in the doorway of the house, madness dancing in his eyes. He walked away, ignoring Alfie and Meg completely.

"There's nowhere for you to go," Alfie called out when he saw that the man meant to head up out of the valley.

The Revelator's voice called back, loud and clear.

"And God shall wipe away all tears from their eyes and there shall be no more death, neither sorrow nor crying, nor shall there be any more pain: for the former things are passed away. And I saw the holy city, a new Jerusalem, coming down from God out of heaven, prepared as a bride adorned for her husband."

The Revelator turned back and smiled at them, although Alfie thought there seemed to be little humor in it—and just for a second it had seemed that John's eyes were red—like fiery embers.

"I go to find the New Jerusalem, in this green and pleasant land," the Revelator said.

"And what about us?" Meg shouted back, squeezing Alfie's hand tight. The guitar at his back rang in answer.

"I don't know," the Revelator said, laughing—and now the red in his eyes was clear to see. "Sing some songs."

His last words echoed around the valley as he started to climb up and away from them.

"Eat some apples."